LEE BROOK

The Footballer and the Wife

MIDDLETON
PARK PRESS

First published by Middleton Park Press 2023

Copyright © 2023 by Lee Brook

All rights reserved. No part of this publication may be reproduced, stored or transmitted in any form or by any means, electronic, mechanical, photocopying, recording, scanning, or otherwise without written permission from the publisher. It is illegal to copy this book, post it to a website, or distribute it by any other means without permission.

This novel is entirely a work of fiction. The names, characters and incidents portrayed in it are the work of the author's imagination. Any resemblance to actual persons, living or dead, events or localities is entirely coincidental.

Lee Brook asserts the moral right to be identified as the author of this work.

Lee Brook has no responsibility for the persistence or accuracy of URLs for external or third-party Internet Websites referred to in this publication and does not guarantee that any content on such Websites is, or will remain, accurate or appropriate.

Designations used by companies to distinguish their products are often claimed as trademarks. All brand names and product names used in this book and on its cover are trade names, service marks, trademarks and registered trademarks of their respective owners. The publishers and the book are not associated with any product or vendor mentioned in this book. None of the companies referenced within the book have endorsed the book.

First edition

*This book was professionally typeset on Reedsy.
Find out more at reedsy.com*

For Malc—
For everything.
Thank you.

Contents

Chapter One	1
Chapter Two	9
Chapter Three	19
Chapter Four	30
Chapter Five	38
Chapter Six	46
Chapter Seven	53
Chapter Eight	57
Chapter Nine	62
Chapter Ten	73
Chapter Eleven	79
Chapter Twelve	81
Chapter Thirteen	89
Chapter Fourteen	96
Chapter Fifteen	104
Chapter Sixteen	111
Chapter Seventeen	120
Chapter Eighteen	126
Chapter Nineteen	133
Chapter Twenty	139
Chapter Twenty-one	147
Chapter Twenty-two	151
Chapter Twenty-three	159
Chapter Twenty-four	168

Chapter Twenty-five	179
Chapter Twenty-six	186
Chapter Twenty-seven	193
Chapter Twenty-eight	200
Chapter Twenty-nine	207
Chapter Thirty	212
Chapter Thirty-one	217
Chapter Thirty-two	222
Chapter Thirty-three	230
Chapter Thirty-four	238
Chapter Thirty-five	244
Chapter Thirty-six	251
Chapter Thirty-seven	258
Chapter Thirty-eight	267
Chapter Thirty-nine	276
Afterword	280
Also by Lee Brook	281

Chapter One

Paxton Cole threw open the blinds and looked across the Linton rooftops towards the horizon hidden by storm clouds. It was pissing it down. Again. Not that Cole cared. He did his job no matter the weather.

A teenager on a pale horse trotted past his house, and Cole thought about The Four Horsemen of the Apocalypse and the aptly named horse Hades, which he lost fifty grand on last night.

Fucking Johann told me it was a sure bet; he thought and clenched his fists. *Fucking wanker will pay later on. Arsehole!*

His head was thumping from the lack of sleep. Last night, after losing that money, he felt like he had a heart attack. Though worryingly, he was becoming numb to it. A tenner? A hundred? A grand, or ten. They were all the same bet to him.

But Cole needed coffee and quick. So he tugged on his trackies, pulled on a jacket and slipped his feet into socks and flip-flops. Amanda stirred in her sleep, but he left her to it, knowing she would appreciate a double Americano from the Inn on Main Street. They used locally roasted beans, and whilst, for the regular punter, they were expensive, the Coles thought they were worth it.

Cole stretched, his back hurting from a crunching tackle

in training yesterday as he poked his head out of the house and peered down the street. The coast seemed clear from the paparazzi, so he grabbed his wallet, phone, and keys and headed out of the house.

The coast was still clear as he made his way down Trip Lane, but as he stepped onto the path from the road, just past the junction to Northcote Fold, he heard a voice and stopped dead.

"Good morning, Mr Cole."

His heart hammered in his chest. He felt sick. This was not what he needed right now.

Jürgen Schmidt strutted out from the junction, casually checking his mobile, a cigar wedged between his teeth. He wore a sharp suit with black pinstripes, a white shirt open at the neck, and shiny black shoes. His greying hair was pushed back in a pompadour, exposing a forehead with various scars from old knife wounds. But it was his bristly moustache that made him so recognisable.

Paxton heard car doors slamming, and two huge lumps appeared around the corner, built like bouncers, wearing black suits.

Cole scanned the street, which was dead at this time. There was nowhere to run. Nowhere to hide. He was fucked.

Jürgen put his phone away. "I can't believe I had to come out here in this, Mr Cole." The man spread out his arms, palms up. "I guess they're right about British weather. Always fucking raining. Am I right?"

Paxton clenched his fists, but more out of habit than an urge to fight. "Nice to see you. Jurgy. How are you?"

"Don't you fucking 'Jurgy' me, Paxton!" Jürgen said as he squared up to Paxton. "I think me and you need to have words. That OK?"

CHAPTER ONE

Cole looked at the muscle. "I don't think I have much choice, do I?"

Jurgy sucked his cigar, then plucked it from his mouth before nodding. "That's true, Mr Cole. No fucking choice."

Cole gave Jürgen a polite smile despite his thumping heart and sore head. He was also feeling sick and wanted to escape. "How can I help you this fine, drizzly morning?"

"I'm here about the tiny matter of your loan. Specifically, you being four instalments late."

Paxton closed his eyes. He knew it was going to catch up with him eventually.

Cole swallowed down the bile rising in his throat. "You know I'm good for it. Got a game tonight. I should score, which means I get a bonus. I'll make sure you get every penny."

"You see, Mr Cole, that's what you told me after you'd missed the first payment. And the second and third." Jürgen smacked Paxton's arm hard enough to hurt. "You haven't scored in months. Do you not get paid if you don't score?" He turned to his men. "Is that right, boys? Star striker here only gets paid if he scores?"

"Nah, boss, these wankers are on like millions a year whether they score or not," a lump covered with spots said.

"Exactly!" Jurgen said, turning back to Cole. "I was a fool to trust you. And then I was a fool to trust that you'd follow through on your promises. But I won't be a fool again, Mr Cole. I want my money."

Paxton felt the gravity of the situation pushing him down into the ground. He'd been paid yesterday, and after paying the mortgage and his other bills and losing money on that fucking nag, he had nothing left. "Next week, Mr Schmidt. Please."

The man laughed and turned to his men. "Hear this, lads.

It's Mr Schmidt now, not Jurgen." The two lumps laughed as they stepped closer towards Paxton.

"It's a cup game. We're playing against a team in non-league. The boss is making me play the whole ninety because I haven't scored for a while. Should be fucking easy."

Jürgen took another puff of his cigar before exhaling the smoke over Paxton's face. "We had an arrangement, kid. I fulfilled my side of the arrangement when I gave you capital after you lost it all on the slots and nags."

"I know—"

"Shut the fuck up!" Jurgy interrupted. "You said your sexy wife Amanda would divorce you if she found out. Remember?"

"I've still got her topless picture on my wall, boss," one of the lumps said, a smirk on his face. There was a great big yellow head on the tip of his nose. "I choked the chicken to that picture a lot."

"Maybe the wife should go back to work, lad? Maybe she can look after you for a bit. You know what I'm saying?" But he didn't let Cole reply. "The truth is, you're a waste of fucking space. I loaned you that money because you said you were good for it. But it turns out you were only good for ten payments. So you've missed four, and we have another eleven payments after that." He shook his head. "Twenty-five payments. Two and a half mil. I want my money, Paxton, and I want it now."

"I don't have it right now."

Jürgen took a deep breath. "When we got into this arrangement, I explained how it worked, right? Men like you, who the public can't see as asking for loans, have no choice but to come to me. So you begged me, pleaded with me to lend you some cash. And fuck me, lad; I helped you. I like to see the best in people, Mr Cole, and I like to help them out. But when people

CHAPTER ONE

miss payments, it fucks me off."

"And I'm extremely grateful, Mr Schmidt, it's just..." Paxton's throat was dry. "I can get you all four payments next week."

Jürgen stood there, sucking deep on his cigar and exhaling the smoke all over Paxton. "No. I want it all."

"What, all of it all of it?" Jürgen nodded. "It'll be a few months. I have fifteen payments left, right?"

"Wrong. I need it by Friday."

"But it's Saturday!"

Jürgen grinned. "Not my fucking problem."

"Please, Mr Schmidt, I—" Paxton was beginning to see spots dance around the edge of his vision and was struggling to breathe. There was no way he could have the entire balance paid by off by next week. It was too deep a hole. "Other than pay it all off, what can I do?"

"You can start by giving me the four missed payments plus a fifth. Get me to trust you a little bit. Today."

"I can't do that, Mr Schmidt."

Jürgen took a long draw of his cigar, swished it around his palate, and then let it slowly out of his nostrils. "I really hate this position you've put me in, Mr Cole. You've exploited my trust. You've let me down, Mr Cole." He grabbed Paxton's arm with a vice-like grip. "So here's the deal. Make sure you're listening." Cole nodded, and Jurgy grinned. "You need to lose the game tonight."

"It's a team game, Mr Cole; I can't exactly—"

"Lose the match. And don't score, either. I've checked the odds, and the bookies think you'll make mincemeat out of those yellow bellies. Scunthorpe are a fucking shite team."

"But—"

"No excuses, Paxton, or I'll have no choice but to get my two friends here to break your legs. That won't do your career any good, will it?"

Paxton wanted to headbutt Jürgen and run away but knew he couldn't. He had his wife Amanda to think of and his daughter Alicia, too. A man like Schmidt would target Paxton's nearest and dearest.

"Fine. I won't score. I'll find a way to make us lose."

The greasy bastard grinned and held out his hand. "Good." Paxton took it and immediately regretted it as the loan shark crushed his fingers. "You'd better, otherwise..."

* * *

Later that night, as the team bus slowly weaved through the streets of Leeds towards the stadium, Paxton was silent with a mixture of dread and nerves. He was going to fix the match to gain back the trust of the loan shark.

He looked out of the window and sipped from his water bottle, breathing deeply between swigs and skipping songs on his phone. But he couldn't concentrate on the music, and it only got worse as he started to see the fans lining the street, waving flags and cheering as they caught sight of the bus. Eventually, the usual excitement erupted in his stomach as he saw lots of 'Cole 9' shirts.

They had no idea he had to let them down tonight. All because he couldn't control his addiction.

A tap on his shoulder from his captain, Johann, made him jump. Paxton took off his headphones. "Ready to go, Pax?" Johann asked, grinning.

"That bet didn't come in, you prick," Pax said.

CHAPTER ONE

"That's why it's called gambling, Pax," Johann said. "You earn enough that it was probably a drop in the ocean."

Paxton couldn't tell Johann the truth about his debt or addiction, so he smiled and nodded. He pointed towards his headphones and then closed his eyes.

Soon he was warming up on the pitch, going through his usual pre-game routine. He had done the hard work during the week to get his body into shape, knowing he needed to score goals today to get the bonuses. All that was for nought, especially as in the first few minutes of the match, Johann laid off a perfect ball to their attacking midfielder, Joseph, who slotted a perfect shot past the goalkeeper to make it 1-0. Instead of sprinting over and celebrating with his team, he picked up the ball from the net and ran towards the centre circle.

For Cole, not scoring was the easy part. But they were playing a team who were four leagues lower than them.

Luckily, the opposing team had managed to equalise by half-time, gifted via a stray pass from Cole. "Fucking stay focused, Cole!" the manager reminded him. "We should be two or three up by now!"

For the next half an hour, Cole bolted the ball over the net with each strike, calling for the pass from his teammates so they wouldn't score. But the clock was ticking, and he couldn't exactly score for the other team.

Or could he?

During the next corner, Cole moved out of position and tripped, which allowed their defender to get a head on the ball, and the goal bulged.

They were now losing 1-2, and Paxton hadn't scored yet, which was the arrangement with Jürgen. But their opponents were looking shaky, and Paxton sensed plenty of opportunities for the team to equalise. So it was his job to obstruct them so they lost.

But a giveaway in midfield fell to Johann, and Cole immediately knew where the winger would pass. He powered forward, hoping to get the ball and launch it over the bar, and smiled as he saw Johann's through ball flying into his path. Cole had one thought in his mind: miss. But it had to be believable. So he used his left foot to change direction and used his signature pace to get away from his marker before coming to the last defender, where he relied on his strength to brush off the last-gasp challenge.

It was just him and the keeper now. And Johann to his right, screaming for the ball. "Pass, Pax! Pass!"

But Cole ignored Johann and dribbled the ball closer to the goalkeeper, giving the gloved man a chance at saving the goal. He had Jürgen's voice in his head. "*Lose the match. And don't score, either.*" And Johann's. "*Pass me the fucking ball, Pax!*" And his daughter's, too. "*Make sure you score today, Daddy!*"

Cole knew if he passed the ball now, Johann would equalise. It meant he still wasn't on the scoresheet, and that would be acceptable, right?

"*Lose the match. And don't score, either.*"

He was fucked if he scored. Fucked if he let Johann score. Fucked if he didn't.

Cole made a choice, stepped over the ball, and used his left foot to change direction when the goalkeeper brought him down.

The ref awarded a penalty. He picked up the ball and headed to the spot.

Chapter Two

Two weeks later

"You heard about Paxton Cole, George?" DS Luke Mason asked, a mug of coffee in each hand, one of which he gave to DI George Beaumont.

George shook his head. "No. Should I have?"

"Let me guess," DC Tashan Blackburn said. "A big bid's come in for him that we can't refuse?"

It was early January, and the transfer market was in full swing. "No," Luke said. "Yolanda was on her way to work this morning from Wetherby and saw an RTA. She got out to see if she could help. The car's driver was dead, but luckily DI White knew whose car it was. Paxton Cole's. He was killed instantly as the airbag didn't go off. Basically, he wasn't belted and went through the windscreen. Cole hit the tree skull first. He didn't stand a chance."

"Christ," George said. "I've worked with James before. He's on the Major Collision Enquiry Team, right?" Luke nodded. "Does he think it was an accident?"

Luke rocked his head from side to side as if he was unsure. "James told Yolanda that Cole's mobile was in the footwell. Could be he dropped it and was trying to pick it up, and wham..." George grimaced. "There're some pretty narrow roads in

Wetherby, boss."

George narrowed his eyes but then smiled. "You still haven't answered my question, DS Mason."

"The forensic collision investigator hadn't finished and collated their findings when Yolanda left." Luke shrugged. "But Yolanda said there weren't any skid marks which means he either fell asleep or did it on purpose. Could have been pissed up?"

"Yeah, maybe. Could also have been a suicide?" If it were a suicide, not just a road traffic accident, it would be passed onto the Homicide and Major Enquiry Team on which George and the team served. They were finished with all their major cases, so they would most likely get it.

"Aye, boss. Something like that. Or a murder disguised as one."

* * *

Later that day, George and his team were finishing off paperwork for the 'Naughty List' case. Isabella was finally allowed back shortly after the new year, and the team were finalising the other minor cases they were involved in. The two young DCs were trawling through handwritten evidential notes from the usual spate of burglaries that happened in the winter.

George watched as Detective Inspector James White appeared on the television in the office, speaking to the press about the death of Paxton Cole.

"We have spoken to several witnesses but are keen to speak to anyone else who has witnessed the collision or the events leading up to it. If you were in the area around the time of this collision, please check your dashcam footage and get in touch."

A reporter interrupted James with a question which he dodged. "Anyone with information is asked to contact the Major Collision Enquiry Team by using 101 Live Chat online or by calling 101, quoting log 11 of 08/01. The road remains closed currently as enquiries continue at the scene."

* * *

"I'm so sorry for visiting late, Amanda," Detective Inspector James White said as he walked past a pink and white Mini Cooper displayed proudly on the drive, "but it couldn't wait." She nodded and allowed him to enter the property. "Thank you."

The blonde Detective Constable Holly Hambleton entered after him, having moved from HMET to the MCET. James thought she was a decent detective with a keen eye for detail. Plus, she was proper fit, and he fancied himself a bit of a ladies' man.

But Holly wasn't anywhere near as fit as Amanda Cole. Even with her pallid, stunned expression that showed James, she was still in shock; Amanda was stunning. Like many others, he'd had posters of her adorning his walls in his teens and early twenties, collected from the many popular 'men's magazines' of the times.

The two detectives followed the blonde beauty, her golden curls bouncing against her pert arse. James couldn't keep his eyes off it. *What a result,* he thought. He could give it a couple of weeks, maybe a month, and then ask her if she wanted to go out for a drink. She'd be loaded, too. A right catch. Perfect for a man as good-looking and charming as he was.

"Take a seat," Amanda said. Her voice was unsteady and so soft the pair had to strain to hear what was being said. "I'd offer you a drink, but I haven't got any milk."

"No bother," James said, putting on his 'winning smile'. "We need to ask you some questions about your late husband. Some of the questions may seem…"

James wasn't sure how to word it, but Holly saved his blushes by adding, "harsh. But we're just doing our jobs. OK?"

"OK."

"Our current theory is that Paxton deliberately crashed into that tree, Mrs Cole." He paused for a moment and saw the shock reappear. "Was Paxton happy at work?"

"Of course, he was. Football was his life. The lads, the banter, the money… I also suppose it gave him a break from our troubles." She stifled a sniffle.

"Troubles?" The DI gave her a moment.

She nodded. "Pax tried to keep it from me, but we had money problems. He told me he was spending a fortune on lawyers to get his mother back into the UK, but Pax was spending much more than he was telling me. She was a Windrush child."

The DI nodded and said, "Money trouble is one of the many reasons a person would commit suicide." Then he winced. He hated using that word.

But Amanda was shaking her head. "He wouldn't do that."

"Do what?" Holly asked.

"Commit suicide." Amanda blew a loose blonde curl away from her face. "Pax loved life. He cherished it. I don't believe for one minute, he took his own life. It went against everything he stood for."

The DI nodded. "Whilst I appreciate that it's one line of enquiry we are looking into. So what's your theory, Amanda."

CHAPTER TWO

She looked taken back, both at the formal use of her name and the fact that he wanted her opinion. It caused her to burst into tears once more.

"Are you OK, Amanda? Do you need anything?" Holly asked.

Amanda shook her head. "I'm OK. I just—I just can't believe he's dead."

The DI continued with his line of questioning. "After looking at the evidence found at the scene, we've spoken with Huddersfield University, who has an expert in psychological autopsy named Dr Shah." Amanda frowned. "It's popular in America and useful, apparently."

"What is it?" Amanda asked.

"When a suspicious death occurs, we are required to look into the mental state of the deceased person," James explained. "The expert will evaluate what sort of person Paxton was, what kind of personality he had, his thought process and other factors like that to determine whether he could have been involved in his own death. Essentially, the expert will attempt to reconstruct a person's psychological state before death."

"Because you believe he committed suicide?"

"Correct," the DC said. "A forensic collision investigator was at the scene with us. She examined the wrecked McLaren and created plans of the scene, which assisted her with a time and distance study. This helped her work out the vehicle speed through the amount of crush damage, alongside the tachograph information from the vehicle. She also liaised with McLaren, who shared technical information. Then, using all that, she produced a report suggesting that, unfortunately, your late husband crashed on purpose." Holly allowed the information to sink in for a moment.

More tears fell from Amanda's eyes. "Which is why you think

13

he took his own life?" Both detectives nodded. "Fine, do the psychological thing. It'll prove he didn't take his own life. I guarantee it!"

"Thank you, Amanda," James said. "I must warn you that if the expert has any doubt as to whether the death was accidental, meaning it was self-inflicted or malicious, then a different team of detectives will take over the case.

Amanda nodded her understanding, then said, "When is the post-mortem?"

"In the morning. That's when we'll also invite you to identify Paxton formally." Amanda nodded once more. "Now, part of the post-mortem will involve toxicology, which can take at most, six to eight weeks to be fully completed. In the meantime, Dr Shah and her team will be conducting interviews with relatives, friends, employers, doctors, teachers, and, in some cases, even people Paxton would have seen and spoken to regularly."

"What do you mean by 'regularly'?"

"People who could provide relevant information in an attempt to reconstruct Paxton's background, personal relationships, personality traits and lifestyle." Amanda shrugged, so James went into more detail. "His favourite restaurants. Shopping centres. Shops. Did he like a drink and have a certain bar he went to? That kind of thing. I know they cracked a case in America by speaking to a bartender."

"He spent a lot of time in Miggy. I was born there, and he liked the café there. They prepared his food for him. Proper healthy stuff. And it's not far from the stadium."

"Miggy?" James asked.

"Middleton. LS10," Holly explained.

"Oh, that shithole?" Both women turned to him, and he

blushed. "Sorry, it doesn't exactly have the best of reputations, does it?"

"No, it doesn't, Detective," Amanda said, "but you'll find the community is filled with incredible people. I'd live back there in a heartbeat. In fact, once the life insurance pays out," she said as she looked around the house, "I think I'll move back there. The New Forest Village is very nice. My daughter and I could live there happily."

James didn't want to say it but had to. "I do need to be frank with you about that, actually, Amanda." She furrowed her eyes. "Most life insurance claims are void if the death was suicide."

"Well, that's fine because he didn't commit suicide. You'll see."

"I also have to be honest and say that the claim might also be void if he was drunk. In my vast experience, fatal accident investigations, in which the technicalities of what actually led to the accident are difficult to resolve. We may decide it was an accident of his own doing."

"That's fucking bullshit," Amanda said before realising the curse and covering her mouth.

"I'm sorry, Amanda, but I have to be honest."

"Do you have any more questions for me, Detective?" Her fists were clenched, as was her jaw.

"When was the last time you saw Paxton?" James asked.

She ran a manicured hand through her curls. "This morning. He was going into Wetherby to do some shopping."

"Did he seem normal? Was he annoyed, anxious, or upset at all?"

She bit her lip, the tears in her eyes overflowing by the minute. "Pax was fine. Match's tomorrow, so he needed to be at training for noon."

James nodded. "Other than the money problems, how was your relationship?"

"Fine."

"Just fine?"

"We married young. Pax is... was a famous footballer." She shrugged. "It's a difficult lifestyle. People think money is happiness, but it isn't."

"So you weren't happy?" Holly asked.

"I didn't say that. I said money isn't happiness."

"So, no cheating?"

Amanda hesitated, and both detectives saw it. It was only quick, but it was enough. "No."

"Neither of you?" James asked.

Her eyes widened. "Not that I'm aware of. Is there something you know that I don't?"

"Of course not. "

James could see that Amanda was worried now. Her forehead wrinkled, and her eyes looked cold. "Then why say it?"

"Because asking difficult questions is part of our job, Mrs Cole," Holly explained.

James was getting impatient. This wasn't his forte. It was why he was on this team rather than the Homicide and Major Enquiry Team. Yolanda Williams, one of George Beaumont's team, had been sniffing about. He thought it may have been best to offload the case onto him. They were pretty sure the death wasn't accidental anyway, which brought HMET into play. "Was he ever violent towards you, Amanda?"

That's when the dam broke. James wanted to console her, but he didn't quite know how. He was a charming bastard and could easily work his way into a pair of knickers, but this was beyond him. So he stayed silent until she spoke.

"He'd hit me if I spent too much money. That kind of thing. Or if we argued. Though we usually argued about money," Amanda said. She looked defeated. "I don't know what I'm going to do now with a mortgage and bills. And the bloody cost of living. Especially if our claim is void."

Holly's heart went out to the poor woman. Not only did she have her grief to deal with, but she also had to deal with their finances and loss of income. They had one more question, and she thought it would be best to get it over and done with.

"From the conversation, you think your husband was murdered?"

"Not necessarily. It could have been an accident. Maybe another car ran him off the road?" Amanda said.

There was no evidence at the scene to suggest that, but the two detectives knew to keep their minds open. So Holly asked, "Can you think of anyone who would have the motive to harm your husband?"

She blinked the tears away from her already tear-streaked face. "No. He had his flaws did Pax, but overall, he was a decent man and mostly a good husband. I can't imagine anyone would want to hurt him."

"OK, thank you." He reached over and patted her arm. She recoiled, and James stepped back. "We will be in touch with the bank and phone network to get your late husband's records, are you fine with that?"

She shrugged. "Of course."

"Well, I think that's everything for now. Thank you for allowing us in, Mrs Cole. I appreciate that this is a tough time for you."

She gave a slight nod and glanced at Holly. Her eyes had changed again. This time, there was a pleading expression in her eyes. It was as if she was begging her to find evidence that it had all been an accident.

Chapter Three

An insistent buzzing of his mobile on the bedside table woke Detective Inspector George Beaumont the following day. He fumbled for it, mistaking the buzzing for the morning alarm, blindly swiping at the screen to turn the bloody alarm off, and finally opened his eyes when he heard a booming voice coming from the speaker.

It was Detective Superintendent Jim Smith. "Hello? Beaumont?"

The realisation that his boss was on the phone made him sit upright in bed and push the phone against his ear. "Morning, sir," he said.

"Are you on your way into the station?"

"Not yet, sir. Just got out of the shower," he lied. "Everything OK?"

"The Paxton Cole case. You know it?" George confirmed that he did. "Tech's finished with his phone. Lots of text messages from various burner phones. There's a lot of talk about money, a loan, and missed repayments."

Picking sleep from his eyes, George said, "Shite. Guessing the case is being passed over to me?" Then he added, "Sir."

"I don't have much information at the moment," Smith said. "But correct. Whether it's a suicide, or a murder dressed up as one, the Major Collision Enquiry Team are not equipped for it."

"OK, sir," Beaumont said. "Who from my team is already in?"

"DCs Blackburn and Scott. DS Williams," Smith said. "DS Wood and DS Mason aren't in yet."

George yawned whilst thanking his superior before tapping instructions to the three team members already in. The two lads were to get in touch with the phone network and see what they could get from them regarding location data. They could also chase up the bank statements. DS Williams was to start doing background checks on Paxton Cole and everybody he knew.

He had barely finished texting orders when another phone buzzed on the opposite side of the bed. A slender shape stirred underneath the sheets, giggling at the second awakening. Then a manicured hand reached out. A voice spoke with a Lancashire twang. "DS Isabella Wood."

She listened to the same booming voice George had just heard on the other end while George swung his legs out of bed.

"I'll be in very soon, sir," she said and giggled at George once more. She pulled off the duvet in time to see George almost fully naked. She grinned and said, "Morning."

"Morning," he said. "Fancy a shower?"

"Do I ever!" she said as she threw herself out of bed and into his arms.

* * *

George and his team, who had moved from the shared office

and into the largest Incident Room, were looking at DS Wood, standing by the Big Board. Somebody had tacked a map of Wetherby and the surrounding areas, which took up a third of the board. The middle third was currently empty. Photographs of Paxton Cole, his wife Amanda, and various friends and family members filled the space between the two-thirds. Stuck around the pictures were a few Post-it notes that had various comments and questions on them.

"This is Paxton Cole, aged twenty-eight at the time of death," Isabella announced. "His wife, Amanda Cole, was the last to see him before he headed off to the shops in Wetherby yesterday morning. Paxton took his burnt-orange coloured McLaren from Linton, where they lived, and crashed. He had no seatbelt on, his airbag didn't deploy, and he flew out of the windscreen, hitting the tree headfirst. His death was instant." She looked around the room to make sure everybody was following. "Initially, the Major Collision Enquiry Team took over the case, but they believe it was no accident. You all should have read the report in the shared inbox from the forensic collision investigator."

There were nods all around, and Wood went back to her seat. "What have we got then?" George asked.

DC Jason Scott stood up first and stuck what looked like a spreadsheet on the board. "No bank statements yet, boss, but I managed to isolate all of Paxton's regular contacts. That includes friends, family, work, and even takeaways and endorsements. His agent was extremely good about everything. It leaves these four numbers. All are Asda or Tesco pay-as-you-go SIMs." George could see three colour-coded green for Asda and the final one blue for Tesco. "We're working on trying to trace their last known locations but haven't had a hit yet, boss."

"OK. Well, keep doing what you're doing, Jay," George said. He pointed towards the paperwork pinned to the board. "And great work on this."

DC Scott walked back to his seat, struggling to contain the smug look on his face.

"Who's next?" George asked, looking between Tashan and Yolanda.

Yolanda smiled and stood up. "Besides Amanda Cole's two younger brothers, they're all clean."

George raised his brows. "Clean?"

"Correct, sir. Not even on CID's radar."

George sat back with his hands behind his head, tongue peeping through his lips. "Tell me about the brothers, then."

"Damon and Declan Lomax. Twins. Twenty-four. Little bastards from what I can see, though nothing major." George raised his brows again. "No drugs or anything like that, but they're always scrapping. They'll fight anybody. Having a famous sister and brother-in-law is the reason. The twins are easily wound up."

"OK, investigate their relationship with Paxton, will you, Yolanda? It could be they didn't like him and wanted him out of the way, though that seems unlikely. I've got a meeting with that Dr Shah on Monday to see how the psychological autopsy is going. So fire off an email to ensure she looks into the twins."

Yolanda, who was furiously scribbling notes, looked up and nodded her understanding. George then looked at Tashan, who had been syphoning through the data DI James White's press release had garnered. "Same old stuff, sir," Tashan said. "Not much to go on. From what I can gather, there were no witnesses to the crash. We've got people to come forward with footage of the aftermath. The same is true for witness statements. But we have nothing of the crash itself, which is frustrating."

"Sounds set up, doesn't it?" George asked. His team nodded. "No witnesses. No skid marks. The airbag didn't deploy. No seatbelt." He scratched his beard. "But who set it up? Was it Paxton Cole or somebody else?"

"I was thinking about the messages, boss," Jay cut in. "About the loan and the missed payments. Could a loan shark be involved?"

"Yeah, I was thinking the same," Wood added.

The rest of the team, including George, nodded. "We need to figure out who those burner phones belong to," he said. "But first, get your coat DS Wood; you're coming with me to see the twins."

* * *

Middleton wasn't too far away from the station but seemed to take an age as George manoeuvred the Mercedes through the traffic. The two detectives discussed the case and what they were having for tea that night.

George and Wood soon pulled up outside the Lomax house.

"Someone's watching us from the window," Wood whispered as the twitching net curtains fell back into place. A moment later, an older, overweight woman in her fifties opened the door, puffing on a cigarette. She had blonde, straggly hair and a pale complexion.

George and Wood got out of the car and approached her. They held up their warrant cards. "I'm Detective Inspector Beaumont, and this is Detective Sergeant Wood."

"Fucking knew you were the pigs," she said with a smile, though her eyes remained cold and hard. "What do you want?"

"We're here to speak to the twins regarding the death of Paxton Cole," George said. Then he indicated to the house. "Can we come in?"

The woman frowned but said, "Fine." She glanced up and down Intake Lane before ushering them in. "We were very sorry to hear about Pax." She smiled. "What a shitshow."

"Indeed," George said.

"The boys are in there," she said, pointing towards a yellow-stained door.

George entered and saw the boys; each slumped on a separate tattered, cream leather sofa. An overflowing bin stood in the corner, and the coffee table was covered in empty beer bottles and cider cans. A large flat-screen TV was on the wall with the latest Xbox perched next to it. The once cream carpet was stained and dirty, the walls stained by nicotine. He noticed there were no pictures on the walls.

One of them glared at George. "What do you want?"

"We've come to have a chat about Paxton Cole." Wood said as she plopped herself down in an armchair whilst George stood blocking the door.

"Well, we did assume this isn't a social call," the other twin said.

George eyed him carefully. He was bigger than his brother, his blond hair cropped close to his head. Tattoos covered his hands, arms and neck. "We need to ask you both some questions."

"We're grieving dickhead. Me and Dec, we just lost our brother. Our hero. Pax was a legend. How about you leave us be for a bit?" the tattooed twin said.

"We can't do that, I'm afraid," George said. "When was the last time you saw Paxton?"

"Dunno," Declan said. "Bro?"

Damon said nothing. It seemed he was the leader—the stronger of the two, both mentally and physically. However, the way Declan deflected the question towards his brother made George suspicious. "I'm waiting, Damon," George said.

"Oh, I see?" Damon said. He stretched his arms behind his head, and George could see the stretch marks that indicated rapid muscle growth. It made George wary. "You think we've got something to do with it." He stood up and squared up to George. "Let me be clear, pig. It's got nothing to do with us."

George kept his expression blank as he said, "Then you'll have no problem telling us when you last saw Paxton then. Will you?"

Mrs Lomax tapped George on the shoulder, a beaming smile on her face. "Do the boys really have to answer these questions, young man?"

George laughed inside at the completely contrasting personality she showed earlier. "They're not obligated to answer any questions, but if we feel like they're not telling us the truth," he said, his tone hardening, "we can take them down to the station and continue formally. With solicitors present if necessary." He let that sink in and turned to the lads. "It's up to them."

Declan stayed silent, as did George, his hard stare doing the work for him.

Eventually, Wood broke the silence when she asked, "When was the last time you saw Pax? Come on. Answer and we'll leave you in peace."

"Friday," the lads said in unison.

"Do either of you own a mobile phone?"

Damon frowned, puzzled. "Aye. Why?"

"One each?" Wood asked, and both lads nodded.

"Any other mobiles?"

"No. *Why?*" Damon asked.

"A pay-as-you-go SIM inside a separate mobile phone, or anything like that?"

"Oh, I see," said Damon, an annoyance to his tone. "You think we have burner phones? You think we're druggies. Fuck me, man. I get it, alright. It's because of where we live." George was about to protest when he was interrupted. "Well fuck you, man, we don't touch that shit. Friends of ours died from that filth. Some were murdered for dealing. It's not fucking worth it. Check the fucking house if you want. We got nothing to hide, right bro?"

Declan stood this time, a stern look on his face. "Right."

"To be clear, we're not accusing you of anything," Wood assured them. "But, we need to be clear that we're investigating your brother-in-law's death, and so we need you to be honest. We're not here to try and trip you up; we just want information." She smiled at the lads, who softened before George's eyes. It probably helped that she was a stunner, but she also had a way with people. "So, tell me, both of you, where were you between 6 am and 9 am yesterday."

"Sleeping," Damon said with a scowl.

"Both of you?" Wood asked.

"Aye," Declan confirmed.

"Can anyone verify that?" Wood asked.

"I can," Mrs Lomax said. "Boys didn't get up until noon. In fact, I had to wake them up to tell them the news."

George nodded and then looked directly at Declan. "Fancy

showing me around?"

But Damon shook his head. "I'm already up; I'll take you."

George then shook his own head, a grin on his face. "I asked Declan, not you."

"Then I guess we revoke our invitation, pig. So get the fuck out!"

George could feel Damon's breath on his face. It stunk of stale cigarettes and alcohol. Like a nightclub dance floor from the nineties. Fucking disgusting. "So you do have something to hide?" George smirked and held his ground, trying his best to stay loose. As a boxer, he'd squared off against many an opponent, but fighting in a suit was brutal, and George had Mrs Lomax standing right behind him. "We can do this the easy way, or the hard way, Damon." George paused to let the words sink in. "We can arrest you for obstructing an investigation, or you can play nice and let me search the house." George made a show of slowly putting on the shoe covers and gloves he kept in his jacket pocket but said nothing more.

"Piss off, pig; you've got nothing on us." George held eye contact but said nothing. "Fine then." Damon looked at his brother. "Show the pig around." Declan got up, and Damon then turned back to George. "You won't find anything."

"I hope I don't," George said as he left the room and waited for Declan to lead him upstairs.

Despite the house being a three-bed semi-detached, the upstairs was a cramped affair, and George didn't enjoy having Declan so close to him in a confined space.

George checked the bathroom first, noticing the different spray cans of Lynx scattered around the various tops, before moving on to the room to the right. "That's my mum's bedroom," Declan said with a sneer. "Doubt you'll find

27

anything interesting in there. Well, not unless you're into older women."

Declan winked, but George ignored the remark and scanned the room. He then gently opened each drawer, and the wardrobe, noticing designer outfits were hung on hangers. He turned to Declan, a frown on his face.

"They're Mandy's," he explained. "She sometimes sleeps here when she's had a row with Pax." Then his face turned forlorn. "I guess she won't need to do that any more."

George nodded and then checked the boys' rooms. They were exactly how he expected them to be. Pig sties. Both stunk of a mixture of BO, Lynx Africa, nicotine and lager. Declan's also had a half-eaten donner kebab, the spicy, sour meat and sauce adding to the room's fragrance.

Feeling as if he was going to be sick, George returned downstairs with Declan at his heel. When they got to the bottom, George turned to face him. "You don't seem very concerned about your sister. Why is that?"

"She's a big girl. And she's rich." Declan shrugged. "She never shared her money with us. Pax did, though. He was always buying us stuff. He was a good guy." George had noticed both lads had PS5s in their bedrooms, something even he hadn't managed to get a hold of yet. "But I guess she'll get the life insurance and fuck off somewhere." He looked down at the floor. "Guess that means we won't see much of our niece, will we?"

"That's not for me to say, Declan. Plus, I doubt your sister will receive any life insurance." Declan looked up, confused. "Suicide voids any cover. She won't get anything."

Declan scratched his head and whispered, "Oh shit. What's she gonna do then?"

George shrugged as he took a quick look in the kitchen. He didn't find anything besides a mixture of dirty plates, empty cups, and ashtrays on the kitchen counters. The oven was dirty, with food encrusted onto the ceramic hob, and a pile of dirty clothes were heaped in front of a grimy washing machine. When he returned to the living room, Declan followed him and plonked himself back on the sofa.

"That's it for now, lads, but I expect we'll need to speak to you again."

George turned to leave, but Damon said, "Whatever, pig. Get the fuck out before I lose my temper."

George turned to Wood as soon as they were outside and said, "Declan mentioned the life insurance and looked disappointed when I explained it would be void if Paxton had committed suicide."

"Now that's suspicious, don't you agree?"

Chapter Four

Amanda Cole arranged to meet them at her home in Linton, so George drove along Trip Lane while Wood tried to make out the numbers.

"Look at the size of some of these places," Wood said.

"This is what being married to a professional football player gets you, I guess," George said. "You sure you want to marry me, babe?"

"I think it's the next house," Wood said and pointed before smiling. "I wouldn't put you on anybody else. I'm a glutton for punishment, after all."

George laughed and pulled into the circular drive. In the centre, a statue of a famous Brazilian footballer stood among white pebbles; the foot of the statue stood on a golden ball. With bay windows and a double garage to the side, the house was impressive. A silver Bentley was parked in front of the garage door. A Mini Cooper next to it.

"Nice place," Wood said, getting out of the car and heading towards the door.

George followed, looking up at the house. "Aye," George agreed. "If I remember rightly, Mrs Cole was a glamour model. *Nuts*, *Zoo*, *FHM*, *Maxim*, the lot."

Isabella stopped and turned on her heel. "You seem to know

a lot about her, Detective Inspector. Something you need to share with me?"

George decided he did not and laughed his way out of the question, his cheeks red.

Amanda Cole appeared at the door before George could knock. She wore black leather rounded-toe boots and was dressed in a black jersey dress with a round neck and long sleeves that showed off her curves and highlighted her blonde curls that hung over her shoulders and down her back. George wasn't expecting Amanda to look this way. He knew if he had lost his spouse, he would have been wearing lounge wear and probably looking like shite. Yet Amanda looked freshly tanned, and her makeup was flawless. Her eyebrows were perfectly plucked, her eyes a sparkling cornflower blue, and her lips crimson. George thought she looked like a blonde *Morticia Addams*.

"I'm DS Wood, we spoke on the phone, and this is DI Beaumont."

"You better come in." She turned and led them inside.

They entered a hallway where a large floral arrangement stood on a table against the wall. Cards offering condolences were propped up around the vases. On the opposite wall, a floor-to-ceiling mirror reflected the flowers. A wide staircase ran up the centre. A black leather bag with an oversized metal F-shaped clasp was perched on the bottom step.

It made George wonder whether she was going out.

Amanda led them to a formal living room, where George felt the urge to remove his shoes before stepping onto the thick pile cream carpet. Looking up at the high ceiling, George appreciated the ornate coving. But the place lacked the warmth of a family home. There were no pictures. No TV. Nothing but two large, elegant potted trees that had trumpet-shaped flowers that bathed in the sunlight.

Still, how the other half lived, eh? George thought.

"Please take a seat. I'd offer you a drink, but I haven't got any milk."

George sat on one of the two matching cream leather sofas next to Wood and watched Amanda take a seat. She crossed her legs and folded her manicured hands on her lap. "We can do coffee black if that's easier."

"It is, but I really don't have the time."

"It's a charming home," Wood said, trying to pierce through the atmosphere.

Without a smile and rather too quickly, Amanda said, "Thank you." She ran a hand through her curls. "How can I help you both, as I've already told that other detective everything."

"We've read the transcripts," George explained. "But, we would prefer to hear it from you personally."

Amanda's shoulders stiffened. "Fine, but I don't have long."

"Are you going out?" Wood asked.

"Correct, so please ask your questions so we can all get on."

"As you know," George said, "Dr Shah will be interviewing everybody known to Paxton in the coming weeks so she can carry out a psychological autopsy." Amanda nodded. "We understand you believe your late husband was involved in an accident rather than taking his own life."

Amanda's hands clenched on her lap. "That's right."

"Yet you've been made aware of the Major Collision Enquiry Team's findings." Amanda nodded. "For us, the lack of skid marks raises questions."

"I appreciate that Detective, but I know my husband. He wouldn't have taken his own life."

George nodded. "I understand."

Wood then took over. "You mentioned you two were having troubles. That he was spending a lot of money on lawyers, right?"

"Right."

"Well, on the way over from Middleton, our team received Paxton's bank statements and have been checking through them. Did you know about your husband's gambling?"

She shrugged. "Pax used to go on the slots now and then. And bet on the horses. As long as he avoids football betting, there's nothing wrong. Right?"

"Right." Wood looked at George.

"From the information, we have so far, Paxton was in debt."

"In debt?" Amanda looked down at her hands and pursed her lips. "What?"

The DI nodded and said, "He was depositing a lot of money daily into various gambling websites."

Amanda paled. "How much money?"

"Tens of thousands. And we have to be frank with you. Money trouble is high on the list of reasons a person would commit suicide. There are about sixty-three pence in your late husband's bank account."

Amanda bristled. "That's bullshit, surely." Then she winced and placed her hand over her mouth.

"I'm afraid it isn't, Amanda," Wood said. "Now, I need to ask you about something you shared with DI White. That Paxton would hit you if you spent too much money."

A shaky hand pushed another stray curl away. "Yes."

"Can you elaborate for us?" George asked, shuffling. He'd sunk into the comfy sofa, and with the heat of the house, was struggling to concentrate.

"As I already said, he'd hit me if I spent too much money.

We would always argue about money, and he'd hit me if he lost his temper."

"How bad did he hit you?" Wood asked.

"It would always be a punch to places I could hide. Never my face. Can you imagine the paparazzi if they found out?"

"Did you never see a doctor or confide in a friend?"

Amanda looked towards the cream marble fireplace. "No. Never. It was nobody's business but ours."

"I see," Wood said. "When was the last time he hit you?"

Amanda stood up, and George noticed her hands were shaking. "Why on earth do you need to know?"

"We need to understand what kind of person Paxton was, Mrs Cole," George said. "That's it. There's no judgement. Honest." He smiled, but she didn't return it.

Eventually, she said, "After the cup match two weeks ago."

George remembered the match. He'd watched it on *ITV*. Well, he'd recorded it and watched it on his day off. Paxton Cole had scored the winning goal in the last minute. A penalty if he remembered correctly. "Why did he hit you that night?"

"Because I wanted a new outfit. Pax had scored the winning goal. He gets a bonus when they win and another depending on how many goals he scores." She shrugged. "At the time, I thought he could afford it. But it makes sense now if what you say is true."

"It is true," Wood confirmed.

"I can only guess he hit me because he lost all that money. But I don't remember him being on his phone or laptop that night. In fact, I remember him turning his phone off, which was unusual. He said something about wanting to be left alone. People were calling him up, congratulating him on breaking his duck. He didn't seem very happy, though." Then she realised what she had said and tried to take it back. "I meant about the people calling him. Annoying him. Not that he wasn't happy in general."

"OK, Mrs Cole," George said. "And have you thought yet about any person who may have reason to hurt your late husband?"

"I have, and I can't. Pax was well-loved. Popular." She shrugged again. "I don't know who did it, but somebody did something to him. I'm sure about that."

The two detectives shared a look. They knew all about the life insurance conversation. George imagined it would be a rather hefty sum that Amanda could live on forever.

George was about to thank Mrs Cole for her time and get up to leave when his phone buzzed in his pocket. It was an email from Tashan. George read it and clicked open the attachment. Wood read it over his shoulder.

Amanda looked at the pair, her eyes narrowed. "Is everything OK, Detectives?"

"No," George eventually said. He stood up, walked over, and handed over his phone. "This is a bank statement from ten months ago where a large sum of money was deposited."

"That's not unusual. Paxton played in the Premier League."

"Whilst I appreciate that, Mrs Cole if you look at this image here," George said as he swiped the screen, "you'll see that Paxton's wages are all referenced this way." George pointed at the numbers, and Amanda nodded. "This one," he said, swiping back, "is a direct deposit. As if he went into the bank himself and deposited the cash." Amanda raised her brows at this.

"You didn't know about this?" Wood asked.

Amanda shook her head. "I had no idea he'd put two million

pounds into his account. So why did he need to? And how did he get it?"

"You tell us, Mrs Cole," Wood said.

"Well, I've no idea, do I?"

~~But George knew.~~ "Paxton's account was in the red until that deposit finally cleared it." Both women nodded. "We found messages on your late husband's phone about a loan. A loan that Paxton had missed instalments of, apparently."

Amanda closed her eyes. "Honestly, I had no idea."

"You have no idea at all?" George asked.

"None. Check my bank statements. You'll see. I still get money from old modelling shots, plus I do a lot of consulting. Anyway, I've just had a thought. If you find out who loaned Pax that money, then you find his killer," Amanda said, a smug grin on her face.

"I was thinking the same, George said as he stood. "Thanks for that, Amanda."

"We may need to speak with you again," Wood said. "We'll be in touch if that's the case. I know you have already rejected a Family Liaison Officer, Mrs Cole, but they are beneficial. Especially when we need to update you on the case."

"There's really no need for one," Amanda said as she stood up. "I'll see you out."

"Well, that was suspicious," Isabella said once they'd left, and George looked at her, his eyebrows arched. "She was head to foot in FENDI, both dress and boots. That stuff's not cheap. And she had a handbag slung casually on the stairs. Those bags alone cost over two and a half grand."

"Well, she *was* married to a Premier League football player, Wood. I don't think a WAG would think twice about spending that much money.

"Yeah, I guess, but if my husband had just died, I'm not sure I'd be parading around the house looking like that. I'd probably have bags under my eyes and look like utter shite."

"That's so sweet of you, my love," George said.

She turned, a coy smile on her face. "Who said I was talking about you?" She waited a minute for George to grin. "In all seriousness, though, she mentioned how he'd hit her if she spent too much money. And she also said they'd constantly argued about money. Was that because he was losing the money and had to resort to a loan shark?"

"Probably, though it looks to me like they were just as bad as each other for spending money," George said.

"True, but why would she say those things and then parade around in expensive designer gear? It just doesn't make sense."

"As you said, the only word that comes to mind is suspicious."

Chapter Five

The footballer lived closer to Wetherby than he did Linton, and on a normal road, the journey would've taken forty minutes, tops. Though on that narrow, twisting, pot-holed monstrosity the council called a road, George knew it would take substantially longer.

The media circus had hounded George since he'd taken over the case. He hadn't told them much because he hadn't much to tell them.

It was approaching dinner time, and George realised he hadn't eaten anything since breakfast, which now seemed like a lifetime ago.

The sun was low in the sky, blinding George as he guided the Mercedes up and down the hills and around the curves as more rain fell from the dark sky.

"It's a bit rough," Tashan said. "The road, I mean, not the area." He grinned. "The area's pretty nice." It was unusual for George to take DC Blackburn with him, with DS Wood being his usual partner, but she was working different shifts to him and, if truth be told, feeling a bit under the weather.

"It's lovely," George agreed, though he barely glanced at the scenery. Some of his father's family members lived out this way, and he remembered being dragged up this way as a kid. He used to get car sick, and the winding roads didn't help. "It's better in the summer."

"How's DS Wood doing, sir?" Tashan asked.

"She's fine, Tashan. Why?" He risked a glance at the young DC.

"But is she fine? How's she really doing, sir?"

George frowned. "Spit it out, Constable."

"It's just..."

George shook his head. "Just what?"

"After, you know, sir... Everything that happened to her during the last case. How's she coping?"

George thought about what Tashan was saying, which brought back memories of what had happened to her, the things the monster may have done to her, and he shuddered. "Thanks, Tashan. But why are you asking me? Shouldn't you be asking her?"

"You're right, sir. But she always looks so professional, like nothing ever bothers her. I guess... I guess I didn't want to embarrass her."

It got George thinking about something Mia, his ex and mother of his son Jack, had said after the Blonde Delilah nearly killed her. Apparently, he tended to assume things were fine. Then, he remembered when he shared what Mia had said with Isabella, and she had agreed. But Isabella was fine with that because she preferred to play her cards closer to her chest than Mia. But that wasn't how it worked for most people. And George knew that which was why he'd brought the subject up just after the new year.

He remembered Isabella was sitting next to him and began fidgeting with her seat belt once George had asked her how she was coping after Miller had tried to kill her.

Eventually, once she had finished fidgeting, she gave the tiniest of shrugs and said, "I have good days and bad."

George remembered he'd said nothing, his favourite technique, and had waited for the silence to be filled.

"I'm suffering from sleep paralysis," she'd told him. "During the night, I sometimes wake up frozen and think Miller is in the house with me. That it's happening all over again."

He'd noticed that she'd been struggling with sleep and had even broached the subject, only to be fobbed off with excuses. Finally, he smiled and said, "Let's go see a doctor about it then. Together."

That's when the bombshell hit that she'd already been. Without him. "They ran tests." She'd shrugged. "They reckon it's psychological."

"I'm sorry, George; I know I should've told you," Isabella admitted. "I just thought I was being silly." She shrugged again. "But now I see how serious it was." Then she corrected herself. "How serious it is."

And whilst George was both angry and upset that she'd kept it from him, her fiancé, he understood why and bit his tongue. For George, you couldn't run a relationship on secrets and lies.

He turned to the young DC. "I appreciate that, Tashan. And so will Isabella." George smiled. "Thank you."

"Well, if she ever wants to talk to somebody, you both know where I am, sir."

"Thanks," George said.

They turned into the driveway of what looked like a Manor House and almost ploughed straight into the back of an orange McLaren that stood proudly on the cobbles. Next to it was a shiny, black Range Rover with a rather recognisable private plate.

CHAPTER FIVE

* * *

Johann Gruber, one of Paxton Cole's teammates and Paxton's best friend, was having lunch when they were met at the door. His wife, a woman in her twenties who was dolled up to the nines, had initially told them in her scouse accent to 'Fuck right off!' otherwise, she'd set the dogs upon them. And George believed it, too. He reckoned they'd be big bastards, explicitly bred to get rid of unwanted visitors.

She'd apologised straight away as soon as George and Tashan pulled out their warrant cards, explaining how the media had been hounding them since Paxton's death, and showed them through to the dining room where her husband was enjoying what looked like brown rice and salmon. Sky Sports News was on the large TV that George reckoned would, at the push of a button, integrate itself into the decor and be hidden away. He'd dealt with women like Mrs Gruber—if she'd taken his surname—before.

Like his wife, Johann seemed overdressed in a black shirt, crisply pressed cream trousers, and shoes so polished that the detectives could see the grand ceiling reflected in them. George thought whilst the man looked well-presented, he also looked as if he were trying too hard. But who was Johann trying to impress? His wife was lovely looking, and he wasn't exactly short a bob or two.

"Who are these people, Megan?" the footballer asked, staring at George but not addressing him. It was clear who wore the trousers in that marriage.

"They're with the police, love," his wife explained and raised her brows. Then, she grinned a perfect smile. "They want to ask you some questions about Pax."

"Fine," Johann said, his smile not meeting his eyes. "How can I help?" George was sure the man had lost quite a lot of his accent; it replaced with the affluent north Leeds accent that grated on his nerves. But if you listened closely enough, there were hints of Johann's Austrian heritage. He held out a hand, which George took, and crushed it. George had been expecting it, so he slid his hand back slightly, so he was the one in control. He gripped harder than was necessary and didn't break eye contact.

"Detective Inspector Beaumont, West Yorkshire Police Homicide and Major Enquiry Team. This is my colleague, Detective Constable Blackburn."

"Johann. It is nice to meet you." He brought up an arm and checked the time on his watch.

It probably, George mused, cost as much as his salary. But then, to a Premier League footballer, it would have cost nothing. Especially a decorated international such as Johann. That's what Tashan had told him, anyway.

"I have to be at the training ground in an hour, so let's be quick. Yes?"

"We're here about Paxton Cole."

"Dreadful news," the footballer said. "We're all hurting over the loss. I sent lovely Amanda a plant."

George nodded. "As are the entire city and many more around the world," he said.

"Have you made a decision on whether to classify Paxton's death as suicide yet?" Johann asked.

George raised a brow. He respected the man for his confidence. "Not yet, which is why I'm here today." George was thirsty and was rather offended he hadn't yet been offered a drink. "At the training ground this week, you'll have a psychologist interview you. Dr Shah. She will ask you questions relating to Paxton's mental health and demeanour in the weeks leading up to his death. We'll be asking similar questions."

Johann grinned. He knew it was a threat. Tell us the truth, the detective was telling him.

The two detectives were still standing up, and Johann took another look at his watch. Again, he was playing mind games.

"OK, so Johann, how long have you known Paxton Cole?"

Johann shrugged. "Since I joined the club."

"And when was that?" George asked.

"Ten years? Maybe more. I forget."

"And you've been friends for how long?"

The Austrian frowned, then looked at his wife, a scowl on his face. When George and Tashan said nothing, Johann repeated, "Ten years? Maybe more. I forget."

"So you've known him as long as you've been at the club." The footballer nodded. "How did he seem in the weeks leading up to his death?"

Johann thought long and hard. "No different from usual." He stuck out his tongue and played with his blond moustache. "Well, he was worried about being replaced on the team. Pax didn't show it, but he confided in me how stressed he was. Amanda would probably confirm this with you. But that's it."

"OK," George said. "But other than that, he was no different?"

"Correct." Johann closed his eyes. "Wait." He paused for a moment. "He had a, how do you say it, a 'training ground bust up'. Yes, that's right."

"With?"

"Rodríguez."

"What, the young striker, Luis Rodríguez?" Tashan asked.

George was more into his rugby league than football, though he watched it on TV when his job allowed it. Tashan, however, was obsessed with the Premier League.

"Correct, son," Johann said. "You a fan?"

Tashan nodded and only stopped nodding when he noticed his boss was staring at him. "Sorry, sir, I'm a bit star-struck."

That made Johann grin. "I'll sign something for you before you go. I have some pictures somewhere." He looked at his wife, who nodded at him. "Yes, he had a... a scrap with Luis. Very nasty business. The Colombian is a right piece of work. Have you spoken with him at all?"

"No," George said. "Should we have?"

Johann shrugged. "I mean, you're the detective. I just know if I were investigating a man's death, I'd want to know who he'd been fighting before he died."

George nodded. Tashan was making notes. George said, "Would you describe Paxton as your best friend?"

"No," Johann said, then grinned. "I consider him family."

"Did he ever confide in you about his financial situation?"

"What, like how much money he was on per week?"

"No," George said. "More about how much he was spending. Whether he was in debt."

Johann's face darkened. "He did. Yes. It's what he and Luis were fighting about." Johann's eyes wandered towards the ceiling. "Well, that and the fact Luis was out for his job. As I said earlier, poor Pax was out of form."

George said, "Tell me more about Luis Rodríguez and the fight. You said it was to do with debt?"

"Yes. I believe Luis put him in touch with a guy who could help him. A short-term loan or something. Get him out of the shit if you excuse my English." Then Johann checked his watch. "I apologise, gents, but I must go." He grinned, got up and took the image from his wife. He signed it, passed it to Tashan and then said, "Duty calls."

George looked around at the dining room, with its expensive old furniture, then gave the footballer a nod. "Keep your phone on for us," he instructed. They now had another link to money. Luis Rodríguez. "Because I've got a feeling we'll be talking to each other again very, very soon."

Chapter Six

The footballer, Luis Rodríguez, was waiting for George as he got into the main reception area, and by his side was his agent, a tall, slim man with dark, greasy hair.

"Hola. Por aqui por favor," George said to him, his arm outstretched. *Hello. This way, please.*

Luis regarded him impassively, then smiled at the use of his native language. The Colombian looked fresh and far too young to be a professional footballer.

Despite Luis' agent advising he could interpret for them, George had secured a Spanish-to-English translator from the police translation service, waiting on the telephone in the interview room. George waited as Luis and his agent sat on the chairs opposite him before he, too, sat, with DC Blackburn filing in to sit next to him.

"Do you want a hot drink?" George asked first, to which the agent translated. It seemed he was the type of guy who didn't take no for an answer.

Luis shook his head.

"Mr Rodríguez, you're not in any trouble, but we'd like to record this conversation," George started by saying. The agent whispered to Luis, who nodded his head.

"Do you know why you're here, Luis?" But before allowing

the translator to speak, George looked at the agent. "I'd appreciate it if you stayed silent. Thank you."

After listening to the young interpreter on the phone, Rodríguez nodded and spoke. The interpreter then translated it as, "To talk to you about Paxton Cole."

"Correct. What was your relationship like with him?"

After listening to the interpreter, Luis looked confused at first. Then he replied, "He was a teammate. One I looked up to. I wanted to be like him one day."

"Would you describe your relationship as friendly?"

"Sometimes." Luis smiled. "Competitive is what I prefer, though. In football, you never know if you will be sold, subbed, or promoted to a starter."

George nodded. It certainly made sense what Luis was saying. Football clubs were essentially businesses; if you weren't pulling your weight, then you were done. "So, Mr Rodríguez, we've already established that you and Paxton Cole were more competitive teammates than friends. Did you two ever argue?"

Luis grinned, clearly knowing where the conversation was headed. "Yes. All the time. I take it you are referring to the fight we had just before his death?"

"Correct. Can you explain?"

"Of course." Luis grinned again, the corners of his lips meeting his eyes. "I was talking shit about his wife. She is very beautiful. Far too beautiful for a man like him." Luis began to laugh. "I told him I'd take her off his hands as he couldn't seem to find the right hole to score in these days."

George was about to reply when more Spanish came from Luis' mouth. "You've seen her, yes? Gorgeous. I wonder how she's doing?"

"Well, I imagine she's not in a good place considering her

husband died, Mr Rodríguez. I think I'd leave her to mourn if I were you."

Luis shrugged, that grin still plastered to his face. He turned to his agent and spoke. "Is that it? Can I go now?" the translator advised.

"Where were you between 6 am and 9 am the morning Paxton Cole died?"

Luis coughed and looked nervously between George and Blackburn. It was the first time during the interview that Luis looked like he wasn't in control. Luis had never been in control; of course, George had only allowed him to think that.

Luis crossed his arms. "I'd have to check." He turned to his agent, who pulled out his phone.

"Training," the agent eventually said. "I was there with him." He eyed the senior detective. "It's a good job he was training, too, because he started the game on Sunday because of Cole's death."

That comment sealed it for George. Luis Rodríguez was involved somehow. He wasn't sure how and why, but he doubted Luis was training then. "Where was your client training, Mr..."

"Montero. Nicolás Montero." The agent looked back down at his phone and then advised it would have been at the training ground in Wetherby.

George noticed Tashan was scribbling notes and hoped the young DC would follow that up after the interview without being asked.

"We'll check."

"Of course."

George then turned back to Luis. "How did Paxton Cole react to those words about his wife, Luis?" He turned to Tashan.

"I don't know about you, Detective Constable, but I know if my colleague were talking shit about my wife, I wouldn't be thrilled. Would you?"

"Not at all, sir. But then, I wouldn't do that. Not to a colleague." Tashan turned towards Luis. "Who started the fight?"

"I don't really remember," said the Colombian, suddenly sounding desperate, the interpreter translating his words into English. "I just remember mentioning Paxton's beautiful wife, Amanda, and then we were fighting." He looked rattled, his eyes slightly wide, his movements agitated as he shifted on the seat.

George berated himself for not asking Johann Gruber about who started the fight. After hearing what Luis had said about Amanda, George assumed Paxton had started the fight, but from Luis' body language, he was now unsure. "You don't remember?" Luis shook his head. "I'm sure your colleagues do," George explained. "I think we should take a break and then meet back here in fifteen minutes."

* * *

When George and Tashan returned to the interview room and continued the recording, it was clear to everybody, from the look on George's face, that he'd found something. "I've just spoken with Gruber and Barnes, two of your teammates who witnessed your 'scrap' with Paxton Cole. They both told me you 'sucker punched' him after he told you to 'fuck off' in Spanish."

"I guess." Luis met George's eyes briefly before they returned to the table. "If that's what they're saying, then I believe them. I just don't remember doing it."

"There must have been a reason?"

Luis shrugged. "No."

"So, you wound up your colleague, talking about his wife, and then proceeded to punch him in the face for absolutely no reason?"

"Yes."

George shook his head, making it clear he didn't believe a word the man was saying. "You're aware that sounds ridiculous, right?"

"I do." He shrugged again. "The club pay for me to have therapy. They like the aggression but want it only on the field."

Again, George noticed Tashan was writing notes. He was getting better with each case.

Luis took a deep breath before he said, "Wait, I remember something," Luis said. "He called me a joto."

"That means homosexual male in Spanish," the translator explained. "It's a derogatory term."

Annoyance niggled at George. "Your teammates never mentioned this," George explained. He looked at Tashan, who shook his head.

"Ask them. He did. That's why I punched him. I remember now."

"You see, your teammates only mentioned that you were fighting over a bet." George turned to his DC. "That's right, isn't it, Detective Constable?"

"Correct, sir. Barnes and Gruber both confirmed you'd given Paxton a sure bet on the horses that lost him a lot of money."

"We're footballers. We can't bet on football, so we bet on horses." Luis shrugged. "It's what we do with all that money burning in our pockets."

CHAPTER SIX

"OK, let's talk about Amanda Cole," George said. "Have you ever met her?"

"Of course."

"Describe your relationship with her."

"I don't have one," Luis said, then he grinned. "Not yet, anyway."

"So, where have you met her? How do you know her?"

"Through Paxton, of course. Club dinners and events. I don't know her personally."

"I see." So there was no link there, not that Luis was admitting to. Isabella believed that Amanda was seeing someone, especially with how she was dressed the last time they visited her. And from how Luis talked about Amanda, he wondered whether they were having an affair. "So you and Amanda Cole weren't having an affair?"

Luis Rodríguez nodded unhappily. "I wish that was the case."

"You do realise this gives you motive, Luis," George explained.

Luis deliberated. "No, it doesn't. Fancying his wife does not mean I'd kill him. How ridiculous. And anyway, I thought he committed suicide. I thought he crashed into that tree on purpose?" He looked at his agent, who shrugged.

"We have a duty to investigate all suspicious deaths," George explained.

Luis met his eyes and frowned. "So I'm a suspect, am I?" asked Luis quietly, his eyes flickering towards the CCTV camera above George's head.

"I'm not saying that, Mr Rodríguez. But we're looking into everybody who knew Paxton Cole and investigating their relationships." George folded his arms across his chest. "Your relationship with Cole is suspicious. You've admitted to assaulting him days before his death, which gives you means. You've also admitted to fancying his wife, which gives you motive. So now it's my job to investigate the opportunity. You say you were training the morning of his death, and as I said before, we will be checking that information."

Luis laughed mirthlessly as Tashan's pen scribbled across the page.

George ground his teeth together. "It's in your best interest to tell us now if you had anything to do with his death."

"I didn't. I'm not a murderer," the footballer explained.

George nodded. He wasn't expecting a confession, but he was more suspicious now of Luis than ever. "Do you know who it is?" He looked sharply between the two Colombians for any tells, fidgeting, or indication hinting at lies or avoidance.

"Sorry, but I've no idea. As much as I hate to admit it, Paxton Cole was a decent man. Other than calling me a joto, of course." Luis grinned again. "He was popular. The fans and the city of Leeds have been hit hard. And that's a shame."

"Is there anything else you can tell us? Anything at all that can help us investigate Paxton Cole's death?"

Luis hung his head and shook it as if he knew he was now their prime suspect.

George sighed and leaned back in his chair. "OK. Thank you for your cooperation; I appreciate it. We will be in touch. Interview terminated."

Chapter Seven

George, Isabella, and Jack pulled into Langdales Wharf Car Park in Bridlington the day after Jack's first birthday. The two detectives had managed to convince DSU Smith to allow them the same day off as leave.

It was chilly, and barely any places were open because it was January. But that was the charm of the seaside in the winter.

As they walked by the harbour, the trio were wrapped up against the bitter cold. George pushed Jack, who was in his pram, and Wood linked her arm with George's. They were a perfect family, and George thought he couldn't be happier. Probably not until the day they got married, anyway.

They took it slow, enjoying the freezing wind on their faces, talking about life rather than work, and enjoying their alone time as a trio. Jack was babbling away, grinning up at his dad and Isabella.

Heading towards the north pier, George could smell his favourite chippy, his mouth salivating as they passed it, continuing past the Gansey Girl towards the Harbour Cannon.

George and Wood sat on the pier's walls, watching the boats go in and out of the harbour, hot drinks warming their frozen hands. For George, this was bliss.

After they'd finished drinking and watching the boats, they

walked around the coastal town for a little bit, picking up rock, fudge and toffee for their colleagues back at work. George had even picked up some rock with Mummy adorned through the middle. It would be from Jack, of course. And he hoped she'd appreciate the gesture.

And then it was time to head back to the chippy on the north bay – George's favourite.

This time they took their fish and chips to the benches opposite rather than taking them back to the pier. For some reason, a chippy dinner always tasted better straight out of the paper, surrounded by the sea air.

As he munched the fresh fish that had been enrobed in crispy batter – with Jack sat in between the pair – George didn't think life could get any better. Then he watched as Isabella blew on the soft, succulent chips before handing them over to his son, who then stuffed said chip into his mouth. His eyes lit up, and George's heart melted.

Later on, after their chippy dinner, George had opted – stupidly – for ice cream.

"How's your ice cream?" Wood asked. They were at a parlour next to the leisure centre, looking out of the windows at the ocean which gorged up the beach. She'd opted for a hot pudding and custard, something George wished he'd thought of.

George jabbed at the contents of his sundae, the ice cream still solid despite the heating. *That's what you get for choosing ice cream in January,* George thought. Jack was munching away at Isabella's pudding, making an absolute mess but loving every minute.

"I still can't believe you went for vanilla," Wood said, grinning. "Who comes to an ice cream parlour and has vanilla."

She pointed at the wall. "Look at all of those flavours!"

"Says the woman eating treacle sponge."

Isabella grinned and plunged her spoon into the warm custard. "Aye, well, I'm not stupid enough to eat ice cream in January." She turned to Jack. "We're not stupid like Daddy, are we?"

George watched as his son nuzzled closely into Isabella's neck. That moment made his stomach flutter. He loved them both so much! "You having a good time?" he asked.

She grinned. "I am. It's not often we get the same day off. And with all the cases we've had this past year, it's been even more difficult." She ran a manicured hand through Jack's blond hair. "It's nice, though, isn't it? To get away for a bit. Get away from... murder." She whispered the final word as if it would offend Jack's ears.

The trio moved into the arcades next, filling up the 2 pence machines – George playing and Jack watching. As they moved from machine to machine, Jack kept pointing at a specific claw machine, and George thought he was up to the task.

But he wasn't. He hadn't come close to getting the Igglepiggle that Jack was babbling away at. But Isabella did. Somehow, with a practised, steady hand, she manoeuvred the claw to the exact blue teddy that Jack was furiously pointing at. He'd started walking two weeks ago, so George picked him up and held him so Jack could see Isabella playing the machine.

Five minutes later, Jack had the Igglepiggle, and Isabella was the apple of his eye.

But by then, it was time to go. And as George dropped Jack off with his mum in East Ardsley, the numb feeling where his heart usually was returned. It would gradually ease between the days he was without Jack and then hit him full force like a truck when he eventually had to give his son back.

George hadn't even told Mia about his engagement yet, nor had he told her he'd moved in with Isabella in Morley. Of course, the less Mia knew, the better, and whilst George felt guilty about keeping the truth from her, he knew how she'd react.

Mia still wanted them to live together. To be a family together. To be lovers again. She'd backed off a bit recently, but George always felt it when he dropped Jack off. It was the way her hand lingered on George's arm as she said goodbye. It was the way Mia held eye contact. The sultry grin on her face as she answered the door. And she always seemed dressed up when he picked up Jack and even late at night when he dropped Jack off.

It was ridiculous, George knew, but he didn't want to inflict any more trauma upon the woman he once loved. She'd suffered enough at the hands of the Miss Murderer and the Blonde Delilah. And she was still struggling to come to terms with the fact that she had a secret half-brother.

But at some point, he would have to tell her.

He just didn't know how.

Chapter Eight

A *week after the crash*
George, Sergeant Greenwood and his Uniforms slowed each car as they passed by the mock wreck they had set up. What they were doing was called an anniversary visit, a technique used by police when seeking further witnesses who had yet to come forward. They were doing it because they had nothing. Dr Shah's ongoing psychological autopsy wasn't helping them at all. Nor was the fact that DSU Smith strongly believed Paxton Cole caused his own death and was putting pressure on George to close the case.

"Morning, Officer, is everything OK?" one concerned driver asked. George could see her hands turning white as they gripped the steering wheel. He flashed his warrant card and introduced himself. "Morning, Detective. Apologies."

"No problem. We're in the area on the anniversary of the death of Paxton Cole seeking to learn more from the community and to talk to any witnesses who have yet to come forward."

"The footballer?"

"That's right," George said.

"I remember hearing about it on the news and reading it in

the paper, love, but I didn't witness it. The crash, I mean."

George nodded. They'd already stopped a hundred cars that morning, and many gave George and the other officers the same story.

His stomach rumbled at about 1 pm, and George was about to leave and put Sergeant Greenwood in charge when he heard a "Sir," coming from across the road. He looked up to see a police constable beckoning him over to a red Ford Fiesta.

"Constable Mullins, sir," the young lad said. "This is Mrs Devons. She has some information for you about Paxton Cole."

George flashed his best smile and his warrant card. "Detective Inspector Beaumont. Do you mind if I record this conversation?"

"No bother, love," Mrs Devons said, so George pulled out his trusty Dictaphone and pressed record.

"Detective Inspector Beaumont with PC Mullins interviewing Mrs..."

"Adela."

"Adela Devons, regarding the death of Paxton Cole." He smiled at her again. "You have some information for us?"

Adela switched off her engine, took off her seat belt and took her phone out of her handbag. She scrolled through it for a minute, her glasses on the edge of her nose. When she finally found what she was looking for, she blew a stray strand of shiny black hair away from her face. "Take a look at this."

George took the mobile from Adela and looked at the image. It showed Paxton Cole surrounded by three men, all wearing dark suits. Only one of the faces was visible. He turned to the constable. "Recognise this man?"

Mullins shook his head. "No clue, sir, but that looks like Paxton Cole."

CHAPTER EIGHT

"I agree," he said before turning to Adela. "When did you take this picture?" She shrugged, but George could see that guilt was written all over her face. He took the phone from her and checked the details. She'd taken it three weeks ago. Beaumont clenched his jaw, tightened his fists, and desperately tried to change his facial expression from anger to disappointment. "This was taken three weeks ago, Mrs Devons. Why haven't you come forward with it?"

"I didn't know it was Paxton Cole. I'm not into football. I was just being nosey, and so I took the picture because it looked dodgy." She shrugged again, and George believed her. "It definitely looks dodgy. Right?" George nodded. "It was only last night when my husband looked through our holiday photos we took last week when he mentioned it to me."

"So why didn't you contact us last night?"

"I didn't know if it would help." She began to sob. "You've got to believe me, Detective. I had no idea. I just... I'm telling you about it now. That counts for something, right?"

"Yes, of course." George smiled. "Thank you for bringing it to our attention." She could easily have said she knew nothing, to be fair. "Do you know any of the other three men?" She shook her head. "Could you describe them to me?"

"I literally only saw what you see in the picture. Paxton Cole," she said, pointing, "and that big fella. That's it."

"Thanks, Mrs Devons." He turned to PC Mullins and handed him his card. "Get that picture from her phone and email it directly to me."

* * *

George flew back to the station in his Mercedes, desperately hoping that one of his team would have the answers he needed. For Amanda Cole's sake, he hoped the three men in the image were involved in Paxton's death. But, for his own sake and that of DSU Smith's, he hoped they weren't. Everything was pointing at suicide. Yet there was a nagging feeling he couldn't escape.

"Incident Room, please," George ordered his team as he entered the shared office. "Chop chop, we don't have all day." He rubbed his hands together to ward off the cold and ushered each team member inside the warm room. "Where's Jason?"

"Looking for Yolanda. He wants to sign out Paxton's mobile," DS Wood said.

Once they were all seated, he tacked a printout of the image Mrs Devons had provided to the Big Board. "This image was taken three weeks ago by a woman named Adela Devons," George explained. "The man in the picture is Paxton Cole. Agreed?" He saw a collection of nodded heads and continued. "We must figure out who these three men are and then find them. From the suits and the way they're surrounding Paxton, I assume it's the loan shark and his muscle." He turned to Wood. "Did you have a look on the PNC and HOLMES for any known loan sharks in the area?"

"I did, George. There are too many to bring in. DSU Smith wouldn't allow it. Budget reasons."

George nodded. They were even more strapped for cash than last year. "Does anybody recognise anyone?" A collection of shaken heads greeted him. He then passed around copies of the image he'd made on the way in. "What about now?"

"Sorry, sir," Tashan said.

Luke shrugged.

Wood shook her head.

CHAPTER EIGHT

DC Jason Scott then entered the room and picked up the image Tashan slid across a desk. Usually the joker of the department, Jay went deadly serious when he looked at it. "I know that guy. It's Colby Raggett."

"You're joking," Tashan said.

"I wish I was, Tashan." Jay shook his head. "Nasty piece of work. I remember him from when I was in Uniform. He was always in trouble for kicking the shit out of people."

Jay explained that from a young age, Raggett specialised in illegal cash loans that preyed on vulnerable victims. He'd set high-interest rates, and if a person didn't pay on time, then he'd batter them.

"I can't believe Paxton Cole was daft enough to get in with that crowd. What an idiot," Tashan said.

"Thanks for the information, Jay," George said. "But it doesn't look to me like he's the boss." George tapped on the slimmer and shorter man. "I'm guessing he's the boss and those two his lackeys."

"Maybe, boss," Jay said. "I guess the only way to find out is to bring him in and see if he'll talk."

Chapter Nine

Instead of sending Uniform to collect Colby Raggett and bring him back to the station, George decided to surprise him at home. They had his address on file alongside his colourful criminal record, and as DC Jay Scott recognised Colby from his days as a bobby on the beat, the DI brought the young DC with him.

Jason hammered on the frail, rotting front door of the house, and the sound of barking and snarling greeted him. Jay banged again. "Answer the bloody door; it's freezing," he whispered.

The dog stopped barking, and Jay looked up at his boss. But still, there was no answer.

He was about to knock for a third time when he heard the sound of a lock turning, and the door opened slightly. Jay listened to the distinctive metal rattle and assumed the security chain was being pulled tight.

A spotty face appeared in the gap. "Yes?"

"Colby Raggett?" Jay asked. He knew it was Colby, and the spotty man frowned at the sound of his name.

"Who's asking?"

"I am." Jay produced his warrant card. "Detective Constable Scott." He pointed to his boss. "This is Detective Inspector Beaumont. We'd like to come in and ask you a few questions if

CHAPTER NINE

that's OK?"

George grinned. His subordinate had managed to be both assured and lacked confidence simultaneously. He wouldn't have asked the cretin if it was OK to be allowed in.

Colby's living room was a shithole. Not literally—the dog shit that dotted the garden didn't make an appearance here—but it was, in every other conceivable sense, a shithole.

"Take a seat," Colby instructed, and whilst George and Jay attempted to find one—the threadbare carpet was covered with empty bottles and cans—they both decided it was probably best to stand.

Nicotine had yellowed the magnolia walls and turned the white skirting boards into a sickly cream.

But the worst part of the living room was the smell. As a teen, Jay had asked his dickhead uncle Pete for a cheeky swig of beer from one of the many cans that had been left on the table of his father's birthday party. Weirdly, Uncle Pete had said yes and grinned as Jay discovered the half-empty can had been used as a makeshift ashtray. And that's exactly the same smell and taste Jay was suffering through now, a sour, stale bitter taste with a nicotine aftertaste.

George coughed, and he swore he could chew on the stale air in the property. The place was bloody disgusting.

Colby eyed the two detectives, and when it was clear they were both choosing to stand, he sat in an armchair facing the television and sparked up a cigarette.

"So?" the spotty man said, exhaling smoke. "What do you two want?"

"We're here to ask you some questions about Paxton Cole," Jay explained.

George took the Dictaphone from his pocket. "We're going

to record this conversation. OK?"

After Colby finally allowed DI Beaumont to record the conversation, Jay made the necessary introductions and was about to get started on his questions when Colby jumped in.

"I'd like to clarify now that I'm not in trouble, right?"

"That's right," Jay confirmed. "Unless you've done something wrong, that is." The spotty man shrugged. "Tell us about Paxton Cole."

"Cracking footballer. Or he was. Next question."

"Did you ever meet the man?" Jay asked.

"I did. Next question."

Jay licked his lips. "When." Colby shrugged. "Recently?"

"Possibly."

"You know he's dead, right?"

"I do. Is that why you're here? I had nothing to do with it! Definitely not! Honest!"

Jay turned to his boss. "Colby looks like he's panicking to me, boss," he said.

"Aye, I agree, Detective Constable."

"You see, that surprises me, Colby," Jay said. "Innocent people don't panic. So why are you panicking?" This wasn't true, of course. He'd known civilians tell stories about how despite driving to the speed limit, reducing their speed whenever they saw a police car. He'd known grown men to be brought to tears at the thought of being brought into the station to be questioned, despite protesting their innocence. Some people just got nervous around authority figures, he guessed.

"I suffer from anxiety, OK? I'm on tablets for it." He got up and pulled a strip of Sertraline from a drawer. It treats my panic attacks. Speak to my doctor. So if I'm acting nervous, it's because I am, OK? Doesn't mean I did anything."

CHAPTER NINE

"We never said you did, did we boss?" Jay said with a grin.

"That's right, Detective Constable."

"Why would you assume we thought you were involved, Colby?" He said nothing, so Jay continued. "Where were you between 6 am and 9 am last Saturday?"

"Last week?" Colby stuttered. The two detectives nodded. "In bed." Then he added, "Probably."

"Probably?" Jay asked.

"I'm usually in bed until noon on a Saturday." He shrugged. "That's when Cole died, right?"

"Right," Jay said. "When was the last time you saw Cole?"

"I dunno?"

"What about three weeks ago?" George asked. Jay grinned.

"In bed, probably," Colby said again.

"Are you sure?" George asked.

Colby sunk back into the armchair. "I don't know, but I already told you I didn't do it."

"You didn't do what?" Jay asked.

"Kill Paxton Cole."

"Maybe not," George added. "But you met with him three weeks ago, right?"

"What?"

"Answer the question," Jay said.

Colby blinked. "I don't know how to."

"Easy," Jay said. "Just tell us the truth."

George rubbed the stubble on his chin. He'd shaved the beard off three weeks ago, but it was growing back. Isabella had been mortified.

"Three weeks ago?" Colby asked, and the two detectives nodded. "Yeah, I might have bumped into him. What of it?"

"Did you see him on your own, or were you with other

people?" Jay asked.

"What?"

"Answer the question, Colby," Jay demanded, but the man stayed silent. Because of that, Jay decided it was time to show him the photo.

Colby's face tightened, his mouth becoming a thin, narrow slit. "Shite."

Jay grinned. "Shite indeed." He let gravity take hold. "Who are your friends, Colby?"

"No comment."

"Unbelievable!" George roared. "Do we need to take you into the station, Colby?" He stepped closer. "Because we will. Trust me."

"There's no need for that, Detective."

"Tell us who the two men are, then," Jay said.

"I can't."

"Can't or won't?"

"Both. Either. Does it make a difference?"

"It does because you and your friends were seen with Paxton Cole under very suspicious circumstances. Then a week later, he's dead." Jay said. "Who killed him?"

"I don't know!" the man insisted. "If I knew, I'd tell you!"

"I don't believe you!" Jay added.

"I don't give a shit!" Colby said. Whatever anxiety he was suffering from earlier had been replaced by rage. Colby's sudden change in demeanour was sharp enough to cut through steel. But why? Were the two men in the picture really that scary? Was one of them his boss? They must be.

"I believe you," George added, and Jay frowned.

They hadn't discussed good cop bad cop on the way over; the boss had simply asked him to take the lead.

CHAPTER NINE

"Why might someone want to kill Paxton Cole then?"

"How the hell would I know?"

George shrugged. "But you know who these two men are, right?"

"Yes."

"Do you have names?" George asked.

The man in the armchair frowned and glanced uncertainly at the detectives.

Both men fixed their gazes on the spotty man. If he could have sunk further into his chair, he almost certainly would have. "I need their names," George warned him. "Now."

"He's..." he said, pointing at the shorter and thinner man. "If he finds out, I grassed him up; he'll... Well, he won't be happy." Colby's eyes darted around the room in fear. "I'll tell you, but only if he doesn't find out it was me. OK?"

"Fine," George promised. "He won't hear about it from me." George stepped even closer. "Name."

George could see the inner battle Colby was having with himself. Eventually, he said the name, though it only came out as a whisper.

"I didn't quite catch that, Colby," George said."

Tears welled up in Colby's eyes. "I don't know the other lad, but our boss is called Jürgen Schmidt," he said between whimpers. "But please, If he finds out I grassed, there's no saying what he might do to me."

"Oh, and I'm gonna need you to tell me what your little meeting was about," George finally said.

* * *

After successfully twisting Colby Raggett's arm, it took a

surprisingly short amount of time to track Jürgen Schmidt down. George wasn't stupid enough to give the man advance notice that he was coming. For a man like Schmidt, he needed to be caught unaware.

Wood had spoken to the council and handed in the necessary forms to check Academy, the system they used to store details of liable residents who paid council tax in Leeds. That information, cross-referenced with information from the PNC, meant that as soon as George tapped on the door of Schmidt's last known address, the man himself answered.

Jürgen Schmidt lived in Middleton, on New Lane, in a decent-sized house that blended into the neighbourhood. It had been extended, from the look of it, with tall, thick hedges grown high to block the view from the road. There were a couple of expensive SUVs on the drive—an oversized garage with a camera looking down at George.

And whilst it certainly didn't look like the kind of house a loan shark would live in, he was reasonably sure the neighbours would know who he was. Middleton was that kind of area. Everyone knew everyone. And George should know; that's where he grew up. As a kid, he'd always wanted to live in one of these houses.

With a frown on his face, Schmidt stopped dead at the sight of George. The frown turned into a smirk as if he somehow recognised George. "Police, right? Not interested. Come back with a warrant."

He went to shut the door in George's face and winced when Beaumont stuck his foot in the door to keep it open and said, "I don't need a warrant to ask you a few quick questions, Jürgen. You know that as well as I do." George looked around at the neighbours' houses for twitching curtains and grinned at the loan shark. "The quicker you answer my questions, the quicker I leave."

Dangerous dark eyes narrowed at him. George's heart began to hammer in his chest, and he wondered whether he'd made a mistake by coming alone. The problem was George hadn't expected to catch the man at home, let alone catch him in his pyjamas and matching slippers. Though, to be fair to the man, George also wore matching pyjamas and slippers when off duty.

"Fine, Detective. Five minutes, then you can fuck off! Alright?"

George nodded, then squeezed inside, careful not to brush up against the loan shark. By the door was a baseball bat wedged underneath an expensive-looking alarm panel. He thought the loan shark should probably get one of those video doorbells like Isabella had just bought; that way, he could have ignored George's knocks, not that he'd tell him that, of course.

The sound of scratching and barking came from George's right, and he stepped back at the sounds. Schmidt laughed and gestured for George to head towards the kitchen that was directly at the end of the lushly carpeted hallway.

George didn't like that he was leading the way instead of following. It would be all too easy for Schmidt to smack him across the back of the head with that bat. But nothing untoward happened. In fact, Schmidt gestured for George to take a seat and even offered him a coffee from his machine. It was one of those you put pods in.

DI Beaumont declined but offered his thanks. He didn't want to stay long, either.

With a scowl, Jürgen asked, "So what do you want, then?"

"Know a man named Paxton Cole?" Jürgen gave him nothing.

Not even a flicker of recognition. He was good. Too good. "Come on, Jürgen. You know Paxton Cole. The professional footballer. Oh, and one of your debtors." Schmidt still didn't react. "You haven't heard about his death?"

Schmidt didn't answer for a moment, but his scowl deepened. "The famous footballer. Of course, I know the name, Paxton Cole. Half of Leeds will know that name. So what? And one of my debtors? Fuck off!"

George handed Schmidt a printout of the picture that showed himself with Paxton Cole and Colby Raggett. "Who's that man then, if not Paxton Cole?"

Again, Jürgen said nothing. "Fine. I admit it. I've met the man, OK? I'm a big fan; I just wanted his autograph."

"Where were you between 6 am and 9 am Saturday?"

There was another awkward silence, and George wondered if Jürgen was considering how best to reply. "In bed. I sleep late on Saturdays. So I wouldn't have been up until ten or eleven. OK?"

"Do you have anybody who can corroborate your story?" George asked. Schmidt's jaw clenched. "I don't care who was in your bed, Mr Schmidt; I only need to know who they are to confirm your alibi."

"I was alone. And I didn't kill Paxton Cole. Why would I?"

"Fine. What about your lads?"

"Lads?" He stared straight at George.

"Aye, like Colby Raggett. I heard on the grapevine that he kicks the shit out of people who don't pay you back. Is that what happened? Did they kick the shit out of Paxton Cole?" George didn't break Schmidt's stare. Schmidt's jaw twitched, but he held his tongue. "Look, Jürgen, you help me, and I help you." George stood up and folded his arms. "Believe me when

I say I can be your worst nightmare. I'll look into everything you and your lads have been up to. OK?" He let the words sink in. "Or, tell me what I need to know, and I'll leave you to it."

Schmidt's scowl deepened, and the atmosphere in the kitchen darkened. Of course, threatening the loan shark was never the plan, but sometimes you needed to act tough against a formidable opponent.

"OK," Schmidt huffed. "Look, Paxton Cole's death has nothing to do with me, OK? Or my men, for that matter." He shrugged. "I'm a businessman. As such, I have no interest in clients being unable to fulfil their contractual obligations. They can't do that if they're dead? Right? So it makes no sense for me to kill them. Is that enough for you? Huh? Because I'm saying nothing else without a solicitor."

George understood the lingo Jürgen was using. He was being clever not to incriminate himself, despite them both knowing full well what he did for a living. He'd acknowledged Paxton was in debt to him without ever uttering the words. Not that it mattered; they had Colby Raggett's confession recorded that confirmed Paxton Cole owed Jürgen a hell of a lot of money. But Jürgen's day would come; George knew that for a fact. They had a growing file on him back at HMET, and one day, they'd have him. "Is there anything else helpful you can tell me?" George kept his tone light and even smiled.

"No." Schmidt got up and gestured towards the door.

"Fine then. If you think of anything else helpful, give me a call, yeah?" said George, handing Schmidt his card, but the man made no move to take it. So instead, George dropped it onto the kitchen counter. "Make sure you call me. And thanks for your time."

George turned to leave and felt eyes on the back of his head.

He wondered how desperately Schmidt wanted to bash his brains in because George was certainly up for a scrap. His right hand had been clenched so hard during the conversation that he'd drawn blood.

Chapter Ten

"Please tell me we've got something on Schmidt?" George asked as he entered the office for a late shift.

But his team looked down at their keyboards, and Luke explained that Jürgen Schmidt had turned from a lead to nothing during the space of a couple of hours as the alibis began arriving. They'd verified everything twice and had even checked out most of his associates. Throughout the day, Jay and Tashan had even triangulated their phone data and, with Yolanda's help, checked through ANPR for their vehicles. That, along with their continued enquiries, had not placed Schmidt nor his associates near Wetherby and Linton on the morning Paxton Cole died or in the days preceding it.

It meant they had nothing, and Paxton Cole causing his own death was looking more likely. He wondered when it was time to give up. To finally close the case. It wasn't necessarily his decision, despite now being SIO. That would be up to the DCS or the DSU, both of whom were currently in a meeting discussing it.

George was due to give them a detailed briefing in half an hour. But first, he needed a coffee.

* * *

"Right," DSU Smith said and sighed. "Advise us of Paxton Cole's last movements."

"We still don't know at this point whether Paxton Cole's death was accidental or deliberate," said DCS Sadiq, "so I'm advising we all keep an open mind. We will then, after this meeting, make an official decision. So, George, what do we know about Cole?"

George cleared his throat. "Paxton Cole, a professional footballer, drove into Wetherby to get some shopping early Saturday morning on the 7th of January. His wife, Amanda Cole, said he seemed his usual self leading up to him crashing his McLaren into a tree. Forensics found Cole's mobile in the footwell, and the forensic collision investigator noticed the airbag was turned off. Cole also wasn't belted, so he went through the windscreen and hit the tree skull first."

"Ouch," DCS Sadiq said.

"Indeed, sir. His death was instant," George explained. "The forensic collision investigator also didn't find any skid marks. Telemetry harvested from the car also suggests the car sped up as it veered off the road. She also liaised with McLaren, who shared technical information. Then, using all that, she produced a report suggesting that Paxton crashed on purpose."

George paused for a moment, allowing the information to sink in. So far, it wasn't looking good for Amanda Cole. "Now, as you both know, HMET weren't initially in charge. Instead, it was DI James White from the Major Collision Enquiry Team." Both senior detectives nodded. "Amanda told him about their money problems. Specifically, Paxton was spending a fortune on lawyers to get his mother back into the UK because she was a Windrush child."

"But you didn't find any evidence of that from his statements, did you?" Smith asked.

"Correct, sir," George said. "I'll go into that in detail later." The DSU nodded. "Anyway, Amanda was adamant Paxton wouldn't commit suicide and that it went against everything he stood for. DI White had decided to use the expertise of Huddersfield University, specifically Dr Shah, an expert in psychological autopsies, which are attempts to reconstruct a person's psychological state before death."

DCS Sadiq said, "James did that because it is a high-profile case."

"Correct, sir." George smiled. "DI White then, for some reason, went back to money. Amanda told him how Paxton would hit her if she spent too much money." He shrugged. "It makes sense, especially if Paxton was in debt and lying to his wife about it. She then began to discuss life insurance, and James decided to be frank with her. Any policies would be void if suicide were ruled as the cause of death. She then became adamant Paxton had been run off the road."

"There's no evidence of that, though, is there?" Sadiq asked.

"No, sir," George replied. "The forensic collision investigator's report is very detailed. And very damning." Sadiq nodded. "That's when the team and I took over the case. We treated it as suspicious from the off and followed the standard policy, starting with Paxton's mobile phone. That's where we found messages from burner phones about money, a loan, and missed repayments. Everything seemed to be coming down to money."

"So where did you steer the investigation next, DI Beaumont?" Smith asked.

George stirred. "We looked into family and friends, as usual, sir," George explained. "Specifically Amanda's twin brothers,

Damon and Declan Lomax, twenty-four, from Middleton. We don't think they're involved now, but like Amanda, they were focused on the life insurance aspect, which we found suspicious. DC Blackburn has tracked their phones and vehicles, and they weren't in the area on the morning Paxton Cole died or in the days preceding it."

"And I take it you personally interviewed Amanda Cole yourself?" Sadiq asked, looking down at the transcripts.

George cleared his throat. "Correct, sir. Because we had Paxton's bank statements, we went into detail about his deposits to various gambling websites. She knew he was gambling, but not quite to the extent that he lost thousands per day. Amanda also confirmed that Paxton would beat her if she wanted to spend money, but DS Wood noticed she was wearing extremely expensive designer gear, so that didn't quite add up. She also had no idea about the direct deposit of two million pounds and that he'd loaned that from somebody." He shrugged. "Dr Shah also had no new information for us. She was working her way through the squad and staff, but everybody she spoke to said he seemed fine."

There was a short silence, and so Sadiq asked, "DI White did a press conference and set up an appeal, correct?"

"That's right, sir." George scratched his chin. "But we got nothing from it, so I decided to set up an anniversary visit. The result of that was a lead from a woman named Adela Devons. She'd taken a picture of Paxton Cole surrounded by three men in black suits a week before his death. DC Jay Scott recognised one of the men as Colby Raggett. So we interviewed Colby Raggett at his home, who not only confirmed the name of his boss as Jürgen Schmidt but also confirmed that Paxton Cole did, in fact, owe Schmidt a lot of money. However, he was adamant he didn't know the other man in the image, and we're still looking into that." George took a long drink from his cup. "I then decided to visit Schmidt at his home. He denied everything until I mentioned the picture, not that it mattered because we've got Raggett's confession on tape."

"That's good. I'd quite like to listen to that, George," Sadiq said, nodding.

"However," George added, "Jürgen Schmidt had turned from a lead to nothing during the space of a couple of hours as the alibis began arriving. The team verified everything twice and had even checked out most of his known associates."

George took another drink. "And lastly, throughout today, DC Scott and DC Blackburn have even triangulated their phone data and, with DS Williams' help, checked ANPR data for their vehicles. That, along with our ongoing enquiries, has not placed Schmidt nor his associates near Wetherby and Linton on the morning Paxton Cole died or in the days preceding it."

"So what do you think, George?" the DCS asked, smiling.

He was surprised. The DCS didn't usually want his opinion, just the facts. "I'll be honest, sir, it looks like a suicide. However, there's just something that doesn't feel right. What that is, though, I don't know. I guess I'll find out once the toxicology comes back."

"I'll look into getting that fast-tracked for you, George," the DCS said.

* * *

It wasn't surprising, but the next day, after discussing the entire case with Detective Chief Superintendent Sadiq, Detective Superintendent Jim Smith had decided to close down the Paxton Cole case, which Mrs Amanda Cole, the deceased's wife, wasn't too pleased about. When she found out, Amanda headed to the station and pleaded with George's superior to keep the case open and investigate it being something other than suicide.

George understood. She'd come away with nothing once the death was officially ruled a suicide.

Chapter Eleven

wo days later

Edmund Flathers groaned as he fell to his knees, the pain contracting every muscle in his body as he desperately tried to expel whatever was doing this to his body. But it was far too late.

He groaned as shock waves plagued him once more. Beads of sweat dripped from his pores. Then the headache started—a blinding pain. Before the drowsiness hit, it was all-encompassing, as if the shadows were swallowing him up. It had all started with a dry mouth and blurred vision.

Edmund fumbled through his pockets to reach his mobile phone, but despite his best efforts, that's when the confusion kicked in. Before him, the blackening kitchen blurred in and out of focus, and as he blinked to fight away the darkness, it only made him dizzier.

He slipped onto his side, his head low against the floor, the cool laminate a momentary relief against the flames that surged through him. With each breath, Edmund took, his breath seemed to stutter and then stall, like a car in the winter. The cold air burnt his throat, and he wanted to scream out in pain, but instead, he gulped down the air desperately, the searing pain helping him fight against the suffocating shadows.

As if like a puppet with its strings cut, when Edmund tried to stand, his world turned sideways, and he crashed to the ground. His heartbeat began to beat harder and faster now as if it rose towards the final crescendo. Edmund Flathers lay there, the laminate cold and wet against his cheek, blinking against his fading vision.

The piece of music that was his life was about to end, and the shadows swamped him.

Chapter Twelve

Because the Paxton Cole case had been officially closed, George had more time to spend on other cases. Specifically, the unexplained death of a man named Edmund Flathers, who lived in Hunslet, that had just landed on his desk. George wasn't sure what to make of the situation and wondered why the Homicide and Major Enquiry Team were even involved. Usually, they were only called if there was something obvious to go on. A knife wound. A blow to the head. A missing child. Drugs. Kidnapping. That kind of thing.

When George arrived at the outer cordon, he recognised the area; behind him and to the left was the Middleton Railway, where his paternal grandparents had regularly taken him as a child. Behind him was a park that was once a lake. He'd seen pictures of it as a child. His grandma had always liked local history and often showed him pictures of what south Leeds used to look like.

He showed his warrant card to an officer at the cordon and headed towards the small back-to-back, red-bricked terraces typical of the area. The street was filled with cars that lined each side of the road, and George imagined parking was a nightmare. Moreover, with the ambulance parked outside the property, the street made George feel claustrophobic.

Isabella was standing by the front door, fully dressed in a white paper suit, waiting for him, looking a bit queasy.

George pulled out his warrant card and flashed it at the PC who guarded the cordon, who nodded and provided George with a suit. The gate that led into a tiny garden was broken. The garden was lined with broken flagstones and a tangle of weeds. The downstairs windows revealed stained net curtains, and George could see movement within. Upstairs, one window was boarded up. He made a mental note to ask who had broken the window.

Isabella groaned. "Do you mind if I give the body a miss, George?" she asked. "Feeling a bit ropey today. I think I ate something dodgy."

"Do you need to go home?" George asked, his face full of concern.

"No. of course not," Isabella insisted. "I'm fine. I just– I just don't fancy getting up close to the body today."

"Right. Fine, DS Wood." He winked. Let me know if you start to feel worse, OK?"

As George went to enter, they bumped into two paramedics. The older one of the two, a slim man with only one ear, nodded a greeting before saying, "Detective?" George was sure he had a South African accent.

George flashed his warrant card and introduced himself. "What have we got then?"

The South African pulled down his mask and stripped off his gloves. "We have a deceased IC1 male, aged in his mid to late thirties, who, unfortunately, we couldn't resuscitate. You need a pathologist to advise on the cause of death because, to be frank with you, we have no idea, do we, Bill?" He looked at his younger colleague, who shook his head. "His wife's in there. Distraught as you can imagine."

George thanked the man and then headed towards the kitchen where the wife was sitting at a kitchen table, sobbing, her words incoherent as she spoke into a mobile phone. The hallway was lined with tall, potted plants that George didn't recognise. They looked nice, though. He turned to Isabella, who was watching him from outside, and nodded towards the wife. George knew she'd be able to tease out more info than he would. Plus, he wanted to see the scene.

A tap on the shoulder caused George to turn to find Bill, the younger paramedic standing there. "Before we go, I thought you should know we called you here because the death is suspicious." George raised his brows, inviting the young man to continue. "The man's pupils were dilated, and despite the cold temperature, his entire body was slick with sweat. I think he died of some kind of illness, but his wife said he was, and I quote, 'as fit as a fiddle'." Bill shrugged and George thanked him. "Oh, and the boss," Bill said, pointing towards his older colleague, "says sorry for contaminating the crime scene. Preservation of life comes first, you know?"

George nodded and stepped into the kitchen. It would be Lindsey Yardley or one of her SOCOs who would end up being pissed off by the mess, not him.

The smell of death hit George as soon as he passed into the living room, so he breathed shallowly through his mouth. *No wonder Isabella hadn't wanted to be in here,* he thought. He stared down at the man on the floor. He was of average height and build, with the beginnings of a beer belly, and had red hair. Edmund Flathers, the DSU had told him. A man roughly George's age, though probably a few years older. Definitely closer to forty than George was.

Besides Edmund lying at an awkward angle, there was nothing untoward that George could see. He bent down to look at the man's face, remembering what the paramedic had said about Edmund's eyes, and immediately regretted it. The dead man's face was contorted, a tribute to whatever suffering he'd endured. Whatever had killed him must have been pure agony.

A leather wallet and one of those folding mobile phones lay discarded next to him. George noticed Wood had finished and was on her way back outside, so he followed her. "So what do we know?"

"His wife called nine-nine-nine and asked for an ambulance as she came home to find her husband unresponsive. That was approximately an hour ago."

"Has she touched the body?"

"Only to check for a pulse," Wood explained, and George raised his brows. "There wasn't one."

"When did she see him last?"

"This morning, George, before she left for work at half-nine. She said he seemed in good health then."

"Strange," George said, and Wood nodded her head. "Whatever it was, he didn't pass gently. Look at the agony on his face."

Wood closed her eyes. "Apparently, Dr Ross is on his way down."

Taking another small breath through his mouth to try and minimise the lingering smell of death in his nostrils, George shifted his weight from one foot to the other. "Of course he is. I forgot that DCS Sadiq has started making pathologists attend crime scenes." He scratched his beard. "Then again, we have Dr Yardley, so I wonder whether he'll show up." Despite being a crime scene manager, Lindsey Yardley was a qualified pathologist who sometimes performed post-mortems for them.

George stepped back inside and took in the view. It seemed Edmund or his wife were fond of plants. Wood saw George looking. "They have a greenhouse in the back garden." She grinned and touched one of the leaves. "I'd have killed these plants if this were me. I'm bloody useless, always forgetting to water them."

George made a mental note to buy her some flowers. Since living together, they had fallen into a bit of a... rut. He hated thinking of it that way, but that's precisely what it was. They were both busy with their careers, with Smith borrowing her regularly to lead teams of detective constables from other teams back at the station. George reckoned he was priming her for DI, which made sense as she had already done the exams. But it was very rare for two DIs to be on the same team, especially in the HMET. That meant Smith was splitting them up or was thinking about promoting him. "Did you get much from Mrs Flathers?"

"Her name's Sally and she's thirty-three.

Thirty-three? George thought the slim, blonde woman looked slightly older than thirty-three, but then she *had* just lost her husband.

"She works for Aldi just up the road. So it's just the two of them that live here. She found Edmund, or Eddy as she calls him when she got in and noticed the house was silent. That was unusual for a Sunday afternoon, as Eddy would usually watch the football on TV with a beer or a cider." She took a deep breath. "Then Sally noticed the smell, and when she went into the living room, she noticed Eddy was on the floor and called an ambulance straight away."

"Tell me what you found out about Edmund," George said.

"Aged thirty and, according to his wife, had no pre-existing medical conditions."

George thought it may have been undiagnosed or even perhaps had come into contact with something he was allergic to. He made a mental note to ask Lindsey to check for any food he'd recently eaten. It could also have been cancer, he thought. He had a family member, a cousin, who works as a carer in Wakefield. She recently told him she only worked for a man for a week before he died. It was harrowing how quickly illness could take you.

"He worked for a company named T. Myles Delivery Experts. It sounded familiar, so I did a Google search."

"It's where Tony Shaw worked," George said, and Wood nodded. "Near the stadium, right?" They'd visited the warehouse during the Bone Saw Ripper case.

"Right."

"Did you notice anything in the kitchen? Like a dirty plate with remnants of his dinner?"

"Nothing," Wood said, confirming what George had already assumed. "There are washed dishes and cups stacked to dry, though." She shrugged. "Nothing suspicious that I could see."

George nodded and looked around the living room, seeing a glass with a golden liquid in it. He remembered what Wood said about Edmund being partial to a beer or a cider whilst he was sure it was whisky in the glass. Once Lindsey arrived, he'd ask her to take it for evidence. Perhaps toxicology could tell them something, though he doubted it. There was nothing out of the ordinary and nothing suspicious, apart from the fact there was a dead man who appeared to have suffered an agonisingly inexplicable death. George would be relying heavily on the SOC team and pathology to get to the bottom of it.

"No signs of forced entry at all then?" George asked, and Wood shook her head. They had to make sure that someone else hadn't done it, even if that possibility already seemed slim.

"No windows left open, no locks busted? You know the drill."

"Yeah, which is why I know, George," Wood said with a wink. "I walked around the house with Sergeant Greenwood before you got here, both of us suited up. I think it's why I felt so queasy. Plus, there's no sign of foul play regarding the deceased."

"Aye, which is making this rather difficult." George stuck his tongue through his teeth. It was the face he pulled when he was frustrated, and Isabella found it rather cute. "Did you ask Mrs Flathers what Edmund was up to today before he died?"

"Playing his PlayStation apparently. With the death of Paxton Cole, the FIFA football game removed him, and he needed to try and win back some coins or something."

She shrugged, but George knew exactly what she was saying. EA, the game's creators, respectfully removed players from the database and their FIFA Ultimate Team mode when a player passed away. With Paxton being a decent striker playing for a decent team, he would have been worth a lot of coins. Instead, upon death, Paxton would have been untradable and worth nothing. George thought it strange that Paxton was still being brought up weeks after his death.

"Sally did mention he usually orders a takeaway when he has a gaming day because, in her words, 'he can't be arsed to cook'."

George made another mental note to ask Lindsey to look into it. He also asked Wood to speak with Mrs Flathers before they left for access to their bank accounts. Then, unless he paid cash, they'd be able to figure out his last meal, not that George thought Edmund had died from food poisoning. They didn't have much else to go on.

A banging on the door interrupted both detectives, and Mrs Flathers hovered by the door, her eyes closed. "I'll get it, Mrs Flathers," George said, "you go back and sit in the kitchen, OK?"

She turned on her heel as George opened the door to Lindsey Yardley and one of his least-favourite colleagues, SOCO Hayden Wyatt. "He's in the living room," George said. The blond American grinned as he followed Lindsey into the living room, putting his mask on and pulling his paper hood up.

Before shutting the door, George glanced outside to find another vehicle had been allowed through the cordon. It was there to take the body away to the mortuary to be examined by Dr Ross and his pathology team. It probably meant the elderly pathologist wasn't coming. Still, he knew they would be speaking soon as George was keen to understand what had happened because, as far as he could see, Edmund Flathers had died inexplicably. And George was baffled.

Chapter Thirteen

The following morning, George reluctantly hauled himself out of bed, the freezing, dark January mornings not helping. Of course, it didn't help that Isabella was beside him, wrapped up to the neck, looking gorgeous. She wasn't in until later, which was good, considering she'd been up about a hundred times in the night to go to the toilet.

After a hot shower and two mugs of coffee, George finally felt awake enough to drive from Morley into the station. But before he found his keys, his mobile phone rang.

"George, it's Dr Ross." The voice that came from out of the speaker sounded stressed. "I'm not happy about this body that you sent me."

George said nothing. Last night, before coming home, he and Wood had combed through the meagre details they had so far, loading up the Big Board in a separate Incident Room with the information they'd need to make a running start if it turned out foul play had been involved in Edmund Flathers' death. So he understood Ross' stress.

"I'd estimate the time of death to be around two yesterday afternoon though I'd probably say between one and three to be more confident," Dr Ross said.

Mrs Flathers was at work between ten and four, which Wood had confirmed last night by getting in touch with her manager.

"I can't determine an exact cause of death yet, son," the pathologist said, "but it looks like respiratory failure. The paramedics noted that he had symptoms inconsistent with a typical non-suspicious death. Other than that, there's nothing else to tell you. Nothing obvious at first glance, anyway."

Whilst he was listening, George's yawn got the better of him, and his feeble attempt to suppress it only made it longer and more powerful.

"Are you OK, son?" Dr Ross asked. "Late night?"

"Not really," George said. "Isabella's been up and down to the toilet all night. When she wakes, so do I."

"Tell her to go to a doctor, George," Dr Ross eventually said. "Going to the toilet frequently during the night is a sign of diabetes." He went silent for a moment. "Anyway, sorry I don't have more for you, son."

"That's OK. I'll speak with CSI and see if they have anything else for me."

"Aye, you do that. You speak with my Lindsey and see what she found."

George smiled at the fondness in the pathologist's voice for Lindsey Yardley. "Before I go, do you think there's been any foul play?" George asked.

It took Dr Ross almost half a minute to answer, and if not for the heavy breathing George could hear, he would have assumed the elderly doctor had cut him off. "Whilst I'm not happy that Edmund Flathers died by natural causes, I can't say there's been foul play. Not yet. Not definitively, anyway."

A politician's answer, but George expected nothing else. The pathologist was holding his cards close to his chest, and George didn't blame him. "OK, Dr Ross, thanks for that," George said, going to take a sip of coffee before realising his mug was empty. It was one of the worst feelings in the world, and he considered flicking the kettle back on whilst talking to Lindsey. "I'll wait for the full report then. Then, hopefully, you find something for me to go on."

He hung up and closed his eyes as he processed what the pathologist had just said. Dr Ross' full report would be with them by the afternoon with, he hoped, answers.

But first, DI Beaumont opened his contacts and clicked Lindsey's name.

"Dr Yardley speaking."

"Morning, Lindsey. George Beaumont. How are you?"

"I'm good, George; thank you for asking."

"Do you have anything for us?"

"Not much," she said. "I checked out everything you asked. It was whisky in the glass like you thought. We've sent that off to be tested. There were no prints."

"None at all?"

"Nope, which is suspicious." George agreed with her. "A McDonald's paper bag in the bin and a receipt suggesting he'd ordered it via Uber Eats. There are no signs of forced entry nor any signs that anybody else was present. Though, the house has a lot of different prints and DNA. I'm guessing they were a popular couple?"

George grimaced and remembered the conversation he'd had with Mrs Flathers. He'd asked her about the boarded-up window, and she explained they'd had a house party, and one of their friends had fallen into it whilst being incredibly drunk. He explained this to Lindsey.

Even weirder, it turned out that friend was no other than

Paxton Cole. He'd offered to buy them a replacement but, up until his death, hadn't fulfilled his promise.

"There were a few fries left in that bag, and we found the burger box so we can test samples in case there's anything relevant there. But honestly, there's nothing really to go on. Are you sure this is murder?"

"No, and that's exactly the issue," George said. He thought about the contorted look on Edmund's face and how he looked in agony. Then, George thought about what Dr Ross had just said. "But I'm also not sure he died of natural causes, so it must remain suspicious. DSU Smith ordered us to investigate, so here we are." The problem was that forensics and pathology had turned up nothing so far, pointing to no foul play. Usually, twelve hours into a case, they had something to go on, but this time they had nothing other than that Mr Flathers had died suddenly and in agony.

* * *

With a coffee in hand, George pushed his way into the office, only to be met by a smiling DC Jason Scott.

"Morning, boss," Jay said. He waited for the DI to nod his head before he bent his head down and continued making notes at his desk.

George put his belongings in his office, then grabbed an empty chair and wheeled it towards Jay. "Can you please request Flathers' medical records for me, Jay?"

"Sure thing, boss," Jay said as DS Luke Mason also rolled his chair over.

"Dr Ross says he can't see anything obvious, but he's not finished with the PM yet, so who knows? Same for the SOC team. Yardley hasn't got anything." Tashan entered the office, stretching. George was sure the lad was getting taller each day. He nodded the young man over to Jay's desk. It was just the four of them until Wood arrived later. "So, I think Flathers' death was via natural causes." He was pretty sure there was an unknown medical condition at play, though he didn't know what that was. "Anybody got anything to share?" He'd left instructions for them in the shared inbox.

"Got Flathers' criminal record, boss." Jay grinned and ran a hand through his hair. It was getting longer, and he was starting to tie it up in a Man Bun. George thought it looked ridiculous, but Isabella had said it suited the young man. He hated to admit it, but that had made him jealous. It also made him consider his own hairstyle. Did he change it up or leave it?

"You seen this, sir?" Tashan asked, breaking George out of his own head. He looked at Tashan's screen to find he was on a search engine, looking for more details. Various newspaper articles from ten years ago populated the screen. Tashan clicked on the top one and then read the article. "Looks like a woman named Lena Schneider, an Austrian national visiting England, died from a drug overdose, and Edmund Flathers was accused of supplying them."

"Did he do it?"

"Dunno, sir," Tashan said. "It says here not guilty."

"That doesn't mean he didn't supply them, though. It just means they didn't have the evidence to convict," Jay added.

"True," George agreed. "But, Flathers was found not guilty in a court of law, and that's all we have to go on. Looking at the PNC, Flathers has no other criminal history, not even any points on his licence, which makes sense as he drives for a job."

"It could be possible he was in the wrong place at the wrong time," Tashan explained. "They only had one witness, and she placed Flathers at the scene. The CCTV was too blurry, though. So it could have been somebody else."

George looked at the photo on Flathers' driving licence and the CCTV footage. There was no way to be sure whether it was the same man. And they would never know because both parties had passed. What he did know, though, was that the man looking up at him from the photo looked entirely different to the agony-contorted face he had encountered the previous evening. Did Flathers supply the drugs that killed Lena Schneider?

George didn't know. Life was so rarely black and white. But, whatever had happened a decade ago did not change the facts of now. Edmund Flathers had died, and DI Beaumont and his team were duty-bound to investigate his death. And fairly, too. Because he was innocent until proven guilty. Right?

George wasn't sure but looked at his team. "Find out more about Lena Schneider, yeah? I want to speak with her family."

All three detectives nodded at their boss and returned to their respective desks. Then Luke turned back. "Sergeant Greenwood and his Uniforms are on house-to-house today, son. I'll let you know if they find anything."

"Cheers, Luke," George said as he headed towards his own office. He needed to update HOLMES, but it wasn't as easy as just logging in any more. They had to allocate actions to a detective, in this case, DS Yolanda Williams, who would write everything up and send it to another detective, the receiver, who would read it and raise any actions required. The receiver would then send it to the indexers, who would type it up on HOLMES so they could search through it when needed. It sounded boring, but it meant George and his team could focus on finding criminals rather than typing up reports and filing them.

He'd do that until Wood got in, and then they'd go and see Edmund's boss.

Chapter Fourteen

Isabella Wood turned the radio off to answer her phone whilst George drove. They were on their way to see Flathers' boss, Tommy Myles, a confident, cocky man they'd met during the Bone Saw Ripper case. According to Mrs Flathers, Tommy and Eddy were excellent friends and often went to football together. It would kill two birds with one stone, especially considering the complete lack of leads they had thus far.

Steaming travel cups of coffee sat in the cupholders between them from the McDonald's on their route. George yawned as he listened to DC Scott relay the details to Wood, who had put him on speaker.

"Basically, his wife was right, DS Wood," Jay confirmed. His wife had reported Edmund had no health problems, and sure enough, no health conditions were showing on the medical report. Not that related to his death, anyway. "Only surgery he had was as a kid. His tonsils. Other than that, his only medication was Omeprazole for reflux."

"Shit." After the criminal record they'd found, George had been hoping for an easy solution. Yet he should have known better. "No allergies or anything, Jay?"

"No, boss. Nothing. Not even hay fever."

CHAPTER FOURTEEN

George sighed. He was truly stumped. And terrified, too. Whatever killed Edmund Flathers was dangerous, and he needed answers.

***

DI Beaumont slowed his Mercedes and turned into the centre of the industrial estate near South Leeds Stadium, remembering the address from a year ago. The place was ugly with its orange brick buildings that contrasted against the newer blue and silver prefab warehouses that were made of stone and corrugated metal.

George knew that the courier company Edmund Flathers worked for was based out of one of the newer prefabs. New signage was fixed on the spiked metal fencing, proudly displaying the words T. Myles Delivery Experts on a white background in blue writing. Various sized delivery vans clogged the yard, though the road leading up to a large warehouse with huge open roller doors was kept clear, which was where the vans were parked up to be loaded or unloaded.

George parked on the road outside due to the lack of visitor parking. The pair got out and walked through the open gates. It was freezing, and he could smell fuel in the air. George hated these kinds of places, preferring to be out in the open with nature around him.

Wood took the lead, directing George towards the small building to the right of the warehouse, which contained the reception and back office. She held the door for him, and smiled at George as he entered.

Inside was the same elderly woman waiting behind the desk as last year. "DI Beaumont and DS Wood here to see Tommy

Myles." They both held out their warrant cards.

She raised a brow at the two detectives. A look of recollection, perhaps? Wood, her brown hair in loose curls, said nothing and stared through the rude woman. George did the same with a slight smirk on his face. The silence lasted for no more than thirty seconds but must have felt like a lifetime for the older lady as she soon made a quick call to Tommy. Then, with a quiet voice, she explained two detectives were here to see him. Wood grinned as the lady hung up.

"OK, follow me," she said as she opened a waist-height wooden swinging door and moved to the side to allow them in. "He's upstairs in his office. You know the way." It wasn't a question.

They entered and headed up the steps, the sound of the pattering rain on the metal familiar to George. So far, January had been one of the driest on record but also one of the coldest. In fact, George was adamant it was colder inside than it was outside, an impressive feat to be sure, and was glad he wore a coat.

The door was open this time, so they entered, the golden plaque on the door stating 'Tommy Myles CEO' catching George's eye again.

Wearing a suit this time, Tommy Myles stood up, his balding head glinting in the harsh light. He'd lost some weight and built more muscle. He offered a tattooed arm and hand to George and Wood, crushing George's hand and lightly shaking Wood's.

"Despite the circumstances, it's nice to see you both again," Myles said in his baritone Yorkshire accent. Then, when neither George nor Wood spoke, Myles clarified, "I heard what happened to Eddy." He shook his head. "Sally called me. I can't believe it, I only saw him on Saturday, and he seemed absolutely fine."

George nodded, walked past Myles and then took a seat. Wood followed suit. They sat there in silence, waiting for Tommy to take his seat. When he did, George said, "We have a few questions to try and understand what happened to Edmund Flathers. OK?"

Tommy's face twisted as he looked down at George, horrified. "So you think somebody killed him then?" George didn't answer. He was the one asking questions, not Tommy Myles. "I mean, from how sudden it was and from what little Sally told me, I assumed it was an accident. A heart attack, or a sudden illness or something. But you're here, asking questions."

George met Tommy's eyes. "I'm afraid we can't comment on an ongoing investigation, Mr Myles, but we are investigating his death." Tommy nodded. "How long did you know Edmund?"

Myles ignored the question and turned to Wood. "Congratulations, who's the lucky guy?" Then he held up his hands. "Or girl?"

"Excuse me?" Wood asked.

Tommy didn't take his eyes away from Wood. He was leering at her, and whilst George wasn't usually jealous, he clenched his fists, counting down from ten in his head.

Tommy pointed at the engagement ring. "You didn't have that on last year." Then he shrugged.

"Let's get back to Edmund Flathers, shall we?" George cut in, trying to hide the annoyance on his face. "How long did you know him?"

"Since we were kids, mate. We were next-door neighbours. Thick as thieves. It's why I gave him a job despite his criminal record."

"You knew about that then?" Myles nodded. "But he was found not guilty," Wood said.

He grinned at her. "True, but that stain does not ever go away. He couldn't get a job anywhere with that on his record."

"Did he ever talk to you about the accusations?" Wood asked.

Myles thought about it for a moment, then shook his head. "No, not really. He tried his best just to get on with life and move on. But whenever I asked, he was adamant he was innocent." He shrugged. "As I said, we've been mates since we were kids."

"The news of his passing must have been hard on you, then," George said.

The bald man took in a deep breath. "Correct."

Wood said, "We're trying to build a picture of Edmund's life. What can you tell us about him?"

Tommy nodded but said nothing. His eyes showed a sadness George didn't expect. Perhaps the guy had feelings, after all. "Edmund had a day off yesterday, is that right?"

"Aye, though I'd have liked him in, truth be told." Tommy winced and shook his head. "We're always swamped in January. I think I told you this last year?"

George nodded. "We need a list of his weekly hours and anybody he worked with."

"Of course. Let me email Patty. She'll print December and January out for you."

The muscled man began clacking away at his computer, and George asked another question. "You mentioned earlier that Edmund seemed alright to you?" Tommy looked up and nodded. "So there was nothing different about his appearance or his behaviour?"

"Nothing that I noticed, no. Ed was delivering parcels all day on Saturday, and when he came back to clock out, he was laughing and joking with the other lads and lasses."

"So, no injuries or illnesses that you know about?"

"Nope." Tommy shook his head emphatically. "Sorry."

"When was the last time you saw him socially?" Wood asked.

Tommy leaned heavily on the back of his chair, the plastic straining under the weight of his muscle. "A couple of weeks ago. It was a cup game at the stadium. We saw our team win and then had a few beers. We've been so busy. Which is normal." He scratched his chin. "We're jam-packed from the end of October until the end of January. Plus, the fucking Royal Mail had some strike days, if you remember?" George and Wood nodded. "That put pressure on us, too."

George was about to ask another question when Tommy pulled out his mobile. He showed George and Wood something with a QR code on it. "We got tickets for the midweek cup game. It's been rearranged because of what happened to Paxton Cole. We were going to get there early to sign the book of condolence to pay our respects. Eddy said to do it online, but I wanted to go in person. You do know that Eddy was close with Cole. Right?"

They did not. "What do you mean by close?" George asked.

"I'm not sure it's any of my business to tell you, is it?" Tommy said, his tone defensive.

"Then why mention it at all?" Wood asked. "We need to know everything about Edmund leading up to his death." Maybe Edmund was so affected by Cole's death that he, too, took his own life. She wasn't sure, but it was feasible, though how he took his own life was a mystery. "Was Eddy affected by Paxton Cole's death?"

Myles had dark shadows under his eyes. As George watched,

the man blinked rapidly as if trying to keep himself awake. "Of course, he was. We all were. He was a brilliant player. But you know, Eddy was affected most because they were friends. Have been for years."

George sent a text to Luke asking him to look into connections between Cole and Flathers. He wanted to know everything there was to know about their relationship. "Anything you can tell us about Paxton and Edmund would be great. Thanks."

Tommy glanced at him, then back to Wood, as though confused that they had changed direction and George had taken charge again. "Erm..." Tommy looked like he didn't have much more to say. Then he shrugged. "He didn't share much about Paxton, to be honest. Said the man liked his privacy, which was understandable. He'd get us amazing tickets whenever we asked, though. And I know for a fact Eddy was invited up to their house in Linton regularly. I think the Flathers even had Christmas dinner with the Coles. Sally will know more."

George thought it was strange they hadn't known about the connection before. But then, why would they have? They didn't know about Edmund Flathers until yesterday evening. Yet if the man was as close to Cole as Myles was saying he was, then why hadn't they interviewed him and his wife? Why hadn't Dr Shah interviewed them for the psychological autopsy? It didn't make sense. Somehow, they'd dropped the ball, and George wondered whether the two deaths were connected.

A knock at the door interrupted George's thoughts. It was Patty with the printouts. Myles thanked her, and George asked his final question. "Is there anything else you can tell us that might be able to help us shed any light on what happened to Edmund?"

CHAPTER FOURTEEN

Tommy looked down and cleared his throat, his eyes closed. "No. The man was as right as rain Saturday. Sorry. But I'd go and speak to Sean Bishop. They were both off yesterday and were going to play FIFA together."

Wood asked for his address, and Myles pondered for a moment before providing it.

The lack of information frustrated George, but there was nothing else he could do. There were no more questions to be asked. "OK, well, thank you for your time, Mr Myles. We'll be in touch if we need anything else."

Tommy nodded as the two detectives left the office, and George noticed Myles' gaze was troubled as he went.

Chapter Fifteen

Sean Bishop lived in a property at the end of Rosedale Bank in Belle Isle. When the pair of detectives got out of the Mercedes, a voice from under a jacked-up car said, "What do you two want?"

"Sean Bishop?" George asked.

"Depends on who's asking?" A man slid out from under the car, covered in grime. He was tall and wore blue overalls that were tight against his chest. He looked them both up and down before a frown laced with suspicion settled on his face.

It was evident to George that the man didn't like the police, and he wondered why. It was usually due to them having some prior offence or they felt victimised by the police. On the way over, Wood had called the station and asked Tashan to search the PNC for Sean Bishop. George was glad she did because George was immediately suspicious. "We are," George said, and both detectives pulled out their warrant cards. "I'm Detective Inspector Beaumont, and this is Detective Sergeant Wood."

"Must be serious then," the man said, gripping a wrench tightly in his left hand. Then, when neither detective said anything, and the silence became too much, the man added, "Because they didn't send detective constables." He picked up a rag from the floor and wiped his hands on it. A look that George could only describe as whimsical appeared on Wood's face. "It's usually coal-faced detective constables, right? Which means you're here about something serious."

"Correct."

"So you are, Sean Bishop?"

"I am indeed."

Cutting straight to the point, George asked, "I take it you know about Edmund Flathers?"

Bishop's scowl deepened. "Correct."

"We have a few questions we want to ask you about Edmund. His death is currently being treated as unexplained, so we need to try and understand what happened to him." Sean didn't respond, so George continued. "Can you tell us when you last saw Edmund?"

"In person?" George nodded. "Saturday morning. I loaded his van."

"Did he seem alright? Was he acting differently? That sort of thing."

"Aye." Sean cricked his neck, and George saw him tightly grip the wrench once more. "He was fine. We didn't talk much. It's hard work packing the vans, especially with how busy it is."

"Was he injured or ill?"

"You what?" Sean asked. George waited. "No. He was fine."

Like Tommy Myles, it was like trying to draw blood from a stone. "And did you speak to him after that?"

"Yesterday morning. We played a few games of FIFA. Then, he logged off to eat and didn't sign back online." He shrugged. "Is that everything? As you can see, I'm a bit busy."

"Why aren't you at work today?"

"Eh?" Sean said and narrowed his eyes at George.

"Why aren't you at work today?" George asked once more.

"Worked too many hours," retorted Sean, his glare hardening again. "Universal Credit top up my wages, so any overtime I get paid reduces that. I prefer to have the days off to work on this fucking bastard car."

"Fair enough." George was losing patience. "So you two didn't talk whilst loading his van on Saturday?"

"Yes."

"Yes, you did, or yes, you didn't. Which is it?" Wood asked.

Sean's brows furrowed. He paused for a long moment. "Yes, we did talk." Wood raised her brows, inviting Sean to continue. He eventually got the message and said, "The same old shit, really. What most men talk about at work." He shrugged. "We like to moan about the job, our women, and how shit our footie teams are doing."

Wood's glance flicked from Sean to George, and he immediately knew she would be asking him how true Sean's words were later. He gave her a grin, then turned to Bishop, tactfully ignoring the provoking words. But it still didn't stop George from provoking the grubby giant. "How are you? You feeling OK?"

"Aye, grand. Why?" George and Wood said nothing. They could see the thoughts whirring around his mind. "Is it because Ed was ill?"

"Was he ill?" Wood asked.

"Well, no. Ed was fine. But Tommy told me about his death. It's suspicious, right? How he died? Fit people don't just drop dead suddenly, right?"

"Right, so if you're fine now and you haven't been ill, I wouldn't worry," George said. "But you're sure Mr Flathers was healthy?"

"Correct. He kicked my arse on FIFA. I've played him when he's had a cold, and he was woeful. So I'm telling you he was fine."

"And then he logged out for dinner?" George asked.

Sean drew himself tall and nodded. "Yeah, he got a Maccie's delivered, I think."

All the facts seemed to fit nicely, and George didn't think Bishop was lying. "Is there anything else at all you can tell us that might help with our investigation?" George eventually asked.

Wood added. "We appreciate how difficult this is for you, considering your friend has just passed, but we need to understand what happened to Edmund. If not for Sally's sake, then for your own. And Tommy's."

Sean gritted his teeth, but he nodded. "Yeah, I get that, but I don't know anything else. Honest. We loaded up his van on Saturday, played FIFA yesterday, and then I found out about his death this morning."

"Did Edmund ever share any sensitive information with you?" George asked. Sean frowned, so George rephrased his question. "Did he ever tell you about his criminal record?"

A light relief spread across Bishop's face. "Aye, but he was found not guilty, right?"

"Correct."

"You think that poor lassie's family killed him then?"

George had certainly considered that possibility and had DS Luke Mason working on it. The problem was Lena Schneider's known surviving family all lived in Austria, and according to immigration, not one of them had ever visited England. "We're looking into it, aye."

He grinned at George. "Good. Poor guy suffered because of it, you know? A false accusation like that." Bishop shrugged once more. "He couldn't get a job anywhere with that on his record."

"Was he angry about that, do you think?" George asked.

Bishop thought about it for a moment, then shook his head. "No, I don't believe so. He tried his best just to get on with life and move on. Because he was innocent."

"Right, OK," George said, stepping backwards. "Thanks for your help, Mr Bishop. We'll leave you to fix your car, but we'll be in touch." The tone of George's words was firmer than he'd intended, but when Sean nodded, George was glad. Finally, the man had gotten the message.

"I don't like him at all," Wood said as they sat in the car. "There's something off about him."

"Yeah, I know what you mean," George replied. "I get the feeling he doesn't like us either. The police, I mean. You know how people are. We're all the same to them, and they become guarded. Despite trying to help, I suppose it's hard for people to shake that suspicion and distrust. Let's go and speak with Mrs Flathers whilst we're over this way, anyway." George said as he yawned. "She's at her sister's in Middleton."

* * *

On the way to see Sally Flathers, George's mood brightened when Dr Ross' name flashed up on the screen, and the radio cut off. "Hiya, Dr Ross. Got some good news for me?" George asked, heading up Belle Isle Road.

"Depends on what you mean by good news, son." Silence permeated the car. "My theory is that Mr Flathers was poisoned."

"Poisoned?" George indicated right at the circus, easing off the accelerator as he coasted down Winrose Drive.

"Aye, son. I can find absolutely nothing medical that would have caused Edmund Flathers to die in the way he did. From the pupil dilation, the lack of wounds and the abrupt nature of his death, it's the only conclusion I can draw at this point. I've taken biopsies from his lungs, but it doesn't look like cancer to me." George said nothing, his mind flitting from theory to theory. "This is just a theory, son, and by poisoning, I don't mean the kind you see on TV. I mean that Mr Flathers appears to have encountered or ingested a toxic substance."

"Such as?" George left the question hanging.

"No clue, son." George's heart sank. "I've sent samples off for a full toxicology report, of course, but honestly, as you know, with Mr Cole's death, it could take weeks."

George indicated right to head up the Ring Road, passing by Asda. "Could the deaths be related?"

"Until the toxicology reports are back, I wouldn't know, son. I'm sorry." George grunted thanks. "I'll keep hounding toxicology, son. Don't you worry."

Despite his disappointment, George managed to inject some warmth into his tone. "As always, Dr Ross, it's been a pleasure. Thanks so much."

"Poisoned?" Wood questioned as George hung up.

"Seems like it," George replied grimly.

Wood shook her head. "What, like arsenic or something?"

George sighed. "Dunno. I doubt it, though. I think Dr Ross would have known if it was arsenic poisoning. This is something else." Wood shivered. "You OK?"

"It's just bloody terrifying, George. The medical professional doesn't even know what it is. And not only that, but it also seems you can't even see it, and it could kill you."

"True, though there's plenty of things we *can* see that can kill us too."

Wood frowned and then shook her head. "Well, isn't that a cheerful thought for a Monday afternoon?"

Chapter Sixteen

George and Wood sat in the Mercedes around the corner from Middleton Park Grove, where Sally Flathers' sister lived and where Sally was staying for a few days whilst CSI searched her house. George was stuck on the Ring Road, about seven vehicles back from the traffic lights, cursing. Recently, Middleton had started getting very busy. The sky was alive with fat blobs of rain that thundered down against the windscreen before being squealed away by the wipers.

Neither detective had spoken since they'd got in the car and driven away, and neither was in the mood to start. Not until Wood said, "Can you open a window, George? I feel a bit sick."

George nodded, clicked the button to wind down the window, and cursed when the back window began to slide down, the whir of the motor like a strangled cat in the silence. He cursed again and fumbled with the switches until Wood's window wound down. She looked across at her fiancé and grinned. He was stressed. And rightly so. Sally Flathers wasn't the font of information George had expected or required.

When they'd asked about Edmund's financial situation, she'd told them, between tears, "I knew Tommy had lent us money, but he paid Tommy back though, right?"

When the two detectives deferred the question back to her,

she looked a bit perplexed and assured them that they'd paid Myles back. This was the first they'd heard about any money being owed. So, fancying his chances, George decided to ask about Sean Bishop.

"That's right," she'd said, more resigned this time. "Ed and Sean had, for a while, fallen out over that. But, unfortunately, Ed was a stubborn git, and he was making Sean hang on. I wanted to pay him back straight away, even started working extra shifts. We ended up arguing about it, to be honest. But as I said, Ed was a stubborn man."

Wood had asked the frail woman if she knew whether Edmund owed money to anybody else, and she advised she didn't. As far as she knew, only Tommy and Sean were owed money, and again, she assumed Tommy had been paid.

Obviously, they were hoping for more. Much more. George had even wondered whether Jürgen Schmidt was involved. Maybe there was a further link between Edmund Flathers and Paxton Cole. "Did he owe money to Jürgen Schmidt?" She'd shaken her head. "Do you recognise the name?" George had asked.

"No," she'd said immediately, her voice shaking. "Not that I know of, anyway."

But the way her voice had changed after only the word, 'no', George wasn't convinced. He knew that something was wrong. He could feel it right down in the marrow of his bones. So he'd said, "Are you sure? You're not in any trouble, Sally. We just need to build a picture of what happened to Edmund, and to be able to do that; we need to know what was happening in his life. Who he was speaking to. Do you understand?"

She'd said she understood but knew nothing. Then George had asked her about Edmund's criminal record.

CHAPTER SIXTEEN

She confirmed her husband had been honest with her, but she assumed he was found not guilty. George confirmed that was correct, and like Sean Bishop, she questioned whether Lena Schneider's family were involved in her late husband's death.

George confirmed they were looking into it, but it didn't seem very likely. And Wood questioned why now, after all this time.

Sally couldn't answer that, of course, but did advise she wished the police could have removed the case from his record.

"He couldn't get a job anywhere with that on his record," she'd explained. That was the third time they'd heard that phrase, and whilst she was correct, there was no smoke without a fire. Not when the police were involved.

"Was he angry about that, do you think?" George had asked her.

Sally thought about it for a moment. "No, he got over it. Because he knew he was innocent, my Ed got on with his life as best as he could."

Then she'd had some questions of her own, which she wasn't in any fit state to ask the day she found Edmund.

George had explained as gently as he could that Dr Ross had done the post-mortem, and because the death was being treated as suspicious, they had sent off samples to toxicology. But, unfortunately, that meant a delay in laying him to rest. She'd shed tears at that moment, and they offered an FLO again, but Sally refused.

"I'm not sure if I fully trust Sally," George said as he slid the car into gear, and the car began to creep forward.

"I know what you mean," Wood said. "She seemed better, though. Unlike the other day, she appeared to be holding it together.

George gazed out the window, watching the rain fall as he slowly returned to the station. "True. I think we should have insisted on a liaison, though. I might speak with Cathy Hoskins and see if she can do a visit." He scratched his beard with one hand and tapped the steering wheel with the other. "And tomorrow, we go see Sean Bishop and Tommy Myles again. They never told us Edmund owed them money." He turned to Wood and smiled. "They both have a lot of explaining to do."

* * *

Whilst Wood and George had been gone, Edmund Flathers' phone records had arrived, and DC Jake Scott had started cross-referencing them against possible contacts of interest.

As promised, Dr Ross emailed his provisional post-mortem report through. Still, without the toxicology report, it didn't tell them much other than that Flathers appeared not to have died of natural causes.

All they could do now was question the right people, build up a case and then wait. Despite being marked as URGENT, similar to Paxton Cole's toxicology, it could take weeks to return. All he could keep doing was the same as he was for Cole's: keep calling the lab based in Calder Park in Wakefield and putting pressure on them.

"Tell me you got something, Jay?" George asked as he passed the young DCs desk with a coffee in hand.

Despite there being no need, Jay cleared his throat as if to get his boss' attention. "I've finally gone through all his phone records, boss. Most of the texts are passcode texts from his bank where he's made a purchase, and they need to confirm it's

CHAPTER SIXTEEN

him, service providers, and the usual spam from food places. It looks like he used WhatsApp for personal messages, but I can't access them without his phone."

"I've put DS Williams in charge of Exhibits. Speak with her to get it signed out. Then, take what you need from it."

"Right. Thanks, boss. In terms of phone calls, there's not much there either. It's the usual, though. Like calls to the wife, his mates, and local takeaways. Nothing unusual."

Disappointed, George nodded. "No calls or texts on Sunday, then?"

"None at all, boss."

George chewed on his lip. *Shit.*

"Fine. Good work." George went to move, then stopped. "Check his bank account, please, see if he spent any money on Sunday. Cross-reference that with previous weeks to check for any patterns. The usual, yeah?"

"OK, boss."

George strode back to his office, pissed off with himself and the world. They were getting nowhere fast. He checked his watch. It was 7 pm. It was time to clock off, go home and try and get some rest for tomorrow. Working his arse off until late would do him no good, especially considering they had no leads to follow up on.

But before he did that, he wanted to speak to the owner of the inn at the end of Amanda Cole's road.

* * *

"The Windmill Inn," a chirpy man answered the phone on the other end.

George put the man on speaker. "Good evening, Detective

Inspector Beaumont from the West Yorkshire Police. Could you put the owner on for me, please?"

"Uh, sure, speaking. How can I help?" The man's tone changed immediately, though a call from the police tended to have that effect on people.

"Do you know Amanda Cole?"

"Of course, she's a regular. I was very sad to hear about her husband passing."

"Have you seen her recently?"

There was silence whilst the man contemplated his answer. "She was here on Saturday night."

"With who?"

"I'm not sure. Certainly not who Amanda usually has drinks with."

"So you didn't recognise the person?"

"No. To tell you the truth, we were swamped. I wouldn't have noticed, except I had to ask the man to leave. He and Amanda had a right row. A proper barney. The man was furious, let me tell you."

"Can you describe him to me please, Mr..."

"Hirst. Chey Hirst. He was a ginner of average height and build, with the beginnings of a beer belly."

From the description, it sounded like Edmund Flathers to George and partially confirmed what Sally had told them, though it seemed Edmund hadn't told his wife about the argument. Well, it was that, or Sally had decided to leave that out of their conversation.

With George's attention now piqued, and another link between the two cases, he asked, "Can you tell me what they were arguing about?"

"I didn't hear much, but my wife did. Elaine." His breathing became rapid. "Elaine told me Amanda was asking for money—it was as though he owed it to her."

"Thanks for that. Is there anything else you or your wife noticed that could be helpful?"

"Look, can I ask why you're calling? Amanda is someone we see a lot of. Is she in some kind of trouble?

George was about to advise the man of the usual we can't comment spiel when he stopped himself. "We're currently investigating the death of the man you and your wife saw speaking and arguing with Amanda Cole."

"Bloody hell, what happened to him?"

"I can't comment on that, I'm afraid."

"Right. I understand. Well, I don't have much else to tell you, I'm afraid."

"Thanks for that, Mr Hirst," George said. He wondered how much the Flathers owed the Coles, especially as he knew the Coles were in debt to Jürgen Schmidt. "Before you hang up, could you get your wife on, please? I could do with taking a statement from her, too."

After, as George sat in his Mercedes pondering the case, he knew for sure that Amanda Cole, and possibly Sally Flathers, had some answering to do. So he looked up Trip Lane on his phone and, after realising it would only take about forty minutes to get there, decided to pay Amanda Cole a visit.

***

The hammering at the door was almost as loud as the thundering of Amanda Cole's heart. As she glanced at the windows again, it sounded like the front door was about to come off its hinges. Luckily for her, she'd already drawn all the curtains, and the lights were off. But her car was outside. Which meant they knew she was home.

The door shook again, and Amanda thought about retiring upstairs and locking herself in the bedroom. It didn't matter if they got inside and turned the whole house upside down; she would be safe in her bedroom. Paxton had made sure of that. She was just glad her daughter, Alicia, was at her gran's.

Bang, bang, bang!

For the next ten minutes, the banging was constant but without the usual muffled shouts coming through the letterbox, which she found strange. In the days since Paxton had passed, those bangs had always been followed by threatening words.

From Him.

Because of what Paxton had promised Him.

Amanda sobbed as she got into bed and pulled up the quilt. As a child, hiding under the quilt was akin to Harry Potter's Invisibility Cloak. Despite being mocked for her love of reading, Harry had been her hero. He still was, in many ways. So every year, she pulled out the battered copies her grandma had bought her as a teen and devoured the pages.

The banging continued, and Amanda considered calling the police. They were adamant Paxton had committed suicide, something she knew for sure he hadn't. The police would know what to do about Him. Then they'd see sense. That Paxton was murdered.

Bang, bang, bang!

Amanda Cole cowered, pulling the quilt over her head while crying silent tears, biting against the cushioned duvet to stop any sound from escaping while she waited for Him to leave.

Eventually, the hammering stopped, but she didn't move. Not until the early hours of the morning, when her only choice was to sneak to the loo or, like she had done so many times as a child, wet the bed.

You're a woman now, Amanda, she told herself. *Grow up!*

Yet as she crept along the landing, she didn't dare switch the lights on. She'd also crawled along the bathroom floor, not daring to go near the bathroom window just in case He was still lurking outside, waiting for her. She was unsure whether He was alone or with his lackeys.

But what Amanda Cole did know was that as soon as it was daylight, she was packing a bag and going to her mum's. There was no way she was going to stay here another night.

Chapter Seventeen

The following day, George left Isabella in bed and made the trip to Hunslet to see Tommy Myles again. He knew it would have been easier to phone Myles, but he also knew you could never see the look on someone's face when you spoke over the phone. You couldn't read their body language, either. And both posture and expression could give a lot away.

This time, George had called ahead to check Tommy was around and found the man waiting for him in the car park. As before, George parked by the road, and when the two men met at the gate, he noticed Tommy's concerned expression and clenched fists.

"With Edmund gone, we're proper fucking busy, Detective," he said, ushering George through to the warehouse. "I'll have to lift and talk if that's OK with you?"

George nodded and took out his Dictaphone. "Only if you're OK with me recording the conversation."

"Got nothing to hide, pal." Myles grinned, though the smile didn't meet his eyes. George thought he looked nervous. "Shoot."

"I spoke with Sally Flathers last night, and she mentioned that Edmund owed you money." He let the words sink in as

Tommy frowned. "Why didn't you mention this?"

Tommy picked up a stack of parcels and slid them into the van. "Because the loan was squared away. He paid me it a while back. I didn't think it was important." He shrugged before lifting another stack.

"Fair enough. Were you aware Edmund owed Sean Bishop money, too?"

Myles stopped in his tracks and turned towards George, the parcels straining his bulging arms and shoulders. "Yeah, but wasn't that paid too?"

"You know more than I do," George said with a shrug.

Tommy's face filled with annoyance as he turned away. "Yeah, OK. I knew about it. As far as I'm aware, he was dicking Sean about.

"How do you know that?"

"Because I witnessed Edmund and Sean having a bit of a scrap, alright?"

"A scrap?" Tommy nodded. "About the loan?"

Looking disgruntled as his brows knitted together, Tommy sighed and folded his arms. "Aye. In the warehouse last week." He shuffled uncomfortably and wouldn't meet the detective's eyes. "I had them both up in the office where they made up. Sean gave Ed a proper shiner, though."

George said nothing, inviting the man to continue.

"Ed borrowed money from him and never paid Sean back. The problem was, he went to the Paxton's over Christmas, the footballer's place, and spent an absolute fortune on stuff. Yet he couldn't pay Sean back. That's fucking shifty if you ask me, and Sean thought the same. So if you ask me, Ed deserved the shiner." Tommy then winced. "Sorry, I don't mean to speak ill of the dead."

"Have they come to blows before?"

"Not really." Tommy shrugged. "Not that I know of, anyway."

"What about Sean? Is he the violent type?"

Tommy grimaced as he picked up another heavy-looking parcel, clearly having caught the inference. "Nah. Whilst yeah, he has a bit of a temper, does Sean; they've known each other for years. Like I have. They play video games together. Heart o' gold, that man. He won't have killed Ed if that's what you're asking."

George wasn't asking, but now he would be. "Is Sean in today?"

* * *

"What the fuck do you want now?" Sean Bishop bent to retrieve his rag from the floor, glaring at George, who hovered over him.

"I've come to ask you a few more questions about Edmund Flathers' death."

"I'm busy," said Sean defensively. "I don't have time to chat. I'm back at work tomorrow and need to finish these track rod ends."

Whilst George wasn't sure what a track rod end was, he really didn't give a shit. "A man has died. Your car can wait." Then he paused, locking eyes with Sean. "Or, we can do this at the station?" George raised his brows. "Your choice."

Sean ground his teeth together.

"Good choice," George said, retrieving his Dictaphone. "I'm going to record this conversation." Then, without allowing Sean to reply, he asked, "Tell me about that shiner you gave

Edmund, Sean?"

Sean didn't answer. George waited, trying his best not to shiver against the cold raindrops falling sporadically around them.

"I asked him what he did for Christmas, and he started bragging about Paxton fucking Cole. How Ed had spent over two hundred quid on a turkey. Yet that bastard, he owed me money. It was out of order."

"Whilst I agree he was taking the piss, you've got to appreciate why I'm here." Sean scowled at George. "Why didn't you tell me about this yesterday?"

Sean folded his arms tightly, his biceps bulging. "Because I knew how it would look, OK?" He hawked up and spat at the ground. George grimaced. "I didn't kill him."

"I never said you did, but I find your lack of honesty suspicious. How much did Edmund owe you?"

George waited.

Bishop was not forthcoming.

"Come on, Sean. I've got better things to do, such as finding the killer. Of course, that's if you are being honest with me."

"I am."

"So tell me."

"A grand, OK?" The man clenched his fists. "I got angry when he spent two hundred fucking quid on a fucking turkey, OK?" He paused. "Can you blame me?"

"And you...?"

Sean scoffed and shook his head. "And I punched him in the face ten days ago. So yes. But that's it."

"And did he ever explain why he couldn't pay you back?"

Sean's face darkened. "Aye. I'm not the only person he owes. Or owed..."

"Tommy Myles?"

"Nah, he paid the boss back. Typical, eh?"

The information confirmed George's suspicions, and he filed it away.

"Look, Detective," Sean said as he laughed darkly. "I didn't kill him. Why would I? Killing him wouldn't get me that grand back." He shook his head profusely, then held out his grubby hands, palms up. "I'm not gonna get my money back now, am I?"

"Do you know how Edmund died?"

Sean frowned. "Not really, just that it's being treated as suspicious. Sally's convinced he was poisoned, though."

George nodded his understanding. "We're still investigating the cause."

"Well, there you go. Proves it wasn't me," Sean said. George frowned. "Come on, mate. Does it look like I know anything about poison?"

"I doubt many people do, Sean," George replied flatly.

"Anyway, if that's all, I need to get back to work," Sean said. Then he paused and turned on his heel. "Oh, and if you speak to Sally, tell her I want my money back."

George scoffed. "Her husband just died."

Sean shrugged. "So, she still owes me it."

When George pulled up in Belle Isle fifteen minutes ago, he didn't think there was any way he could like Sean Bishop any less. He was wrong. Sean Bishop was an absolute prick. "If I think you're keeping anything else from me, Sean, then I'll be back," George threatened.

Sean glared at him, then grinned. "Yeah, OK, Arnie. Whatever you say."

CHAPTER SEVENTEEN

* * *

Whilst on the way back to the station, George decided to call Dr Ross for an update. "Got anything for me, Dr Ross?"

"Nothing. Toxicology takes weeks, not days."

"I know, but I really need something."

"I'm pushing as hard as I can, son," Dr Ross assured him, and George didn't doubt it. The pathologist was a good guy, and George thanked him, leaving him to continue his work with the dead.

Next, he called Dr Lindsey Yardley, the head of one of many CSI teams they had at CID, though Lindsey worked solely for the Homicide and Major Enquiry Team, or HMET for short, George served on. They hadn't found much at Flathers' house, even after donning protective gear that looked like they were travelling to the moon.

Lindsey had found nothing they could identify as poisonous, and George leaned back in his seat as he eased the car down Wesley Street and sighed heavily.

Chapter Eighteen

"I've got something, boss," DC Scott said from across the office an hour later. George, who was sitting with DC Blackburn, raised a brow. "I've sent the screenshots to the shared inbox." George raised his brows. "Basically, with the help of Sally Flathers, I managed to get into Edmund's mobile and check his WhatsApp."

"Hurry up, lad," George said.

"There's everything you'd expect on there, like family and friends getting in touch, but a few unknown numbers have sent some pretty nasty messages."

Tashan had already pulled them up on the screen, and George began scanning them. "Do we know who the numbers belong to?"

"Not exactly, boss."

"What do you mean, not exactly."

"They're the same numbers that were contacting Paxton Cole. It looks like Edmund was in deep with a loan shark."

George raised his brows before reading the threads. Jay was right. And George's suspicions had been, too. Tommy and Sean weren't the only people from whom Edmund Flathers borrowed money.

George looked up at Jay, who grinned. "Looks to me like

your friend, Jürgen Schmidt, boss." George nodded, and Jay added, "he's the type of guy who'd send a message if he didn't get paid."

"Aye," George said, "though not with some kind of poison, I wouldn't think."

"Criminals are getting much better at killing, sir. It's not all broken bones and beatings any more."

"Shit. We need to get in touch with Schmidt. I don't know what the hell's happening here, but if Schmidt's somehow tied to Edmund Flathers and Paxton Cole, I want him brought in and pronto. So get on that, will you, Jay? And I'll speak to Flathers' wife to see what she knows about all this. I got the feeling she was withholding information."

DC Scott returned to his desk as George pulled up Sally Flathers' number and dialled. Three attempts went to voicemail before she picked up. "Hello?" her voice was quiet.

DI Beaumont introduced himself and walked into his office. DS Wood followed.

"Oh, hello, Detective." Her voice sounded weak, though George should have expected it. After all, she'd just lost her husband. "Do you have news?"

"No, I just wanted to ask you for more information regarding Edmund's financial situation."

"OK."

"We asked you last time if you knew of a man named Jürgen Schmidt. I need you to think. Do you recognise the name?"

"No."

"Are you sure? As we said before, you won't be in trouble, Sally, but we need all the information we can get to find out what happened to your late husband."

"I–I know Ed borrowed a huge amount of money from

somewhere, and they've – and they've been threatening us to get it back." Her voice dropped to a whisper. "I'm sorry I didn't tell you before, but I was embarrassed."

George said nothing.

"I was so angry when I found out, but he told me everything would be OK." Her voice broke as she started sobbing.

George let her continue, putting her on speaker so he could take notes. DS Wood was listening intently.

"They used to come most weeks and batter the door down if Ed didn't pay. They'd shout and scream, telling us what they'd do to us if we didn't pay. I thought about calling the police, but it's Ed's fault. He got involved with them."

George frowned. "So they threatened you?"

"Yes." She coughed. "Did they – did they kill my Edmund?" she asked before becoming inconsolable.

George wished he had answers for the poor woman, but he had nothing. Not really. He wondered whether Jürgen Schmidt killed Edmund Flathers or whether Schmidt was entirely unaware that his debtor had passed away. He found himself thinking of Sally, knowing that despite the answer, Edmund's death wouldn't stop the loan shark from getting what was owed.

He wasn't sure. Poison didn't seem like Schmidt's thing. If Edmund had been kicked to death or tortured or something similar, then yeah, Schmidt would have been top of his list. But the man was... unharmed.

"We'll look into that for you, Sally." George paused, scribbling more notes. "You said before you didn't recognise the name, Jürgen Schmidt."

"Correct."

"Can you give me any details at all for the people that

Edmund borrowed from?"

"No. Sorry. Ed dealt with it all."

Shit. "OK." George sighed and was sure it had been loud enough for Sally to hear. "Look, if you can tell us anything else that might help, then please do so." He paused. "It can be anything at all, even anything you may think is insignificant. Let us be the judge. OK?"

But Sally Flathers could tell him nothing else. Nothing at all. And as George thanked her and hung up, he was greeted by the sound of muffled crying as a farewell.

But at least they now had a solid lead. And a possible connection between the two deaths he was in charge of investigating. He turned to Isabella and scratched his spiky chin. "Hear me out, OK?" George asked, and Wood nodded. "What if both deaths are linked? Maybe Schmidt poisoned both Flathers and Cole. Maybe the car accident was simply that, an accident and Cole was supposed to die at home? Exactly like Flathers?"

Wood shrugged. "Sounds reasonable to me, but I guess we'll only know when the reports from toxicology come back."

George nodded. Whilst he didn't think that poison was Jürgen Schmidt's style, he wouldn't put anything past the man. As Tashan had said, criminals had to become creative to try and get away with crimes, especially in Schmidt's line of business, after all.

* * *

"This better be fucking good, Detective," Jürgen Schmidt said as he opened the door and allowed DI Beaumont and DC Scott inside. "I don't have time for your bullshit."

"We're here to talk to you about Edmund Flathers."

"Who?" As before, Jürgen gave him nothing. Not even a flicker of recognition. He was good. Too fucking good. George couldn't wait to have a reason to arrest the bastard.

"Edmund Flathers, the man you loaned money to."

Still nothing.

"I suppose you won't have anything to do with the fact that he's lying in the LGI's morgue right now, would you?"

Schmidt scowled and didn't answer for a moment. George wondered what kind of lies he was concocting. Though maybe he'd had no idea. Anything was possible.

He shrugged. "Nothing to do with me, Detective."

"So you do know Edmund Flathers?"

Schmidt nodded. "Aye."

"What about Colby Raggett and Michael Green? Did they put him there?" They'd managed to track down the other man threatening Paxton Cole alongside Schmidt and Raggett. Green had given them a 'no comment' interview, and George terminated it quickly. They had better leads to pursue.

"I don't know what you're talking about."

"Of course, you don't. But I think they've been round the Flathers' recently, threatening them to get your money back?" George didn't break Schmidt's stare.

Nothing.

The two men didn't break the stare until Jay said to George, "Boss, I heard a rumour that Schmidt has been running a bookie out of this property. You think we should do what we normally do?"

"And what's that?" Schmidt asked, staring straight at Jay.

"Well, we pull you to shreds, Mr Schmidt, and investigate you and your men down to the last shit any of you took. Or, you tell us what we want to know, and my boss doesn't have to trouble himself." Jay looked smug.

The loan shark frowned. "A bookie? Me. Piss off. That would be illegal, Detective Constable," Schmidt replied. "As if I'm fucking daft enough for that." Jürgen grinned. "Now, I will admit that Ed and I had an amicable arrangement between two mates. That's all."

"Between mates?" Jay asked, and Jürgen nodded. "The kind of agreement with no interest, then?"

Jürgen snorted. "I said I was his mate, not that I was a fucking mug. Of course, there was interest. But I loaned it to him at a very reasonable rate because he was my pal."

"Which was?" Jay asked. "And how much?"

It was clear from the vein throbbing in his temple that Jürgen didn't like this line of questioning. Jay could see the loan shark clenching his fists as if the motion was the only thing keeping his temper in check. "I can't remember. But I have paperwork somewhere if you'd like to see it?"

"Aye, we'd like that," Jay said. "Did he say what he wanted the money for?"

"Nope, and it was none of my fucking business." He got up from his seat. "Is that all?"

"I find it hard to believe that you didn't ask what it was for."

"As long as he paid it back, it was none of my fucking business, right." Then Schmidt slammed his fist on the table. Jay jumped, but George remained composed. "Guess that's more bastarding money down the drain." He pondered for a minute, then grinned. "Then again, I take from what you said earlier that his wife, Sally, is still alive?"

"I shouldn't need to say, but as Edmund Flathers is dead, you won't be getting your money back," George explained. "So, don't go after it. Don't go after his family." It was a warning, one that he hoped Schmidt would take seriously.

Chapter Nineteen

The following afternoon, as George was on a late shift, George ushered the team into his Incident Room and asked for updates. Last night, for once, he'd gotten home at a reasonable hour and must have slept through Isabella's frequent urination as he managed a whole night's sleep.

Unfortunately, Jürgen Schmidt had turned up no leads. As before, they'd verified his and his prominent associates' phone and vehicle triangulations. Uniform had been out canvassing but also got nothing. He wasn't sure what to make of the situation, especially considering it had seemed a sure thing that a connection with Jürgen Schmidt would lead to something. You didn't simply become involved with that man and escape unscathed. Yet Schmidt was a cautious man, never being directly involved when it came to broken bones and torture.

Now, Tommy Myles and Sean Bishop were their most promising leads, Bishop being their prime suspect, and even that was pushing it. But, in truth, George wasn't convinced Bishop or Myles had killed Edmund Flathers. Not only that, but if he genuinely wanted to link the deaths of Flathers and Cole, then the two men had to be excluded entirely, for

DC Blackburn had taken statements confirming Myles and Bishops' whereabouts on the morning of Cole's death.

Perhaps both deaths weren't linked, and Paxton had committed suicide? It was certainly feasible. And the truth if you asked DCS Sadiq and DSU Smith, yet George wasn't sure. Still, he ordered DC Jason Scott to bring the two men in. "I want both Myles and Bishop in custody by the end of the day. Send Uniform to check their work and home addresses, please."

"Already done, boss." Jay nodded towards Wood, who grinned. She'd been in charge until George was on shift, having started at 7 am that morning. They'd done some excellent work. "Neither man showed up for work this morning, and neither man's answering their doors. Do you want me to go out personally and check?"

George pondered for a moment. It was clear the young detective wanted to prove himself, and it was true, to an extent, that George was beginning to trust him. Maybe it was time to set him loose, let him and Tashan go and start questioning people whilst George stayed at the station running the show. It wasn't necessarily his style, and even as a DS, he would be out and about in the thick of it. But if he wanted to be a DCI, which he certainly did, then he would need to start and trust the junior detectives to do their jobs.

"Good idea, DC Scott. Take DC Blackburn with you. Go to Bishop's first, then Myles'. Check their work last, OK?"

"Brilliant. Thanks, boss."

"Yes, sir."

* * *

He'd felt fine earlier. Perfect, even. Yet now, he'd never felt so ill in his life.

He groaned. He felt so weak. His entire body hurt so much. The pain tore through him, excruciating. He'd gone to bed but couldn't get comfortable. No matter how he moved or writhed or how much padding he wore, he couldn't chase away that pain. The springs felt like they were piercing his skin.

But Christ, he was so hot. Too hot. He needed to strip. But he couldn't.

God, it felt like he was dying.

His lungs were on fire, a fiery pain deep inside them, a burning pain so great he struggled to breathe. As the minutes passed, he became so weak he couldn't even move from the bed. Turning over felt like climbing Everest.

His vision began to fail as if the shadows in the corners of his room were starting to swallow him up, and then the shockwaves started. He hadn't eaten all day, so it couldn't have been food poisoning. And the drink he'd shared with his guest earlier tasted fine. There was no way it was spiked, right? Yet something was wrong.

His thoughts hazed as he tried to remember the identity of his visitor. He couldn't remember. In truth, he couldn't even remember what drink it was.

His memory failed him as the minutes passed, as was his life.

He moaned as pain seared through him again, leaving him quivering in bed, each twitch sending shock-waves throughout his bones.

There was a real chance he was dying. He knew that for sure. But he'd left his phone downstairs, and couldn't even move his head from the pillow now, let alone any other part of his body.

With each breath he took, his breath started to falter, and then he'd sputter, his lungs burning as he tried to take in oxygen.

Soon the darkness swallowed him whole. He'd already lost track of time, and that terrified him.

They say your life flashes before your eyes when you die, but he recalled only one memory, one he regretted more than any other. He'd been involved in a lie. A coverup. For a mate. But who was the mate? And who was the victim? His memory was failing him.

Then his other regret, something about Polaroids and blackmail, came to the forefront of his mind. Was that who his visitor was? The one on their back? Or the one who'd threatened him?

His heartbeat began to beat harder and faster now as if it rose towards the final crescendo, and he found he didn't care any more.

He didn't care about either regret. It was time for him to stop running from the guilt those two regrets had caused him. But as his heart rate rocketed and his breathing became shallow, panic soared through him.

Death was coming for him, its outstretched hand inches away.

His last thought was inevitable... he knew deep down he deserved it. He always knew his two regrets would catch up with him one day.

* * *

Isabella Wood had just about finished the bottle of wine while waiting for George to return home from work. George had installed extra locks on the insides of the house in Morley as a result of the incident before Christmas. Not that it made Isabella feel safe. She would never feel safe alone any more, or that's what she believed.

She checked her phone and confirmed the time. Her fiancé would be back soon. Half an hour. That's if his shift ended on time. It usually didn't. She fired off a text. *I miss you xxx*

Isabella headed upstairs to the bathroom. She'd been feeling queasy recently and was struggling to sleep. The doctor said it was a psychological reaction to being attacked, which made sense; she just wished the nausea would piss off.

Cold water spewed out of the tap, and she waited for it to rapidly heat up before mixing the blistering stream with cold water to bring the temperature back to a tolerable level.

Like Oliver asking for more, she placed her hands under the water, and once enough water had pooled there, she splashed it against her face. Then she made the mistake of looking into the mirror fixed to the wall above the sink.

There was a man there. Behind her. A few metres back. He was half-hidden by the steam, so she could barely make out the form. Then he stepped forward, his eyes wide, a snarl on his face and a Santa hat on his head. She saw a metal cane in one hand and a scalpel in the other.

He lunged at her, grabbed for her with gloved hands and groaned with pleasure. She turned, a scream building in her throat, fists clenched.

And then Santa was gone. She was all alone, her heart hammering in her chest.

Ethan Miller had evaporated like a ghost.

Isabella chastised herself. "Moron."

She turned back to the sink and finished washing her face

before she turned off the taps. Then she dried her hands, making sure to avoid looking in the mirror for fear of what she might see.

Or what she might remember. Her dreams were already filled with vivid recollections of the attacks.

Then her phone went off, and she jumped.

It was George. He'd be ten minutes.

Thank God for that, she thought. And then she cried.

Chapter Twenty

The next morning, the Incident Room at Elland Road station was now a hive of activity. Although granted, much of that activity was centred around the ravaging of Greggs' breakfast sarnies and the consumption of various hot beverages.

It had been Tashan's treat, considering it was his birthday, though being a vegetarian, Tashan had some sort of weird-looking omelette between his breadcake. George wasn't sure how much of a treat that was and considered advising Tashan how lovely McDonald's eggs were when Isabella caught his eye.

She was struggling with her sausage sarnie, dabbing at the corner of her lip to remove a smudge of brown sauce. He saw her look at the sarnie with disgust before dropping it back into the waxy bag and taking a sip of coffee.

He'd never known her not demolish a butty before. "You OK?" he asked her.

"Fine." She smiled.

"Not hungry?"

"No, not really," she confirmed.

Strange. George was about to ask Isabella why when the door to the Incident Room opened, and an out-of-breath constable burst in. He looked around the room until he met eyes with DI Beaumont. "Sir, somebody has reported a dead body."

* * *

George listened as the constable explained. "The deceased's wife arrived home to find the body in the bedroom. My colleague told me it isn't very pleasant."

"Right, well, we have two active cases," George said and winced. Technically they had only one active case. "Who sent you to find me?"

"DSU Smith, sir," the constable said. "It's because the deceased's wife said he was perfectly healthy this morning but obviously dead when she returned. My colleague told me the man didn't look like he was murdered. Does that make sense?"

It made perfect sense, of course. It sounded exactly the same as Edmund Flathers' death. And George did not believe in coincidences. "OK, Constable, we'll go and take a look." He nodded at Wood to put on her coat, then remembered how she felt last time and how she looked eating her sarnie, so he shook his head. "I'll take DC Scott with me, DS Wood. You can stay here and start background checks." George turned back to the constable. "Do we have a name?"

"A name?"

"Aye, of the deceased?"

"Andre Harding."

"Andre Harding?" Tashan asked, and the constable nodded. "As in, a Jamaican named Andre Harding?"

"Well, I dunno," the constable said. "He's got black skin, so I suppose he could be Jamaican." He shrugged.

CHAPTER TWENTY

George looked at his young detective. "You know him, Tashan?"

Tashan shook his head. "No, but when I checked upon Luis Rodríguez and the therapy sessions he advised us of, I was given details for a man named Andre Harding. So I got in touch and took a statement. It turns out he was also Paxton Cole's therapist. In fact, the three of them sometimes went out for drinks. So Andre was embedded into the team, from what it sounded like."

"I mean, it could be a different Andre Harding," George said, and Tashan nodded. "Address, constable," George demanded.

As soon as the police constable told the detectives where Harding had been found, Tashan began nodding. "Check your inbox, sir. I booked another interview with him. He was busy until tomorrow and could fit me in at his home between clients. That's the correct address for him."

"Why didn't you advise me of this before, Detective Constable?" George asked. It probably wouldn't have made any difference, but he needed the young DC to know that George was in charge. He was also responsible for everything his subordinates did.

Tashan looked mortified, but all George could think about were the two men. What did that mean? Two men, who were both linked to Paxton Cole, were now dead. He wasn't sure. All he knew was that they had two dead men and even fewer answers. Without waiting for an obviously hurt DC Blackburn to answer, George, nodded at DC Scott, grabbed his coat and headed straight out.

* * *

Having been allowed to drive through the outer cordon, George arrived at Andre Harding's house in Rothwell just as an ambulance was leaving. He watched it trundle down the narrow lane of Swithen's Street back towards the A654, where it would be needed somewhere else in Leeds.

Two BMWs were in the drive, a blue one and a white one, and George swung his Mercedes next to a Fiat Punto that was blocking the blue BMW.

A female police constable of average height and red hair turned at the noise of George's Mercedes and paused, relief washing over her face as she realised who it was. "Sir," she said.

George introduced himself. "DI Beaumont. This is DC Scott."

The redhead smiled and said, "I know who both of you are. I'm PC Candy Nichols." She couldn't look Jay in the eye, George noticed, who grinned. "This is Penelope Harding, Andre's wife."

"Penny," the woman offered. She smiled, though the smile didn't meet her eyes. George thought she looked exhausted. "Hi."

"Hiya Penny, we are very sorry for your loss," George said. The words felt hollow as they left his mouth, but Penny, to her credit, gave George a watery-eyed smile and mouthed a 'thank you'.

George nodded at DC Scott, chucked the keys to the Merc, then gave him a look that said, 'Interview the woman and find out whatever you can that might be pertinent because we are really fucking clutching at straws for Flathers right now.'

Or so he hoped that's the look he'd given. Then he turned to PC Nichols.

"It's not pretty in there, sir." She looked disgusted.

"It never is." He let the sentence hang in the air. "First time?"

"Not at all, sir. I was just expecting blood, but the smell coming from the body is something else." She grimaced. George understood. A deceased's bowels usually emptied soon after death, and whilst that was fairly standard, it was never pleasant. "Anyway, he's upstairs in bed. Dead. But, I can't see any obvious reason as to why."

"No stab wounds? Bruises? Ligature marks?"

"No, sir, not that I could see."

He'd still get Dr Ross and Dr Lindsey Yardley to confirm, but it looked like whatever killed Edmund Flathers, Andre Harding, too. But, then again, assuming was a rookie mistake, as was believing in coincidences.

"Anything else you can tell me?" George asked.

"Sorry, sir. I've been busy with Penelope, liaising with the paramedics, and keeping the neighbours in check."

"All on your own?" She nodded. George was impressed at her thoroughness. "Well done, constable. Good intuition."

The lass beamed.

"Run me through everything that happened, Constable."

"PC Fletcher and I arrived at the scene after dispatch called us. Penelope was waiting for us outside. She told me as soon as she saw the body, she fled the house."

George nodded. "Did you or PC Fletcher touch the body?"

"No, sir, but I assume the paramedics did."

That meant his crime scene had been contaminated. Candy frowned as if she knew what he was thinking. George allowed himself a wry smile. "OK. Have you called the morgue to pick up the body?"

"Yes, sir."

George smiled. He liked the young lass. She was good. He nodded at her, donned a paper suit, gloves and shoe covers provided by the constable by the front door, and headed upstairs once he was signed in. He was greeted with that weird, unique smell of the mixture of shit and death. It only got more pungent as he made his way towards the only door that was open.

He nudged the door wide open, and the scent of death flowed out. George steeled his stomach, pulled up his mask before breathing through his mouth and stepped in.

Andre Harding lay on top of the duvet, looking like the Michelin Man in his multiple layers. The duvet was covered in shit, piss, and, no doubt, sweat. It certainly smelled that way, and George resisted the urge to throw open the window and let in some blessedly cold, fresh, clean air from outside. One of Andre's arms was wound tightly around his stomach as though he was cradling it. And like Flathers, his face was contorted in agony.

The bedroom was not what George had expected. There was no dirty washing strewn around. In fact, the place was sterile. Other than the corpse on the bed, of course.

George looked around the room, doing his best not to disturb anything that Lindsey and her SOC team could dig up. He didn't think they'd find much, though. There were no wounds that he could see, and like Edmund Flathers, it seemed Andre had just dropped dead.

DS Wood had called him on the way over, advising Andre Harding's medical records showed a clean bill of health. So why, then, were two married men who had seemed fit and healthy without any pressing issues to their health suddenly dead? It made no sense.

CHAPTER TWENTY

He was already getting déjà vu. It was exactly like the scene at the Flathers'. So Harding must have been poisoned too, but with what? That thought didn't comfort him.

George took another look around the room and then had a peak into the ensuite. He then left the bedroom and looked in each room, noting there didn't seem to have been any visitors or signs of breaking and entering.

He made a few quick phone calls whilst on the upstairs landing, asking Isabella for more information. She didn't have much for him other than his record was clean. She was working flat out, looking for answers.

George headed downstairs and stuck his head in the kitchen, where he could see nothing out of the ordinary. It was neat and tidy, with an unopened letter on the kitchen table. There was no lingering smell of food. With a gloved hand, he checked the bin in the corner, but it was empty. On the side were two empty glasses. Harding had had company. But who?

He headed outside and beckoned PC Nichols over. "Candy, call Sergeant Greenwood and get him to come out, please. I need his Uniforms on door-to-door ASAP."

"On it, sir," Candy said, pulling out her mobile.

But he held up a hand to stop her. "CSI will be along shortly, Candy. You said the morgue transport's on their way?" Candy nodded, and a movement caught his eye. George watched DC Scott helping Penelope from out of the Merc. He doubted Lindsey would find much, not if it were like the Flathers case.

"Thank you, DC Scott," George said as the pair got closer. "Mrs Harding, our Crime Scene Investigation team will be along very shortly, so please stay outside the house. Transport will soon arrive for Andre. They'll look after him." He smiled sympathetically and handed her one of his cards. "If you think

145

of anything else, please call me. And again, we're very sorry for your loss." The words rang hollow as they did before.

As George marched Jay back to the Mercedes, he knew they couldn't do much for Andre and Edmund today, but he still wanted to know what Penelope Harding had to say.

Once Jay had divulged all the information he had – which wasn't a great deal – he promised the young DC his extra hours back as time off and dropped him off at the station so he could collect his car. He made no promises when, though, but it was better than Jay working for free.

George, however, wouldn't get the same from his superior. As a DI, George had worked many free hours during the last two years. But that was expected of him. It was part of the job.

He just wished he could switch off as soon as the clock did. But he couldn't. Ever. He knew for sure that as he slept beside Isabella tonight, listening to her breath and watching her chest rise and fall like he usually did, all he'd be able to think about was how Andre and Edmund had died. And why?

Chapter Twenty-one

George woke up feeling like utter shite. Isabella had once again been up to the toilet throughout, though George couldn't blame her for his lack of sleep. He had a cold. He was sure of it. Despite Isabella telling him he had a temperature, he'd spent the entire night shaking.

And it was all confirmed he was ill when he attempted to get out of bed and almost toppled sideways, the wall sparing his blushes.

She was not on the rota today. "You should stay at home, George," Isabella said. He was sure he detected a slight tone. One of warmth but also one of want. After the conversation with Tashan, George spoke with her about the night terrors again, but she assured him she was OK.

"It's nothing. "I'm fine." Plus, duty calls," George insisted. He tried to smile reassuringly, but the grimace that twisted across his green-looking face made Isabella grin.

"You look like you're going to be sick."

"Nah, I can't remember the last time I was sick."

Isabella could. It was last year when he was struggling with his drink. "Luke and Yolanda can take care of everything, George," she pleaded. "Stay home." She grinned and patted the mattress. "Stay in bed with me."

"As much as I'd love that, I have two, maybe three, murders that require my attention. A possible serial killer on our hands." George pinched the bridge of his nose as he took another step, the movement making him sway before he righted himself.

"Well, if you need me, I'll be here," Isabella grinned, "naked."

* * *

After taking a good ten minutes to get dressed because of the room spinning around him, George finally managed to get to the station after downing all the pills he was allowed to take.

The steps leading up to HMET were a bastard, though, and he pushed his way through the door to the shared office space out of breath.

"Christ, it's hot in here. The heating broke or summat?"

"Morning, boss," DC Scott said, not looking up from his computer. "The temperature feels fine to me."

Well, not until DS Mason shouted across the room. "Jesus, look at what the cat dragged in."

"Wow, boss. Are you OK? You look like shite." He turned to Luke. "Doesn't he look like shite, sarge?"

"Aye, he does, son. Like death warmed up."

"Well, that's exactly how I feel," George said. Then suddenly, a sound erupted from somewhere inside George's stomach, like the sound of a grumbling frog that came out of his mouth.

Luke and Jay both winced, moving their necks back.

"False alarm," George eventually said before slapping a hand across his mouth as a similar, less sinister sound forced its way out.

"Go home, son," Luke said. He turned to the two DCs, who

both nodded their heads. "We got this."

"I'm sure you have," George said, "but I'm the boss. I'm expected to be here." He headed towards his office and locked himself in there, sagging against his chair and letting it support his weight.

Every step he'd taken that morning felt like walking on a partially deflated bouncy castle. Soft and spongy. And a fucking nightmare.

He closed his eyes, swallowed back more rising bile, and enjoyed the peace of his office. Maybe he should have stayed at home. His team were good. Very good, in fact. He could trust them to do a great job in his absence. Yet there were at least two people out there who had died by unknown causes, people who had friends and families. And they deserved to know the truth.

So, with exhaustion filling his bones and sick rising up his throat, George phoned Dr Ross to discuss Andre Harding.

"Are you OK, son? You sound a bit peachy," Dr Ross asked as soon as George had said hello.

"Fine, fine. Have you done the post-mortem yet?"

"Not yet, son. Anything I need to know before I start?"

"He was a known associate of Paxton Cole, the deceased footballer, and a known associate of one of our prime suspects. And weirdly, the crime scene was eerily similar to Edmund Flathers'. I think they're connected since nothing obvious caused their deaths."

"OK, that is suspicious," mused Dr Ross.

George sighed heavily down the phone.

"I know you're disappointed, son," Dr Ross said, "but if Flathers was poisoned, which I believe he was, then we have to wait for toxicology. And from what you're saying, that'll be the same for Harding." Dr Ross paused. "I'll check for anything else untoward, however. But I'm going in blind, too."

George could hear the edge of frustration in Dr Ross' voice. "Thanks, Dr Ross," George said. He knew the pathologist wanted answers for himself, too. Despite his old age, he was a professional and wanted to learn.

"Leave Harding with me, son, and I'll do what I can. Oh, and I'll do the same as I did with Flathers and Cole; I'll expedite the toxicology samples.

"Thanks, Dr Ross; I appreciate you." George hung up.

Chapter Twenty-two

Yesterday, George had spent the rest of the morning in the shared office, sweating, trying his best to keep the room from spinning, but by 1 pm, he'd had enough.

It was now the next morning, and he felt much better; whilst not quite raring to go, he knew that he could hobble through the day with the crutch that was strong painkillers.

What he didn't anticipate, though, was the mental strain. They still had nothing. And the cases were stalling. Morale was low, and George needed to do something about that.

He knew exactly what to do. First, he'd buy his team food—nice, greasy, stodgy food to energise them.

* * *

George took DC Blackburn with him to the chippy, and they waited in the car, watching the rain thunder down on the Mercedes' bonnet whilst each team member texted George their orders.

Isabella wanted fish, chips, and curry sauce. He'd read the message twice and frowned. She didn't like chip shop curry sauce. She didn't even like the Irish curry sauce that George had discovered on New Year's Eve. It was phenomenal stuff, and

George had wished he'd only known about the sauce sooner.

He texted her back, asking her to check her order as he knew she didn't like curry sauce. It was something about the smell, the colour, and the consistency she disliked. But she replied that she fancied it, the Irish one he'd been banging on about since New Year's Eve.

George shrugged and was about to get out of the car when his phone pinged again. A follow-up message: And a large, battered sausage and a scallop, please.

* * *

An hour later, the Incident Room positively reeked of fried pork and fish, vinegar, and a spicy bottom note of Irish curry sauce.

George noticed that Wood's appetite had changed. Unlike the Greggs' breakfast, she'd gobbled up the lot with a level of enthusiasm that had drawn strange looks from her colleagues.

"Bloody hell, love," Mason said, "Has he been starving you?" He fired an accusing look at George. "He might be the boss, but you can tell us, you know."

"Of course, he isn't," said Isabella, wiping a smear of curry sauce from her navy blouse with a paper napkin. "I got up late and skipped breakfast," she explained.

Mason furrowed his brows, then covered up his confusion with a smile. "You do look better today, to be fair. I've noticed you looking a bit peaky recently."

"Yeah." She pointed towards George. "Probably had what he's got."

Then, once they'd finished eating, Wood stood up to go through the Big Board, and all eyes were laser-trained on her.

The food had done its job, and George was grateful for that.

"Right," Wood said. "I've pinned up your work on Flathers' and Harding's personal lives and known acquaintances." She pointed towards the top right of the board. "This is Flathers' background check." He turned to Tashan. "We're still waiting on more information regarding Harding, but if anybody needs to know anything, Tashan is your man. OK?"

There were nods all around.

"Good." She accidentally burped and looked instantly mortified. Luke looked down at the floor, and Tashan looked up at the ceiling. George was sure he could smell a tinge of Irish curry. Jay started pissing himself laughing but soon stopped at the ferocious glare he received from his sarge.

"Can I continue?"

"Sorry, Sarge," Jay said, grimacing.

"So from what we know so far, it appears Flathers and Harding were in good standing. There's nothing obvious in terms of any personal or professional grudges, that sort of thing. So other than Lena Schneider's family, which is only relevant to Flathers, there's nobody with a motive." She stared at her colleagues. "In conclusion, I think we're finding nothing there because there's nothing to be found."

George sighed. He knew this was coming. He tapped his fingers on the desk, drumming away, each tap sending pain through his body. It was soothing.

"What do we do next, sir?" DC Scott asked.

George stood up. "What we always so, Jay. We start from scratch and widen the search," George said. "We need to go back and review all the information we have."

Then George's phone pinged, the tone announcing an email had been sent to the shared inbox. It was a report from Lindsey's team detailing Harding's final meal. He explained this to his team. "Chicken in a garlic and cream sauce with pasta. She suggests it was rather fresh and ingested in the few hours before his death as it wasn't heavily digested. Lindsey's sent a sample off to toxicology."

Wood turned to Tashan, who was taking notes. She smiled at him.

"I'll see where Andre got his last meal from, yeah?" Tashan said.

"Aye you do that," George said, smiling at his fiancée. Then he turned to the team. "Anything else?"

"Just the rest of my background check on Andre, sir," Tashan explained.

"Anything else?"

"What about Jürgen Schmidt, boss?" DC Scott asked. "Flathers was in debt to him, as was Cole. That's a clear motive to murder them both. So I really don't think we should rule him out."

"We're not, DC Scott," George said. "My only issue is that poison doesn't seem like his style. They break legs and torture people." George shrugged. "He had no reason to kill either of them because that meant he wouldn't get his money back."

"I agree, boss, but he looks guilty to me."

George sucked the inside of his cheek. They had precious few other options. "Fine, chase it up. OK?"

Jay looked like the cat that got the cream. "Thanks, boss, I appreciate it." Then, as if remembering something, he raised his hand. George, amused, nodded at him to speak. "I spoke with Harding's partner, Penelope, yesterday, but she didn't give me much. She did, however, give me his pin. I've asked DS Fry to download the information from his phone, so I'll let you know once that comes in, boss."

CHAPTER TWENTY-TWO

"Oh, just to let you know, George, Dr Ross called yesterday afternoon advising, like with Edmund Flathers, he has no idea what killed Andre Harding, but that his death occurred between noon and 4 pm on Thursday the 2nd of February."

"OK, thanks for that, Luke." George turned to his team. "Anything else?"

His team shook his head. And then his phone rang. "DI Beaumont," he answered. "I've got you on speaker with my team, Lindsey."

"No worries, George. I've got some information for you that I think you and your team will like."

* * *

Lindsey started by explaining that Andre Harding's house had been turned upside down and marvelled over the thorough job that her SOCOs had done.

Hayden Wyatt, to his credit, or so Lindsey certainly thought, had found the journal whilst rummaging through the dead man's underwear drawer. The SOC team had apparently been taking the piss out of Wyatt, jokingly accusing him of fumbling through a dead man's pants until he'd found gold.

"So you've found a journal. Harding's?"

"Correct, George," Lindsey said. She was out of breath, clearly elated. "We have in our possession a journal of Andre Harding's innermost thoughts and feelings in the run-up to his death."

"Christ, really?"

"Well, I hope so, anyway. We haven't looked through it, obviously. That's your job."

"Aye. Thanks." George didn't want to get his hopes up,

knowing that learning who the killer was through Andre's journal would be far too convenient. "You got anything else for me?"

"Yes. We found two small glasses in the kitchen. We've managed to match the prints from one of the glasses to Andre Harding."

"And the other?" George was getting impatient.

"The prints are not a match for anybody on the database."

"Right, OK." *Shit.* All that meant was once they had a suspect, they could take prints to match against any taken from the glasses because there was no way the budget would stretch to fingerprinting the trios' close acquaintances. And even if it could stretch, DSU Smith wouldn't allow it. He turned to Luke, who nodded his understanding. To bring in Luis Rodríguez and take his prints immediately.

Lindsey must have heard the disappointment in George's voice as she said, "I've already sent the glasses off to the Calder Park lab, so they will check for DNA. I knew you'd ask, so I took the liberty. I hope that's OK."

"No, it's fine. Brilliant, actually. Thanks." He paused for a moment. "Don't suppose those glasses had any remnants left in them. Like whatever the two people were drinking?"

"Already sent off to toxicology."

"Amazing, thank you, Lindsey."

"I just want to let you know before I let you go, George, that we need to take prints and samples from the journal before we hand it over," Lindsey explained.

"Once you've done that, send somebody over here with the journal immediately," George demanded before adding a "please." to the end.

CHAPTER TWENTY-TWO

* * *

Now that they had the journal in their possession, and the SOCO confirmed they had taken prints from it, George sent Tashan and Jay to pick Penelope Harding up and bring her in to identify it.

George, gloved up, flicked through some of the pages, looking at the almost illegible scrawl, before thinking that starting at the back would probably be their best bet. George was sat at Wood's desk alongside her. "You're looking better," she whispered in his ear.

"You are, too," George whispered back. After scoffing her face, she looked a better colour than she did earlier: A more human colour. He pointed to the journal. "Have a read of that whilst I make us a brew."

George had only just placed the tea bags in the mugs and switched on the kettle when Isabella shouted, "George, you really need to come and see this!"

He sprinted out into the shared office, with other HMET detectives looking up from their desks at him as he flew by. "You found something?"

"Yeah, read this." She pointed a blue, gloved finger at one of the entries.

"What am I meant to be looking for?" George asked.

But Wood didn't answer. She didn't need to. Instead, a word jumped off the page at him. He'd been looking above Wood's finger instead of to the side of it.

"Jesus Christ!" he ejected, and then he looked up, the shock evident on his face.

Then immediately, he looked back to the page, making sure what he'd seen was real.

And it was. It was still there, looking up at him, changing everything he knew about the cases.

But before they could talk about what they'd just read, DC Scott called, advising they were pulling into the station.

* * *

George met Penelope Harding and his two Detective Constables down in reception, signed her in, and took her into one of the more friendly interview rooms they used for children.

After they both sat down, George handed over the journal, but he noticed no flicker of recognition from her. "Were you aware that Andrew kept a journal?"

"No," Penelope admitted. Her grip tightened on the book, and she pulled it in against her chest as if she were holding the last piece of Andre and didn't want to let it go. "But he was pretty old-fashioned. He liked writing letters by hand rather than sending emails."

"Do you have anything Andre wrote that we could use to compare to the journal?" George asked.

And, of course, she said she did and would bring it to the station first thing.

"We'll bring you the journal back when we're done with it, of course," George said, and he received a mouthed 'thank you' in return.

Chapter Twenty-three

"Right." George sighed. "We now know that if the journal is genuine, which I believe it is, then Flathers and Harding were friends and had been for a long time.

I'm perturbed about the death of my best friend, Eddy Flathers. His wife, Sally, called me to break the news. The police are investigating, believing the death is suspicious, but do not know the cause. So that's the second friend of mine that has now died this month—the second of our trio who were keeping secrets from the world. Rest in peace, Pax and Eddy.

Tashan turned to George. "As he was Paxton Cole's therapist, Harding was interviewed by Dr Shah. The transcript is in the shared inbox." He looked down at the floor before meeting George's eyes. "I haven't had time to print it for the Big Board, sir."

"No bother, DC Blackburn. Give us the highlights," George said.

"Andre suggests Paxton Cole was fine and wasn't the type of man who would commit suicide."

"That's what the wife said," DC Scott said.

"True. Andre goes on to state that Paxton was his usual, bubbly, confident self. But not once did he advise Dr Shah that he knew Cole personally."

"Which is suspicious," George said.

"I certainly believe so, sir," Tashan said.

"Walk us through Andre's final moments, will you please?" He looked at the two DCs.

"He was working," Jay explained. "He often worked from home, providing sessions over the internet."

"We know he had dinner between two and three but messaged his final two clients of the day apologising. According to them, he needed to cancel because he was feeling ill," Tashan offered.

"Penelope came home and found him in bed, dead," Jay cleared his throat. "We assume from the two glasses he had a visitor during his lunch."

"The food and glasses are at the lab, and we obviously have the journal to read through," George said. "Have we checked Harding's bank accounts?"

"I did, sir," Tashan said. "He was loaded. There's no sign of any loans going into his account."

George turned to Jay. "Does that discount Schmidt from the investigation?" They would find out later through Harding's journal that they could not discount Jürgen Schmidt from the investigation because Harding was Flathers' guarantor. It made no sense to the detectives, especially considering Harding's healthy bank balance, but they couldn't exactly ask Flathers or Harding why. However, he made a mental note to speak with Schmidt again.

"Next steps?" George asked.

"We need to read the journal," Wood said, frowning. Harding's scrawl was challenging to decipher, and they considered asking DSU Smith to bring in an expert. But that would be

CHAPTER TWENTY-THREE

costly and take time. They had no budget and no time.

"OK." He looked around the room, then turned to Wood, who grimaced. "I'll leave that to you."

* * *

"Everything alright, Luke?" George asked.

"Aye, son. Just reading something," Luke said.

"Anything interesting?"

"Not sure yet. Give me a few minutes to finish."

George and Wood locked eyes, shrugged, and then turned their attention back to their own work. Wood was still trying to decipher Harding's journal, looking for clues. The revelation that Andre Harding and Edmund Flathers were also childhood friends was shocking news. It meant they could link all three dead men together. It also meant they could link two of the dead men to the footballer, Luis Rodríguez.

"I've got something," DS Mason said. He beckoned over George and Wood.

"What is it?"

Luke grinned. "I went to the library last night." George raised his brow. He didn't realise Mason was a reader. Luke must have seen the brow because he chuckled. "They have old newspaper microfilms in there."

"Get to the point, Detective Sergeant," George commanded with a grin.

"I found some newspaper articles relating to the death of Lena Schneider. Old South Leeds Live issues that were written by your mate, Johnathan Duke."

"Show me."

And that's precisely what Luke did.

"Jesus Christ," was all George could say.

* * *

DS Wood shared a glance with George and Luke. "How is it possible we missed this?"

They all stared again at the screen.

As well as speaking to Edmund Flathers, nineteen of Hunslet Carr, Leeds, officers from the West Yorkshire Police advised they have spoken with three other individuals related to the drug-related death of Austrian citizen, Lena Schneider.

Luke Mason then scrolled down to another paragraph he'd highlighted.

South Leeds Live have contacted Paxton Cole, seventeen of Middleton, and Andre Harding, seventeen of Beeston, but have so far received no comment. The other individual involved cannot be named for legal reasons.

"The three were questioned regarding the death of Lena Schneider, with Edmund being charged and later found not guilty," George said. "That's what I'm getting from this." He looked at his two sergeants. "What about you two?"

"Same, son," Luke said.

"I agree, George," Isabella said.

"Jesus Christ," George said. "Why didn't we know about this earlier?" He then turned to Luke and clapped him on the shoulder. "Amazing job." Tashan and Jay had searched online for historical newspaper articles regarding the case, yet it seems that only Johnathan Duke, the jolly American giant, knew about them. So why hadn't the other papers mentioned them? It made no sense.

George reread it, and it all clicked. It was there in black

and white. "Harding and Cole were seventeen at the time." Both detectives looked up at George and instantly understood. When the offence had been committed and gone to court, because Harding and Cole were minors, their identities had been safeguarded because, in the eyes of the law, they were children at the time. "I guess that goes for the third individual, too."

"Holy shit," said Wood. "This is just..." She shrugged. "I don't know how to process it. I still don't understand why we didn't know about this earlier. Why isn't it on their criminal records?"

"I think I know why," Luke said, then clicked another file. It was another article written by Johnathan Duke.

My source within the West Yorkshire Police has advised that the two seventeen-year-olds questioned in connection with the drug-related death of Austrian national Lena Schneider have been fully cleared. The other individual involved, who cannot be named for legal reasons, was also cleared. Both teenagers, when questioned, gave evidence against Edmund Flathers, and the West Yorkshire Police are now confident they have reached the charging threshold.

"Fucking hell," George said.

"Aye, son." Luke let the detectives reread the extract. "Looks like Cole, Harding and our unknown dobbed Edmund in."

"That doesn't make sense, though," Wood explained. "Why would Paxton and Edmund stay friends if Pax gave evidence against him?"

George shrugged. "Paxton was a minor, so maybe Edmund had no idea?"

"True," Wood conceded. She read the article extract once more. "So that case links all three victims."

"That's if we believe Paxton Cole was murdered, which I do," George said.

Wood nodded. "And I imagine all three have made enemies because of this?"

George chewed his lip. "I mean, Sally Flathers and Sean Bishop questioned whether Lena's family were involved. I don't think they are because we have no evidence any of her surviving family members has ever come to England. Plus, if anyone wanted revenge, they'd have acted sooner, right?"

The two sergeants shrugged, and then Wood said, "They could have paid somebody to do it."

George had considered that, too. It was expensive if they were going to liaise with the Austrian police, and DSU Smith had been apprehensive. "True, but then, why now?"

Luke checked the date. "Lena's body was found in the summer, and the trial was the following summer. Lena's birthday is also in the summer." He frowned. "There's no connection to the date. No anniversary." He shrugged.

It seemed that's all they were doing. Shrugging. And it was pissing the DI off.

"Maybe they were saving up? Perhaps contract killers are dear?"

"Yeah, maybe." George tapped the corner of the desk. "Do we even know why Lena was here?"

Both sergeants shrugged, and George took a deep breath to calm himself. Then he looked at Mason. "Luke, investigate that for me. Check through the old records on HOLMES. I want to know why she was here. Who she was friends with. Where she lived, you know, the drill."

"No bother, son," Luke said and began clacking away at his keyboard.

Isabella and George got up and walked towards her desk. "I want you to look at any connections between Harding and the loan shark. We know he didn't borrow money from Schmidt, but they may have known each other in some capacity. Find out." He began to walk away, then turned back. "Do the same for Schmidt's acquaintances."

George wanted more information on Lena Schneider, so he read some historical articles. Unfortunately, they didn't have much context to them, which frustrated George, but after an hour of reading, he discovered that a friend had found Lena sparko on the sofa. The friend had assumed Lena was asleep and failed to rouse her. When toxicology came back, it showed she'd overdosed on drugs. Usually, drug-related deaths like that would have been classified as accidental, but Lena was also a minor, so they went after the dealer.

And that dealer was assumed to be Edmund Flathers. Yet they could find no evidence that Flathers had dealt drugs in his life, let alone to Lena. But he was wearing a jacket they tested for ecstasy, which returned positive for the illegal substance, and the prosecutor ran with that despite Flathers' insistence that the coat wasn't his.

Eventually, the trial ended when they couldn't prove he had intended to kill Lena. They had nothing. Nothing at all. And so Flathers was cleared, the case was closed, and Lena's death was classified as an accident.

As for Lena's family back in Austria, George learnt that her father worked at one of the Baroque castles in Vienna and didn't earn much money. At first, the family struggled to get Lena's body home until a fundraising effort raised funds to fly her body home.

As a father himself, he couldn't imagine what Lena's parents went through, and George's stomach curdled; his growing appetite was gone, and he no longer wanted his lunch.

George continued reading for another hour and was about to give up when he clicked on an article from Austria. Clicking the translate button, the words changed to English, and whilst not perfect, George got the gist. Apparently, three or four years after Lena's death, her brother had begged the West Yorkshire Police to reopen the case but had refused. He claimed she had died, whilst the *four* culprits had lived, forged lives, and started families and careers, whilst Lena was snatched away from them cruelly.

Four culprits. Lena's brother knew about Cole, Harding, and the minor.

It was obvious Lena's brother had done his research, so why hadn't the case been reopened?

Nothing was making sense.

He needed to reach out to the brother and see what other information he had. Yet the man didn't show up anywhere. George didn't even have a name for him. Yet for all intents and purposes, Edmund had been found not guilty, and it seemed everybody had moved on with their lives, no matter how fractured they had become. Lena's brother didn't appear in any more articles, and both Lena's parents had died. He wondered whether the Schneiders had ever stopped grieving for their lost child.

The dilemma was evident; they'd wasted enough time on dead ends. Searching for Lena's brother, a needle in an Austrian-sized haystack, wasn't feasible.

Yet he felt the Austrian was the key, that's if he was even alive. An unnamed brother in a foreign country. He almost wished they'd never found the connection between the men.

CHAPTER TWENTY-THREE

George suddenly hit his desk with a heavy fist, his irritation budding into anger at the world for not giving him the answers he required.

He just needed answers.

And fast.

Chapter Twenty-four

They'd decided the best way to get the information they needed was to interview all three wives simultaneously.

So DS Wood and DC Blackburn were interviewing Amanda Cole, DS Mason and DC Scott were interviewing Penelope Harding, and DI Beaumont had asked for PC Candy Nichol's company whilst interviewing Sally Flathers.

"I know we've asked you this before," DS Wood said, "But did Paxton have any enemies?"

"You know, it's funny," she said, although her expression said it was anything but. "I'm sure he's a hated man in some parts of the country. A black football player with a white wife. But in Leeds, he was loved." A tear fell from her eye. "I'm not sure anybody would want to hurt him." Then as if she'd just suddenly remembered, she added, "Other than that bastard loan shark. Have you found him yet?"

"Him?"

She turned and looked at herself reflected in the interview room's two-way mirror and didn't make eye contact. "An assumption. I shouldn't do that, I guess." Amanda then turned and looked at Wood. "Why am I here, Detective?" She blew a blonde strand out of her face. "Are you reopening the case?"

"Not at the moment, no, but as I'm sure you've heard, Edmund Flathers and Andre Harding are also dead."

"I had no idea," Amanda said. "With everything that's happened to Pax, I've not been interested in the news." She paused. "I must give Sally a call. And Penny. They'll be distraught."

"You know their wives?" Tashan asked, jumping in before Wood could respond.

Amanda looked put out. "Of course I do. Pax was very good friends with Eddy. I know that you know that. And as for Andre, he was my husband's sports psychotherapist. I've had drinks with them at their home many times."

Wood slid across the article Luke Mason had found in the library. Amanda took it, frowned, and then read it.

She kept looking up after finishing each sentence with accusing eyes. "As well as speaking to Edmund Flathers, nineteen of Hunslet Carr, Leeds, officers from the West Yorkshire Police advised they have spoken with two other individuals related to the drug-related death of Austrian citizen, Lena Schneider," Amanda read. "Who the hell is Lena Schneider, and what does this have to do with Paxton?"

"If you keep reading, you'll see why we've brought it up, Mrs Cole," Tashan explained.

"South Leeds Live have contacted Paxton Cole, seventeen of Middleton, and Andre Harding, seventeen of Beeston, but have so far received no comment." She looked between detectives. "And? He never mentioned it to me, so I assume he wasn't involved."

"And whilst we agree with you, Mrs Cole," Wood said. "The fact that all three men mentioned in this article are now dead seems like a coincidence to me. And I don't believe in coincidences."

Amanda shrunk into her chair, reacting to Wood's words as if she was somehow being accused of the crime herself.

"We also need to discuss the money that Edmund Flathers loaned from you."

* * *

Mason noted that Penelope Harding, Penny, had been fine since starting the interview. But now that they'd mentioned Lena Schneider and handed over the article he'd found, she'd started acting differently. She'd started mirroring their mannerisms.

If Jay started tapping his pen, then Penny would tap her nails against the table. If Luke smiled, then Penny smiled. If Jay ran a hand through his hair, then Penny ran her own hand through her blonde curls.

"What do you do for a job again?" Luke asked.

Penny frowned. "Why?"

The mirroring she was doing was a de-escalation technique that officers were taught during training. Basically, officers were trained to subtly mimic the behaviour of someone in a confrontation, making them more likely to like you.

Was she hiding something and trying to avoid scrutiny?

"Just curious." He looked at Jay. "Remind me to do a background check on Mrs Harding."

"Will do, Sarge," Jay said. He scribbled it down in his notebook, and Penny looked horrified.

"I'm an accountant," she confessed.

Now the two BMWs and the beautiful house made sense, but the escalation technique did not.

"Thanks for that," Jay said. "He underlined the sentence he'd written just moments before, then looked up and met Penny's eyes. "So, back to Lena Schneider." Penny nodded. "You've never heard that name before?"

The accountant's lips thinned. She chewed at them as if attempting to stop herself from voicing something she had been conditioned not to say.

"Penny?" Jay asked. Then he repeated the question. "Have you heard the name Lena Schneider before?"

But Penelope Harding sat in silence, the tiny flitting movements of her eyes the only outward sign of the processing that was currently happening inside her head.

* * *

Sally Flathers looked like a tired little mouse. A tired, little, blonde mouse. And George understood why.

"He never told me Andre and Paxton were involved," she explained.

"So, to confirm, you've heard the name Lena Schneider before?" George asked.

"Well, of course, I have. She's that poor girl who died, and everybody accused my poor Eddy of being the cause."

Whether Sally's words were accurate or not was irrelevant. It was the fact that she advised she didn't know Paxton and Andre had been dragged in for questioning. And he believed her.

"So Mr Flathers never told you that the West Yorkshire Police had questioned Cole and Harding?" She shook her head. Then George read out the second article Luke Mason had found. "It reads, 'My source within the West Yorkshire Police has advised that the two seventeen-year-olds questioned in connection with the drug-related death of Austrian national Lena Schneider have been fully cleared. Both teenagers, when questioned, gave evidence against Edmund Flathers, and the West Yorkshire Police are now confident they have reached the charging threshold.'" George took a breath. "You don't think Edmund was trying to blackmail them, do you?"

"Absolutely not." She shook her head as tears began to fall from her eyes. "And unless you have any evidence of such a crime, I suggest you keep those accusations to yourself."

"I apologise, Mrs Flathers," George said. "But we have to ask the tough questions; otherwise, we'll never find out what happened to your husband."

"OK."

"You told my sergeant that you didn't think Edmund had any enemies, but when you and I spoke, you wondered whether Lena Schneider's family was involved." He paused. "Has anybody been in contact with you?"

"I'm sorry, no."

"OK," George said before removing a transcript from a manilla envelope. "Please read this, Mrs Flathers."

She picked up the transcript and began to read, her eyes narrowing as they scanned each line and took in the words.

* * *

"What money?" Amanda Cole asked.

"The money you argued with Edmund Flathers about in the Windmill Inn in Linton," Tashan explained. "Money he owed you?"

"We argued, but not about any money he owed me." She

frowned.

"So what did you argue about? Because I have two witnesses, plus another independent witness that says otherwise, Mrs Cole," Wood said.

"Who are these witnesses? Because they're lying to you."

The two detectives produced the printouts of the statements Mr and Mrs Hirst gave DI Beaumont and a third from a punter who witnessed the argument. Laid bare the exchange between her and Edmund, there had been a moment of disbelief, several seconds of denial, and then the silent processing had started.

Wood and Tashan watched her, saying nothing, letting her reach whatever conclusion she needed to get to reach. Eventually, she said, "I did meet with Eddy. And we did argue. But not about any money he owed me."

"So what was it about then?" Tashan asked. "As you can see," he said, pointing at the statements, "you were loud enough to be heard."

Amanda was quick to shake her head. "I can explain," she advised.

Tashan and Wood waited.

And waited.

And waited.

Still nothing.

Her eyes filling with tears, Amanda brought a knuckle to her mouth and sucked on the skin. "He owed Paxton money, OK?" She buried her face in her hands, her shoulders shaking. "I thought—I thought it would help me if Eddy could give me what he owed Pax. Especially with all the issues regarding Pax's life insurance."

"You said you weren't arguing about money," Wood advised.

She looked up and scowled. "I said we weren't arguing

about any money *he* owed *me*." Then she looked horrified and brought her hand up to her mouth. "Oh God, you think it was me, don't you? You think I killed Eddy Flathers?" She was babbling now, unable to stop the words coming. "No, no, no, no, no! It wasn't me, I swear!"

"Think of it from our point of view, Mrs Cole," Wood said, softening her tone. "You're witnessed arguing with a man about money the day before he dies. And Paxton, he hit you." It wasn't a question, and Amanda didn't waste their time by bothering to answer it. "Then he dies under suspicious circumstances, and with the gambling debt, and the mention of life insurance, it all just sounds–"

"Suspicious," Amanda cut in. She shook her head, and all those blinks she'd been holding back came one after the other. "I see that. But it doesn't mean I killed him. Or Pax. Plus, why would I kill Andre? So it's clear you're linking the three deaths." She began to cry once more, emotionally crumbling before their eyes.

Wood thought very hard for a few moments. This was her interview, and the outcome would reflect upon her. "Is there anything else you can tell us about the night you argued with Edmund Flathers?"

"Nothing. He couldn't give me the money," she advised. "He was skint." She shrugged.

"And anything about Lena Schneider?"

"Sorry, I'm clueless about that."

But DS Wood wasn't sure she believed Amanda Cole.

* * *

"Of course I have," Penny confirmed. "Andre and I didn't have any secrets."

"Was he involved?" Luke asked.

"What?"

"Was he involved in Lena Schneider's death?" Luke asked.

For a long time, Penny said nothing. Then the twitching of her lips and the slight intake of breath suggested she was thinking about it, and soon words would come. Or so they hoped. But she remained silent for a full minute before finally settling on what she wanted to say.

"Andre *was* involved, but only that he was in the room when he assumed they were handed over." She paused. "Andre was keen on Lena's friend, and Pax keen on Lena herself. Despite being older, Eddy always used to tag along, the odd one out." She blew a stray blonde strand away from her round face. "Andre thought Eddy was gay. He also thought that somebody else other than Eddy or Pax supplied Lena with the drugs. Or that's what he told me, anyway."

"Do you think he was covering for Pax or Eddy?" Wood asked.

"I don't think so, no," Penny advised.

Jay was about to say something when Penny started speaking. Again, they smiled at each other, this time more at the embarrassment of talking over each other rather than her mimicking him.

"He told the police this, of course. And when they cleared him and Pax, Andre was surprised."

"Why?"

"Because he and Paxton were black, not white." Her cheeks went red, and she lowered her gaze to the table. "But that's all I know," she lamented. "Honestly."

"Did you not try and ask him about it?" Jay asked.

Penny smiled and nodded her head. "Of course I did. He just didn't want to talk about it. I remember him telling me it happened long ago and that *he* wasn't guilty of it." She shrugged. "And so I stopped asking."

* * *

"'He was a ginner of average height and build, with the beginnings of a beer belly'," Sally said, a look of disgust on her face. "My poor Eddy." Tears began to roll down her face. "He was so much more than that. So much more."

George's phone buzzed, and he took it out. It was a message from Isabella. *Amanda confirmed the meeting at the Windmill Inn. Edmund owed Paxton money.*

"Sorry about that, Mrs Flathers," George said. He showed PC Nichols the message, who nodded. "Did you know Edmund had met with Mrs Amanda Cole?"

She shook her head. More tears made their way down her cheeks, the grief carving through her face like a river that broke its banks. "Were they having an affair?"

George was somewhat taken aback by the question. "I don't think so, no," he explained. He pointed towards the three statements. "They were arguing about money. Money, your late husband, owed her late husband."

Sally crumbled again then, her hand shaking as she brought it to her mouth. "That man of mine seemed to owe everybody money."

"Did you know?" George asked. "About the loan, I mean."

"No!" she retorted, horrified by the suggestion. "No, I had no idea. No idea at all."

George allowed her a few moments respite, and she surprised

him when she looked up and asked, "How is any of this relevant to my late husband's death?"

"Because we're looking at people with reasons to hurt your husband."

"And you think that *tart* killed him?"

"Excuse me?" George asked.

Terror flashed across Sally's face, but it was closely followed by embarrassment. "I'm sorry. We're actually very good friends, but I saw the way my husband looked at her." She twisted a blonde curl around her finger. "Most men looked at Amanda that way." Sally looked at Candy. "You seen her?"

Then George narrowed his eyes. Could Flathers and Amanda have had an affair? Wood had mentioned she thought Amanda might have been seeing somebody, but that was based on how she was dressed. It was something they'd have to look into.

"Can you enlighten us as to why Edmund would have been angry with Amanda?" George asked, moving the conversation along.

"I wasn't there, so I have no idea," Sally huffed.

Do you see the sentence highlighted in red pen, Sally?" George asked.

She nodded and read it aloud. "'I wouldn't have noticed, except I had to ask the man to leave. He and Amanda had a right row. A proper barney. The man was furious, let me tell you.'"

"'Furious'," George said. "Would you ever describe Edmund as 'furious'?"

"No," Sally told them. "He was a lovely man with a very gentle demeanour. He never fell out with anybody."

A look passed between George and PC Nichols that was so brief and subtle that Sally missed it completely. They knew for a fact that Edmund had argued with Sean Bishop about money.

When George advised Sally of this, she sniffed, rolled her eyes in embarrassment as the tears began to fall again, and then managed to croak out a final. "That bloody man of mine, always causing trouble."

"Is there anything else you can tell us that may be helpful in our investigation?" George asked.

Sally turned and looked at the mirror, wondering who might be standing there, watching and listening.

Was she afraid of somebody? And if so, who?

"No, nothing," she eventually choked out. "It seems I know nothing at all."

Chapter Twenty-five

The following morning, George and the team discussed their interviews with each wife. As the discussion by the Big Board progressed, George found they hadn't learned much. Not really. Not much other than Amanda Cole had no idea who Lena Schneider was. The other two wives did, with Sally Flathers knowing Edmund's side of the story and Penelope knowing Andre's.

George's phone buzzed in his pocket. He slipped it out and looked at the number. "Hiya, Dr Ross."

George gripped the table at Dr Ross' reply, his knuckles white. "George? I have Paxton Cole's toxicology report."

* * *

DI Beaumont had put the pathologist on speaker. "Scopolamine?"

"Correct, son."

"Never heard of that before. What is it?"

Dr Ross reeled off an answer from a textbook. "Scopolamine, also known as hyoscine, or colloquially as Devil's Breath, is a natural or synthetically produced belladonna alkaloid and anticholinergic drug that is formally used as a medication for treating motion sickness, nausea, and vomiting. It is also sometimes used before surgery to decrease saliva."

"Belladonna?" Wood asked.

"Yes, Isabella," Ross confirmed.

"That's poison, right?"

"Right. Created by certain plants and shrubs."

"I've heard of that," DC Scott piped up. "Deadly nightshade, right?"

"Wrong, son," Dr Ross said. "In this case, at least. Brugmansia suaveolens."

"In English, Doc," George said.

"Paxton Cole was poisoned by Devil's Breath." He paused for effect, but George was getting pissed off. "Devil's Breath is made from several plant species, one of which is called Brugmansia, or Angel's Trumpet, because of its large, trumpet-shaped flowers. They're native to South America, and more commonly Colombia."

The entire team looked at George. "What are you standing around for? Find Luis Rodríguez, and bring him in now!"

***

"Sorry about that, Dr Ross," George said after putting Luke in charge of hunting Luis Rodríguez down. He was to work in tandem with Sergeant Greenwood and his Uniforms to find the footballer. "So you're saying Cole ingested this trumpet Angel-devil-plant-thing?"

"Not at all, son," Dr Ross said. "The chemical scopolamine, toxic at high dosages, was found in his system. And that chemical comes from Brugmansia. Now as you can probably imagine, I'm not particularly green-fingered. So, I did some research before calling you." Dr Ross continued, oblivious to the chill slowly spreading through George's body. "According to a reputable gardening website, all parts of brugmansias are highly toxic and can cause serious illness or death if ingested, but the seeds are the killer. Once ground into a powder, a small amount would kill a person instantly." Ross took a breath. "Worst still, that powder is undetectable. It doesn't have a smell or a taste and dissolves easily."

"So it could have been put in, say, a drink?" George asked, thinking about the glasses they found in the Harding household and the whisky glass they found at the Flathers'. They hadn't received any information from toxicology regarding those two deaths.

"Exactly."

Shit. "Right, well, thanks, Dr Ross. Anything else?"

"Nothing yet, son," Dr Ross explained. "They're working on Flathers and Harding, so we should get them back soon. Though, that could be a week." He paused. "I'm hoping less, though, especially considering they're aware of the scopolamine now."

George turned to Wood once he'd hung up, about to discuss with her his thoughts, when Isabella beat him to it. "There's a greenhouse at the Flathers' house," she explained.

"And potted plants inside," George added.

Wood was already slinging on her jacket as the words left George's mouth. He picked up his car keys. He would gain access to that greenhouse and look around whether Sally Flathers was home or not.

* * *

Scopolamine poisoning. The more George thought about it as he made the trip to Hunslet, the more far-fetched it sounded—like the plot of some Agatha Christie novel, as opposed to the modern-day suburbs of Leeds.

Wood was talking to the forensic collision investigator who had produced the report for them, discussing the effects scopolamine could have had on Paxton. Finally, after hanging up, Wood was convinced, and when she explained it to George, he, too, was convinced.

The forensic collision investigator was convinced the toxin would have turned Cole into a vegetative-like state, which would explain the lack of skid marks and the telemetry taken from the car.

Paxton hadn't crashed on purpose. Instead, the toxin had caused him to lose control.

It was agreed then that Paxton Cole had been murdered.

DI Beaumont pulled outside the terraced house, got out of the car, and knocked on the door. He waited, then knocked again. Then he repeated that routine a third time.

Nothing.

He assumed Sally Flathers was still in Middleton at her sister's place, though he couldn't be sure.

On the way to Hunslet, he and Wood had bounced ideas off each other, wondering that if, indeed, Sally did keep poisonous shrubs, then why. They discussed motives because the opportunity, and the means to kill her husband, were obvious. It was not, however, obvious as to why the wife had possibly killed the footballer and the therapist. If, indeed, she was even involved. Though it seemed anything was possible at the moment, and George wasn't sure where his head was at.

"The greenhouse was around back, George," Isabella said

from the Merc.

George nodded and jogged to the end of the street where he could access the back gardens of the terrace. He scolded himself as he jogged, wondering why he was even here. They had no suspicions about Sally Flathers regarding her husband's death. And they had even less idea why she would kill Paxton Cole.

Once inside the Flathers' back garden, he marched across the grass to the greenhouse. The windows were frosted so that George couldn't see inside. Whatever lived in there was green. After gloving up, he opened the door, which was luckily unlocked, and a green tendril stretched out towards him. The surprise and the warmer air made George's breath stutter, and he hoped he hadn't just inhaled anything insidious.

That thought caused him to pause, and he took out a face mask he kept handy from his coat's inside pocket, one of those disposable ones from the Coronavirus pandemic. Then he entered a place where green living things were curling up the insides and wondered whether he'd ever felt so out of his depth before.

Probably not, he reckoned, as he peered at the tangle of greenery around him. Though luckily for him, many of the plants and herbs were neatly labelled, and he found he'd heard of many of them.

Flicking to the images Dr Ross had sent to the shared inbox, George zoomed in on the Angel's Trumpet, looking around the greenhouse for the obvious-looking hanging trumpet-shaped flowers. But nothing matched. Nothing at all. Nothing was remotely similar.

George chewed the inside of his cheek as he strained his memory, thinking back to the plants that were inside, but truth be told, whilst he knew he'd seen the shrubs before, he wasn't entirely convinced they'd been at the Flathers'.

He remembered nothing and racked his brains as he raced back to the office, calling Yolanda en route and asking her to organise for Uniforms to bring Sally Flathers into the station. Then he thought about the McDonald's and the pasta with chicken and cream sauce they knew Flathers and Harding had eaten before their deaths, respectively.

Then he called DS Williams again. "Change of plan, Yolanda," he explained. "I'm going to go and see Amanda Cole and have a chat with her about the toxicology report. She might be able to remember what he had for breakfast. Meanwhile, pull up the PM report, and let me know if Dr Ross managed to document any stomach contents."

George hung up and then turned to Wood. "Ring Amanda and make sure she's in."

* * *

"You think Amanda Cole is involved?" Wood asked as they entered Linton. She hadn't been able to get in touch with Amanda.

"I do, yeah," George confirmed. "We don't have a link to Harding yet, but we know Amanda was seen having an argument with Edmund Flathers not long before his death. And she was the wife of Paxton Cole, the footballer." He turned to his fiancée. "You know me, I don't believe in coincidences."

They soon pulled up outside the gate of a darkened house. George got out and pressed the buzzer on the gate, but there was no answer. "Looks like we wasted our time," Wood said.

George shook his head. "Nah, it was always a risk coming

here." He had another look up at the house. "Looks secure, but empty. She's probably at her mother's house in Middleton. We can swing by there on the way back."

Chapter Twenty-six

The following morning, DI Beaumont and DC Scott sat knee to knee in an interview room whilst DS Wood watched via a live video link.

Luis Rodríguez entered with his solicitor, trying his best to exude confidence. After Jay and a team of Uniforms had brought Rodríguez in, he'd spent the night in the holding cells at Elland Road Police Station, but how much sleep he had managed was debatable. George thought that the footballer looked like shit.

They sat down, and George handed out the document folders whilst DC Scott started the Digital Interview Recorder. The police translation service had already translated the documents into Spanish so Luis and his Colombian solicitor could read them in their native language.

As before, George had managed to secure a Spanish-to-English translator, a young man waiting on the other end of the telephone, despite the Colombian solicitor offering to interpret for Luis.

"Interview of Luis Rodríguez in the presence of his solicitor by Detective Inspector Beaumont and Detective Constable Scott at 9 am." He asked each participant to identify themselves for the DIR.

"You remain under caution, Mr Rodríguez," DC Scott said. Rodríguez glared at him, but if it affected the young DC, he didn't show it. "Mr Rodríguez, what's your current permanent residence?"

"I live in a rented house in Wetherby," Rodríguez explained, the translation coming via the interpreter.

"Please see document three in your folders," Jay said, and at the sound of the translator, both Colombians looked down. "Document three relates to a legal search of your rented accommodation in the early hours of this morning."

George could feel the tension rising in the sweltering room. They hadn't turned the heating down, and George had begun to sweat. The footballer, though, seemed unaffected.

"Please see document four. Do you recognise the item in document four, Mr Rodríguez?"

"Yes?" he said, more of a question than an answer. "Creatine." A smirk stretched from ear to ear on Rodríguez's face.

Cocky bastard. George knew he'd soon wipe that smirk away. "So to confirm," George said, "those chemicals we found, as documented in document four during our lawful search of the premises, are yours?"

Rodríguez looked at his solicitor, who nodded. "Yes."

George grinned, saying, "A sample has been sent off for testing, and we are awaiting the results."

Both the footballer and the solicitor nodded.

"Please see document twelve in your folders. Document twelve shows an image of a plant." He looked at Luis. "Do you recognise this plant?" It was a printout of the image Dr Ross had given them, and whilst there was no trace of this plant in Luis' property, the white powder was suspicious.

"Borrachero," Luis said.

"A what?" George asked.

"Borrachero," Luis repeated.

"What does Mr Rodríguez mean?" George asked the translator.

"It means drunkard," the interpreter said. "I don't really understand."

"I do," the solicitor said, his accent heavy. "It's the name of a tasteless and odourless drug that blights our homeland, commonly made by grinding down the seeds of plants or shrubs named Angel's Trumpet."

George and Jay looked at each other.

"It's nasty stuff, detectives," the solicitor advised. "I believe you know it by the name, scopolamine?"

George nodded. "That's the toxin we found in toxicology samples taken from Paxton Cole." He looked at Luis. "Did you give Paxton Cole this toxin?" He pointed at the plant, and the interpreter spoke in Spanish.

"Lies!" Rodríguez screamed in English. "Lies! Lies! Lies!"

"Calm down, and less of the shouting, Mr Rodríguez," DC Scott said, raising his brow.

In English, Luis said, "I'll fucking calm down and stop shouting when you stop talking about fucking Borrachero."

"I'm sorry for my client's outburst," the solicitor said. "In our country, Borrachero, or the drunken binge tree, which has beautiful white and yellow blossoms that hang down from the plant's branches, are filled with white seeds. When the seeds are ground down, inhaled or consumed, they can eliminate a person's free will and be fully controlled without inhibitions. It can wipe people's minds and turn them into a zombie-like state. It's horrifying stuff, detectives."

George had already done extensive research on scopolamine,

and whilst stories surrounding the drug are the stuff of urban legends, some stories were very real. There was one story about a person being raped after somebody on the street blew powdered scopolamine into their face. Others had their drinks spiked by the toxin, then forced to empty their bank accounts and even coerced into giving up an organ.

It was truly horrible stuff and would kill at high enough doses.

"Now, if this creatine comes back as scopolamine, I'm going to be very angry, Luis," George threatened. "Tell me the truth. Now!"

"It's not that," said the Colombian, suddenly sounding desperate, the interpreter translating his words into English. He looked shaken, his eyes slightly wide, his movements agitated as he shifted on the seat. "I don't touch the stuff."

"My client is telling the truth. He strenuously denies ownership of scopolamine," his solicitor said.

"So you didn't supply it to Amanda Cole or Paxton Cole?"

After listening to the interpreter, Luis looked confused at first. Then he replied, "Absolutely not."

Weirdly, George believed him. For the moment, anyway, so decided to change tact. He nodded to DC Scott, who knew the drill. "Do you drink whisky, Mr Rodríguez?"

Luis shook his head. "No."

"So we won't find your DNA and prints on this whisky glass, then?" DC Scott asked. They'd taken prints and DNA from Luis when processing him late last night. "Please see document fifteen."

The two Colombians rooted through their pack to find the image. "No," Luis said.

"What's this all about?" the solicitor asked.

Ignoring the solicitor, DC Scott asked, "Document fourteen shows an image of a man. Do you recognise him?"

"Andre Harding," Luis confirmed.

"Correct," Scott said. "What is your relationship with him?"

"He's my friend and my therapist." He looked confused. "I told you about this before. Correct?"

"Correct," DC Scott said. "Are you aware that Andre Harding is dead?"

After listening to the young male interpreter on the phone, Rodríguez nodded and spoke. The young man then translated it as, "He was a good man."

"During our search of Harding's premises, we found those two whisky glasses in the kitchen. We've managed to match the prints from one of the glasses to Andre Harding." George looked at Luis. "Are you sure we won't find your prints on the second one?"

"Of course not," Rodríguez said. "Not unless they'd been there for a while. My last session with him was last week."

"Documents seventeen to twenty show a set of images captured on CCTV. Is that you, Luis?" CSI had managed to access the data from Harding's CCTV camera, which was situated high above his door.

Luis Rodríguez looked gravely down at his copy of the document and scrutinised the images. They showed him knocking on the door of Harding's house. "Yes," he said. "That's the date of my last appointment."

"I agree with you. Mr Rodríguez," Jay said. "Can you explain this one, though?" He pulled out another set of images. "Documents twenty-one to thirty." He pointed to the date and time stamps. "This is the day Andre Harding died."

"That's not me."

"No?" Jay turned to his boss. "That looks like Mr Rodríguez to me, boss; what about you?"

"Looks like Mr Rodríguez to me too, Detective Constable."

Both detectives looked at the footballer.

"I'm being framed. Please, you have to believe me."

"Framed by who?" DC Scott asked. "Why?"

Luis said nothing.

"This is your interview, Mr Rodríguez," George said. "If that's not you, then who is it?"

"That could have been anybody," Rodríguez's solicitor said. "I can't see a resemblance. And I must repeat that my client insists he's innocent."

"It's not me," Luis eventually said.

"Then who is it? And what are they framing you for?"

"You're going too fast for me, detectives. Please slow down and let me think. It's difficult listening to you and the translator."

As if, George thought. The footballer was under pressure and would soon break. They couldn't afford to let him get his composure back.

"Answer us, Luis," George said again. "Who is that person? And what are they framing you for?"

"For the death of Andre Harding." Luis's voice held an edge of panic.

George held out his hands. "Who would frame you, and why?"

"I don't know," Luis said.

George could hear a raw edge to the footballer's voice. "But somebody is?"

"Is what?"

"Framing you?"

"Yes!"

"You see, Mr Rodríguez, I'm not sure I believe you."

Luis swallowed and shook his head, the sharp jerks erratic. "I'm innocent."

"Innocent of what?"

"Are you even listening to me?" He sounded panicked now, and the solicitor placed a calming hand on his shoulder. "I didn't do anything."

"Somebody killed Andre Harding. Just like somebody drugged Paxton Cole." It was time for their final gambit. George produced an image of Edmund Flathers, which they hadn't disclosed to the solicitor.

George slid it across the desk. "Do you know this man?"

The footballer was about to speak when George saw the solicitor grip his shoulder tightly.

"No comment," Luis said.

"Do you recognise this man?" George stabbed his forefinger at the image. He allowed the question to hang, but Luis gave him nothing.

"I probably don't need to remind you, but when this goes to court, we will advise them you answered 'no comment' during questioning.

"Do you recognise this man, Luis?"

"No comment."

After terminating the interview, the two detectives stood up, and George banged on the door to be let out.

"Please... I'm being framed," Luis said in English as they left.

Chapter Twenty-seven

"DS Williams, I've just received some dashcam footage from a member of the public who lives near Linton," DC Blackburn said as he entered the open office of HMET. "It's from the morning of Paxton Cole's death."

Yolanda nodded and held out her hand for the USB stick. Tashan was the kind of guy who would normally want to insert the USB for his superior, but he knew from experience Yolanda was highly independent, so he decided to hand it over.

After Tashan wheeled over his chair, DS Williams hit play once the video file loaded and leaned back in her seat. The screen showed a narrow road and the car's journey down said road.

At first, little happened, not until the driver of the car had to slam on. Then, they watched as an orange McLaren exited the Coles' driveway without a thought for any other traffic.

Because of the narrow road, the driver had to overtake the McLaren by going up the kerb, which gave the dashcam a vantage it usually wouldn't have. And that's when both detectives saw.

Tashan looked at the detective sergeant and asked, "Is that...?"

"Looks like it to me," Yolanda said.

* * *

When George and Wood got back to the station, George finished taking his coat off and then tossed it onto Isabella's desk. "Tashan, get hold of the Uniforms and put out an APB for Amanda Cole. She's disappeared off the face of the earth. Her daughter's with the grandma, Amanda's mum."

"You think something's happened to her, sir?" Yolanda asked.

"No, she's a suspect."

"It's funny that you should say that, sir," Tashan said. "We need to speak to Amanda about this footage we've just received."

"What footage?" He turned to Wood. "See if Josh Fry is in. Jay's out with Uniform looking for the footballer, but I need to see if we can trace Amanda Cole's mobile."

Wood nodded and pulled out her mobile as Yolanda beckoned the two men over to her desk and clicked play.

* * *

Johann answered the door wearing a white tracksuit, the logo of a popular gambling company emblazoned in navy.

"I was just on my way to training, detectives," the Austrian said.

"This won't take long," George advised, stepping inside without being invited.

Wood followed and was sure she could feel Johann's eyes on her as she walked by. The thought of being leered at made her shiver.

"Murdered?" Johann asked once they'd been invited to sit

down. He was still standing up, his head up and shoulders back. "You must be mistaken. I thought you'd declared his death as suicide?"

"Toxicology found traces of scopolamine in the samples taken from Paxton's body. You know of it?"

"No, never heard of it." Johann's eyebrows dipped. "How's Amanda taken it?"

George chose to ignore the question to pursue his own. "The toxin is derived from a plant found in Colombia. Do you have any idea how Paxton could have come into contact with such a plant?"

"I've no clue." Johann shrugged, and then George saw something click. "Edmund Flathers."

"What about him."

"His wife apparently was obsessed with exotic plants. Have you spoken with her?"

"We have," Wood confirmed.

"And?"

"And we cannot comment on an ongoing investigation," Wood explained.

"Of course." He scratched his freshly shaved chin. "Look, detectives, I have no information for you. Really, none at all."

George let the silence hang in the air, and whilst Johann stood to let the detectives out, they stayed put.

Then eventually, Wood asked, "How well do you know Amanda?"

"Excuse me?"

She turned to George. "Was that a difficult question, DI Beaumont?"

"Certainly not, DS Wood."

Both detectives smelt blood in the water and began to circle.

They also had the dashcam footage for leverage.

"What was your relationship with Amanda Cole?" Wood asked.

"Relationship?" Johann scoffed. "She was a WAG. Paxton's wife. That's the extent of our relationship."

"So you never went to visit her at her home? Nothing like that?" Wood asked.

Johann smiled, but it was clear from the rest of his face that he was finding the detectives less amusing by the moment. "She was my mate's wife. Did we necessarily need to forge a relationship?"

"I mean, I have a relationship with my best friend's wife," George pressed. "A friendship." He paused. "A relationship doesn't have to be sexual in nature to be considered a relationship."

"I beg your pardon?" Johann's smile died away completely. "I'm sorry, but I don't think I like what you're implying."

"What exactly am I implying?" George asked.

"That I am having some sort of relationship with my dead friend's wife."

"I wasn't implying that. Were you implying that, Detective Sergeant?"

"I wasn't implying that Detective Inspector," Wood replied. "In fact, just a moment ago, you clarified that a friendship could be considered a relationship." She met Johann's eyes and grinned.

"That's what I thought," George said before turning to Johann. "Are you saying you are involved in a sexual relationship with your dead friend's wife?"

The footballer tutted and then held up both hands as if surrendering. "Of course not." Then the smug smile spread across his face once more. "I apologise for the misunderstanding." He headed towards the door. "As a professional footballer, I must be absolutely clear to avoid scandal. And so, to be clear, I only know Amanda Cole through her late husband, Paxton Cole."

"Oooh, I love a bit of scandal, Detective Inspector," Wood said, grinning at George.

"Me too, Detective Sergeant. Please remind me to check up on past tabloid scandals involving Johann when we're back in the office, will you?" George instructed, not breaking eye contact with the footballer. "Might make for some interesting reading."

"I'm sure it will," she said.

Neither detective moved despite Johann bouncing from one foot to the other.

"Well, you won't find much," Johann advised. "I'm happily married. There are no skeletons in my closet. But *drek* gets written all the time. So all footballers must be on guard."

"*Drek?*"

"Shit, dirt, mud, filth, muck, rubbish. Use whatever word you like." Johann shrugged. "Nonsense!"

"Aye, fair enough," George said. "So, to be clear, you aren't in a sexual relationship with Amanda Cole, nor do you have any kind of relationship with her?"

Johann smiled. Then he lowered his head and clasped his hands in front of him like he was paying his respects. "I just can't believe Paxton was murdered."

"Answer the question."

Johann raised his head. "I'm sorry?"

"So, to be clear, you aren't in a sexual relationship with Amanda Cole, nor do you have any kind of relationship with her?" George repeated.

"Oh, that, sorry, sorry," Johann said, trying to dismiss the whole thing with a laugh and a wave of a hand. "Correct, Detective."

"And you were never at the Cole household without Paxton being there?" Wood asked.

"Never."

"You see, that's very, very interesting that you say that," George said, looking between Isabella and Johann.

"What is?" He checked his watch and was about to point out that he really had to leave before George cut in.

"We have dashcam footage that proves you were at the Cole household the morning Paxton died."

Johann winced and gave his watch a tap. "I've got training to attend, detectives. I really must..." He realised this wasn't carrying any weight with the detectives and sighed. "I really must go."

"Are you really going to pretend DI Beaumont hasn't just advised you that we have dashcam footage that proves you were at the Cole residence the morning Paxton died?"

Johann frowned. "Are you sure it was me?"

"You tell us," George said.

The footballer blew out his cheeks, then edged out of the study door. "Then I think you have a case of mistaken identity." He returned, now wearing a North Face jacket, and retrieved his mobile from a desk drawer. "Now, if you'll excuse me, I need to—"

"Sit down, Johann," George said.

The footballer looked like a deer caught in headlights. "Wait, I know why you're here. You think... You think I had something to do with it. With Pax's death. You think I killed him?"

CHAPTER TWENTY-SEVEN

"The thought hadn't crossed my mind," George said. "But now that you mention it, it makes sense." He turned to Wood. "I just assumed he was having an affair with his mate's wife, not that he'd actually murdered his best mate."

"I don't think Johann would've killed Cole, Detective Inspector," Isabella said.

Johann puffed out his cheeks and then smiled at Wood. "Exactly, Detective Sergeant! Thank you! Thank you!"

Wood grinned. "I think it's more likely he'd have paid someone," Isabella concluded.

George scoffed as he appraised the footballer. "I'd probably agree with you on that, Detective Sergeant."

"No, absolutely not!" Johann said. "This is unacceptable. I'm not having this in my own house. I'm not being accused of... whatever it is I'm being accused of." He turned to the two detectives. "One of my best friends has not long died, and you dare to come here and accuse me of killing him!" He pulled out his phone. "Who is your superior? Please provide their email as I'm going to put in a complaint."

"Aye about that, Johann," George said, standing up. "You can personally submit your complaint to Detective Superintendent Smith at Elland Road station." He turned to DS Wood. "Would you like to do the honours?"

"I am arresting you on suspicion of murder. You do not have to say anything. But, it may harm your defence if you do not mention when questioned something which you later rely on in court. Anything you do say may be given in evidence."

Chapter Twenty-eight

The following morning, Johann Gruber sat stone-faced in the interview room next to his solicitor. He'd spent the night in the holding cells, and George knew what that did to a person. Gruber then yawned,

George reeled off the usual spiel, then said nothing for a long moment. The tension built as he rifled through some documents. Then he slid said papers across the table at a snail's pace. "It says here, Mr Gruber," George eventually said, pointing down at a report he had in front of him, "that you tried very hard to curtail our attempts to take DNA samples and fingerprints from you. Why?"

"I didn't realise I *had* to provide them. I assumed it was my choice. My right!"

"Not when you're arrested, Mr Gruber," George explained. "When that happens, most of your rights go right out of the window." He cleared his throat. "Shall we begin?"

"Where were you between 6 am and 9 am on the 7th of January, the morning Paxton Cole was murdered?" Tashan asked, clearly no longer star-struck.

"I can't remember." He turned to his solicitor. "That's OK, right?"

"I've advised you to say nothing, Mr Gruber. As far as I'm

concerned, that's the only *OK* thing you can do right now."

As with all police interviews, George had disclosed evidence to Gruber's solicitor, who then had time to go through it with his client. George didn't like the rules, especially as it usually resulted in a 'no comment interview,' but it was what they had to follow.

So, the footballer turned to George and Tashan and said, "No comment."

"But you've just told me you can't remember," Tashan said. "You're aware we are being recorded right now?" He pointed towards the tape, and the camera trained on Gruber.

"No comment."

"OK," Tashan said. "I'll tell you where I think you were, and you can confirm or deny it. OK?"

"No comment."

"I believe you were at the Cole household, Mr Gruber," Tashan explained. "I think you were there to commit a heinous crime. I think you poisoned your friend and colleague."

"No comment."

"I'm right, aren't I, Mr Gruber?"

"No comment."

"And I'd quite like to know why you killed Paxton Cole, Mr Gruber, especially as during previous interviews, you said you considered him 'family'." He turned to George. "I'm not sure I'd kill somebody I considered family, sir, would you?"

George stared right at Johann. "Definitely not."

"No comment."

"Please disclose proof that my client killed Paxton Cole because so far, he has denied all accusations," the solicitor asked.

"We're awaiting the DNA profile analysis and are currently

matching Mr Gruber's prints to prints we've found."

"What prints?" Johann piped up.

George grinned. He nodded towards Tashan, who said, "Where were you between 1 and 3 pm on the 29th of January, Mr Gruber?"

"At home."

"Can anybody verify that?"

"No comment."

"And can you confirm where you were between noon and 4 pm on Thursday the 2nd of February, Mr Gruber?"

"Home again."

"And again, can anybody verify that?"

"No comment," Johann snarled.

"Did you kill Andre Harding, Edmund Flathers and Paxton Cole?" Tashan asked.

"Who the hell is Edmund Flathers?" Johann asked.

Tashan stared. "Answer the question."

"Who the hell is Edmund Flathers?" Johann repeated. George produced a picture of him from the pack by his chair and handed it over. "I don't know this man."

"We find that hard to believe," George said. "Just admit it." Despite not knowing how Harding and Flathers had died, it was undoubtedly worth asking Johann Gruber. If only to see the look on his face."

"Admit what?"

"That you killed Andre Harding, Edmund Flathers and Paxton Cole," Tashan said.

"No comment."

"Is that how you're playing this, Mr Gruber?"

"No comment."

It was time to change the questions they were asking, so

George removed another image from his pack and slid it over. "Do you know what this is?"

"A plant."

"Yes, a plant. Do you know the name of this plant?"

"I'm a footballer," Johann said, "not a fucking gardener." He shrugged. "I've not a clue."

"I think you know already, Mr Gruber, but this plant is called Angel's Trumpet. It is named as such because of its large, trumpet-shaped flowers. They're native to South America, and more commonly Colombia." Tashan paused. "We've learnt you grind the seeds of this flower down into a powder which results in a toxin named scopolamine."

"What the hell's that got to do with me?"

"Are you and Luis Rodríguez in this together, Mr Gruber? Did the two of you kill Paxton Cole by giving him scopolamine?" George questioned.

"No comment."

* * *

Beaumont gave DC Scott an encouraging smile. He grinned back and then tacked the papers in his hand to the Big Board, one by one the team could see. The lad seemed nervous, which George thought was unusual.

"Whilst the boss interviewed Johann Gruber, I worked with DS Joshua Fry and the digital forensics team, looking through Gruber's and Harding's mobiles. They're able to access everything on the devices—"

"Great work Jay," George murmured.

"—which means we've been able to examine everything from photos and media to detailed message transcripts." Jay watched his team nodding. Tashan was scribbling notes. "As you can imagine, both primarily used text messages and WhatsApp to communicate. For Andre, he used WhatsApp for friends and family and texts for work and clients. Johann did the same."

"I'll start with Andre." Jay pinned up the penultimate printout from his hand and turned back to the team, who was staring intently at the Big Board. "From WhatsApp, there's nothing of any concern. Most messages are from Penelope. There are some from Luis Rodríguez recently, asking in broken English for details of their next sessions. A few from some of the other footballers, too. And from info provided by Penelope, we've matched numbers to Andre's acquaintances."

"Fair enough," George said. "And his text messages?"

"In Andre's text messages, discounting administrative ones like notifications from his phone network, Just Eat and bank, etc., there's a lot of communication from his boss. But nothing untoward." Jay paused. "Sorry."

"Don't be sorry, lad," George said. "You can't help what you find, even if it's very little." He smiled. "Tell us about Johann."

The interview with Gruber had been challenging, especially considering they had little to go on. George hadn't liked the man instinctively, but that meant little—he often didn't like people instinctively. As a detective, people like Johann set him on edge. It's the vibe they give off that unsettled him. It was probably something unresolved and probably from his childhood, but whatever it was, it troubled him.

"Johann's phone is filled with messages I'd consider banter, boss," Jay explained, tacking his final printout to the board. "Especially when it comes to WhatsApp. There are various groups, each containing different footballers. Then, there are the expected WhatsApp messages from his wife." Jay shrugged. "The text messages are all business, mostly with his agent. It seems the Austrian has a personal chef with whom he keeps in regular contact, and like with Andre, the usual administrative ones from his phone network and bank."

"So, nothing suspicious?" George asked.

"Nothing suspicious at all, boss," Jay said, "which, weirdly, makes me suspicious. Josh tells me he finds the usual porn website in the internet history and stuff like that. Which we did find on Andre's phone." Jay grinned. "Looked as if he had a thing for blondes." He then started smiling more.

"Get on with it, Jay."

"Sorry, boss. But Johann had nothing like that. His phone was so... sterile."

"OK, DC Scott. Go through the network data with us."

"Aye, sure, boss." He shifted his weight from one foot to the other. "GPS data retrieved from Johann's phone suggests that he was at home, at the training ground, and at various restaurants around the city on the days that Edmund Flathers and Andre Harding died." He paused. "If we consider the time of deaths Dr Ross has advised, then Gruber was home when both Flathers and Harding died."

"He could have left his phone at home," Wood said.

"I agree, Sarge," Jay said.

"I think we need to speak with Mrs Gruber. We can ask her where she was and see if she can alibi him." He turned to Jay. "I do agree it sounds suspicious, though. What do you have for Andre?"

"GPS data retrieved from Harding's phone suggests he was at the house all day the day he died. I checked historical data, and when he works from home, he doesn't leave, so that's not suspicious."

"So we got nothing." He looked around at his team, who looked despondent.

"You know what I've been thinking, though, boss?" Jay asked. George raised his brows, inviting the young DC to continue. "We've been advised that Andre Harding delivered sessions at home, and his GPS data confirms that." He looked to Tashan, who nodded. "That would require a tablet or a laptop of some kind. Right?"

"Right," George said. "He could have done it via his mobile, though. They use Zoom."

"I know that, boss. But, Zoom wasn't even installed on his phone. Nor had it ever been."

"So we're missing a laptop or a tablet, then?"

"Aye, boss, I think we are."

Chapter Twenty-nine

It felt strange to return to a dead man's home. Very strange. And as he suited up, icy fingers gripped at his spine. DS Wood and DC Blackburn were interviewing Harding's boss and work colleagues.

Lindsey Yardley's SOC team were busy coming and going. One was already cataloguing the broken side door. Shattered glass was sprinkled across the floor. Unlike the front door, no CCTV camera was looking down at him. He guessed that was why whoever had broken in had chosen this door to smash.

Because Penelope had gone to stay with her parents, not being able to face going back to the house, she had only called it in that afternoon and was unsure when the break-in had happened.

George entered, carefully keeping to the stepping plates the SOCOs had placed. Any diverge from that path could result in the contamination of evidence. And that was never good.

The side door led into the kitchen where they'd found the two whisky glasses during George's previous visit. He remembered the house being much tidier before, whilst now, it looked like a tornado had passed through.

Every drawer, cabinet and cupboard had been opened and ransacked; the contents rifled through before being thrown to the floor. CDs, DVDs, books and Blu-rays, and even cushions from the brown leather sofa had been removed, split open, and the spongy filling tossed aside. The TV remained in place, untouched, as did the surround sound system. George's eyes narrowed. This wasn't a burglary.

In the small office next to the living room, various manilla folders had been emptied all over the desk and floor. George crouched on the plates and peered at them, careful not to disturb any evidence. They were therapy notes taken during meetings with Harding's various clients, and George wondered whether they could get a warrant and look through the ones regarding Paxton Cole and Luis Rodríguez. In addition, there was an open laptop case in the corner, at least proving Jay's theory that Harding had one. But where was it? And why didn't Lindsey's team seize it when they found the journal?

Cables had been pulled away from the monitor and spaced across the desk as though someone had wrenched them from the floor. He followed them with his eyes before stepping further into the office when he found what he was looking for. A laptop charger snaked its way towards a space with an empty laptop stand.

"Lindsey," George called out, but she didn't arrive. "He stepped back into the living room and nodded a SOCO over. "Was there a laptop in this office?"

"No, sir," not today, at least.

"What about when you found the journal?"

"Sorry, sir, I wasn't here. It's my first time in this property."

"Is Hayden Wyatt here?"

"Somewhere, sir." She looked around, then shrugged. "Sorry."

George doubted there had been a laptop in the office during

either search. If it had been there when the body was found, it would have been seized then.

Shit.

George scratched his chin. This was a messy search and hoped the culprit left traces behind. He was certain this wasn't a typical burglary. The TV was a testament to that. Though whoever had broken in could have been searching for small valuables or car keys, he mused. Yet Harding's BMW was sat on the drive.

Nothing made sense.

He moved on, wanting to take a look upstairs. He remembered there being a TV and a PS5 in the bedroom. The game console was still relatively rare in the UK, which would confirm whether this was a simple burglary.

A CSI in a paper suit and mask waited for him to enter Harding's bedroom before she walked past him into the bathroom. He doubted anything was in there. From what he remembered, it was pretty modern and tidy. Almost sterile.

Another SOCO was combing through the room and looked up at George. "I've just found this, sir," he said. He held out an evidence bag containing a mobile phone inside.

"Where did you find it?"

"It was concealed inside that cabinet, there," the SOCO said and pointed towards the built-in cabinet. "You have to depress it, and it clicks out. Clever, really."

George took the evidence bag from him, his interest piqued, and looked at the device. It was an old Nokia that was switched off. "Why didn't you find this during your last search?" George asked.

"I'm unsure, sir; you'll have to ask Dr Yardley." He smiled. "However, I nearly didn't notice it. It's extremely well concealed."

An itch started between his shoulder blades and worked its way up to his neck as George nodded at the SOCO. This was Harding's place, so unless Penelope had hidden the Nokia, then Andre had two phones. That was suspicious and significant. He needed the contents of that phone, and he needed it yesterday, but he'd have to wait for CSI and then digital forensics to process it.

Shit.

He turned to the male SOCO, who found it. "This needs processing ASAP." The young man nodded but didn't approach to take the evidence bag. "I mean it, young man. Find Lindsey Yardley, and get this back. If you have to take it yourself, then so be it. I need you to process it!"

"OK, sir," he said, taking the bag and disappearing from the bedroom.

George looked around the room, realising it was just as messy as the rest of the house, clearly having been subjected to the same tornado as downstairs. Both bedside drawers had been tipped over, their contents spilling all over the floor. The mattress had been pulled off the bed and stripped. Same for the duvet and pillows.

Clothes and shoes had been tossed onto the floor from the still-open wardrobe. An opened jewellery box had been hurled, alongside its contents, into the corner. George used a tile to step closer and saw the glint of gold and silver.

George narrowed his eyes once again. The TV and the PS5 were both where they were last time. This was a search, not a burglary. But who was searching? And why.

Were they looking for the Nokia? Or something else?

He had so many questions but no answers.

CHAPTER TWENTY-NINE

Not until a SOCO shouted out from the bathroom, anyway. "Come quick! I've found something in the bathroom!"

Chapter Thirty

They took Rodríguez out of holding. Their extension was nearly up. It was now or never.

After starting the interview, they informed him he was still under caution. According to the interpreter, the first words out of Rodríguez's mouth were: "I'm being framed."

Wood cleared her throat and shared a look with George. He nodded at her. "What are you being framed for? And by who?" Wood asked.

"I'm being framed," Luis repeated in a whisper. "Please. Let me go. I'm innocent."

"Have you found any evidence that my client was at any of the murder scenes? Because as far as I'm aware, DNA is king." The solicitor smiled a yellow-stained toothy grin.

When George said nothing, the solicitor once again asked, "What forensics do you have linking my client to the crime scene?"

"We are in the process of matching your client's DNA and prints to evidence found at the scenes," George lied. It was a half lie, and he was OK with it.

"You won't because I wasn't there," Luis said.

"Fine, let's move on," George said. "Why did you break into Andre Harding's house?"

"I didn't."

"We have footage of you."

"No," the solicitor cut in. "You have footage of somebody." He looked between the detectives. "That person could be anybody, but it's not my client."

It was true; they didn't have footage of him; they were only hoping he'd incriminate himself.

"Fine, let's move the conversation on," George said. "You mentioned in your interview before that you and Paxton argued about a bet."

Luis nodded.

"You a gambling man?"

"As I said before, we're allowed to bet on the horses."

"How are your finances?" George already knew, but he wanted to hear it from the horse's mouth.

"Fine." He shrugged. "I'm a footballer. I'm better off than most."

"That's why you sent most of your salary back home?"

The footballer chewed on his lip. "That's not illegal, is it?"

"No, I'd say the opposite. It's admiral what you're doing for your family, but I can't help but think you're missing out."

"On what?"

"On the banter." George grinned. "Many of your teammates advise you don't socialise with them. I'm now wondering whether that's because you can't rather than not wanting to."

"What of it?"

"Do you know of a man named Jürgen Schmidt?"

"Yes," he said and winced. Then, he quickly added, "No. Wasn't he a footballer?" He looked towards his solicitor for help, who shook his head. "I get confused easily."

"I'll ask you again, Mr Rodríguez. Do you know of a man

named Jürgen Schmidt?"

"No."

"Your face is telling me you do know Jürgen Schmidt. So why would it be doing that?" George asked with a grin. He nodded to Wood.

Wood mirrored George's grin. Rodríguez was sweating even more. Beads of sweat dripped down his face. "Tell us the truth."

Luis Rodríguez looked confused, so Wood said, "Do you know of a man named Jürgen Schmidt?"

"No."

"Jürgen Schmidt is not a very nice man, not a man I'd want to be associated with," George explained.

"I don't know him," Luis protested.

"It was clearly a slip of the tongue, Detective," Rodríguez's solicitor said, framing George with a furious stare. "He's even told you he got confused. So move the interview on."

"As you wish," George said. But this next set of questions was it. This was all they had. "Tell me about Johann Gruber," George asked.

"What about him?"

"What's your relationship like with him?"

"He's a good man. My captain."

"What kind of relationship do you have outside of work?"

Luis swallowed and closed his eyes. "We don't really have a relationship outside of work."

"Because you send all your money to Colombia?"

"No." He opened his eyes. "I'm here to play football, not make friends."

"Yet we know from statements taken from your teammates that you and Gruber were pretty good mates. That's what the statements suggest, right Detective Sergeant?" He looked at Wood.

"That's exactly the impression I got, Detective Inspector."

"So," George said, grinning. "Tell me." He let the two words hang in the air. "Are you and Gruber in this together?"

"In this together? What do you mean?"

"Did you provide the toxin that caused Paxton Cole's death?"

"No!"

"Tell us the truth!"

"I am!" The footballer began to sob now. He was about to crack; George knew it.

"We have him in custody, you know."

"I know."

They'd purposely allowed each to see the other whilst taking them into the yard for some exercise. "You won't believe the stuff he's telling us."

"So tell us the truth before he blames you for everything."

"Is... Is that what Johann's saying? That it was me?"

George and Wood said nothing.

The solicitor whispered in Luis Rodríguez's ear.

"No comment."

"Tell us the truth."

"No comment."

"Okay, Luis, we'll play it your way. This is your last chance." George watched menacingly. "Answer–"

A loud knock on the door interrupted George's words. George turned to find Luke standing there. "For the DIR, Detective Sergeant Mason has entered the room."

"Can I have a word with you outside, please, boss?"

George slipped out quietly, and Wood notified the DIR. Then she sat and stared at the footballer.

***

"Creatine?" George asked, and Luke nodded. "You're sure?"

"The lab's confirmed it, son," Luke said. "Just like Rodríguez said it was."

"Shit."

"Shit indeed."

"And Greenwood found nothing else?"

"No, nothing at all. And Tashan finally managed to get in touch with the training ground." Luke let out a sigh. "They confirmed his alibi."

They had absolutely nothing to hold him for. "Shit."

***

Luis was sweating profusely as he waited for Detective Beaumont to return. There was a ringing in his ears and an ache in his temple. He looked at the female detective. "What's taking him so long?"

She didn't reply.

Then suddenly, the detective came back in with a custody officer and said, "Please release Mr Rodríguez on bail."

Chapter Thirty-one

The following morning, George and the team were in the Incident Room discussing yesterday's events.

"What else did you get from the receptionist?" George asked DS Wood and DC Blackburn.

Isabella nodded. She'd told him everything last night at home, so this was more for the team's sake. "Well, Andre Harding was a well-respected employee of the firm, and both the boss and Andre's colleagues were shocked to learn of his passing. The receptionist had taken it the worst, weirdly. I think she may have fancied him. Or that was the impression I got."

"I thought the same, Sarge," Tashan said. "She didn't know of anybody who would want to hurt Andre. And it was like Andre's death had affected her personally."

"I've got Andre's professional background here," Wood explained. "He'd only ever worked for them. He did some of his training there whilst at university and never left. They are only a small company, but his relationship with the footballers brought in a lot of money. So from what the receptionist told me, and this is only office gossip, they were going to ask him to be a partner."

George nodded. "How was he personally? Of course, we've

got Penelope's side, but she would naturally be biased."

"Same goes for the receptionist, boss," Jay shouted out.

"True," Wood said. "But Tashan and I spoke with all the staff, and they all said the same: That Andre Harding was one of the loveliest men you could ever meet."

* * *

Later, sitting next to Wood at her desk, George eased back in his chair. His fingers tapped on the desk as he opened up the image files taken by SOCOs of Harding's house.

Arms folded, Jay stood beside him, and Tashan had wheeled his chair over too.

"Whoever did that left it a proper mess, boss," Jay said.

"Indeed. The place had been ransacked, with clear signs of breaking and entering," George explained. "I arrived to a SOCO cataloguing the glass-panelled side door that had been smashed. It was a nightmare." His team nodded. "The problem was I had to let CSI slowly and painstakingly process the scene before getting any results.

Overnight, CSI had swept the whole place, and George had barely slept, his nerves on edge as he waited for their report. Lindsey Yardley's team pulled overtime to ensure it landed that morning, especially with the growing severity of the linked deaths.

Lindsey agreed with George that a laptop was missing from Harding's office. As the team looked through the images, they, too, decided that there must have been a laptop at one point. However, he'd managed to speak with Lindsey last night before leaving, and she explained the laptop hadn't been there during their initial search.

CHAPTER THIRTY-ONE

"Lindsey's SOC team found two crucial pieces of evidence," George explained. "A pay-as-you-go Nokia phone concealed inside a built-in cabinet which digital forensics has just delivered the contents into the shared inbox."

He had been waiting for that report the most, which was why he had barely slept. "I'll tell you about the second piece of evidence later. But first, let's read this."

He opened up the digital forensics report to find it wasn't an old, forgotten phone. In fact, it was the complete opposite. There were recent messages and calls on it leading up to the day Harding died. And, after reading them, George knew Harding had concealed the Nokia with good reason.

"All these texts and calls are to the same two numbers," George said, looking at Jay. "Look them up for me, please."

Jay nodded and returned to his desk whilst George continued reading the text message exchanges.

Andre Harding had been up to something illegal. And the communication between the other two mobile numbers was evident in this. Yet within the messages, there were no names. No identifying features. They only had part of the puzzle.

Andre Harding: Did you receive my email?

Contact 1: I did, and I don't appreciate the threat.

Andre Harding: Well I have been trying to get in contact with you now for weeks.

Contact 1: How can we resolve this?

Andre Harding: I explained everything in the email I sent you.

Contact 1: I don't think you did, Andre. I want you to be clear. Give it to me in black and white.

Andre Harding: It's simple. I want money; otherwise, I go to the press.

Contact 1: So you're blackmailing us?

Andre Harding: I suppose.

Contact 1: You could have faked those photographs.

Andre Harding: They're real. She will remember me taking them. Ask her.

Contact 1: I have. She's distraught with the situation. The situation you've put us in.

Andre Harding: I appreciate that it's difficult for her, but I want money.

Contact 1: Well, you're fucking pissing me off with your demands. I'm not sure I want to pay.

Andre Harding: The press will pay me a lot of cash for these images.

Contact 1: Fuck off!

Andre Harding: You're getting an excellent deal. I suggest you take it.

Contact 1: I need to know that this goes away if I pay the money.

Andre Harding: You have my word.

Contact 1: The work of a blackmailer means fuck all. I want the files and any images you've printed.

Andre Harding: Fine, but we do a mutual exchange.

Contact 1: When?

Andre Harding: Tomorrow. You can come between clients.

Contact 1: Fine, I trust you.

Andre Harding: Come to the side door. I don't have a camera on that one.

Contact 1: Fine, I'll be there tomorrow with the cash.

Andre Harding: Good, you'd better! Or there will be consequences.

Contact 1: Whatever…

CHAPTER THIRTY-ONE

Andre Harding: I'm warning you. Don't push me. You better arrive tomorrow with the money, or I'm done.

Contact 1 had made no reply, and George wondered whether the message had been deleted or whether they hadn't replied. Though one thing George was sure of was that Contact 1 was involved in Andre's death. They had to be.

And then, on cue, George's phone rang. Dr Ross. With a tingle of excitement, George knew what the man would say. Or what he'd hoped the pathologist would say. He was about to get the answer they were waiting for.

And sure enough, Dr Ross' voice held a tremor when he answered the call. "George. I've got the toxicology results back for Harding and Flathers."

Chapter Thirty-two

After they'd taken in the shocking information that both Harding and Flathers had died from scopolamine, the five of them of them—Tashan, Jay, Mason, Wood and the DI—huddled around the Big Board in the Incident Room. They needed to crack this case wide open.

"OK, so far, we have Andre Harding threatening an unknown contact via the use of an unregistered burner phone, who we believe caused his death." George spread his hands wide and raised his brows.

"I'd agree with that, boss," Jay said. "We don't know whether 'Contact 1' killed Andre with the scopolamine or whether they got somebody else to do it. But it seems obvious from the messages 'Contact 1' is involved."

"I'd also add that 'Contact 1' was probably the one who ransacked the house or paid somebody else to do it," Tashan said. "And they were probably looking for the burner phone and the second piece of evidence, whatever that is." He looked at George, who smiled.

"SOCOs found film hidden in the bathroom. Inside the tank, weirdly. The roll of film was in a waterproof tube taped underneath the float ball. They are in the process of being developed. Once I know what the images are of, then so will you."

"Sorry, sir, I didn't mean–"

"No bother." George turned to the team to continue the analysis. "From the messages, we can assume Andre met with somebody on the day he died, but as Jay said, we don't know whether the killer is 'Contact 1' or somebody they hired. We also have 'Contact 2' in Andre's burner phone, which we will get to later, but we can infer that 'Contact 2' is a she from the messages between Harding and 'Contact 1'."

"The woman could have been the killer then, 'Contact 2'," Wood piped up. "When it comes to poison, statistically, it's a woman's weapon of choice."

George nodded his agreement. "Ultimately, these two people have the motive to kill Andre Harding, but why would they kill Edmund Flathers and Paxton Cole?"

"Could 'Contact 1' be Lena Schneider's brother?" Luke Mason asked. "Did she have a sister?"

"it could be her brother, aye," George said. "It's the only link we have, but we haven't found him, whoever he is. It would be a mighty coincidence if 'Contact 1' was Lena Schneider's brother." He thought for a moment. "No sisters, no. She probably had cousins, though. And aunties. She would definitely have female relatives. I still think it's a coincidence."

"But who else could it be, George?" Luke said. "No other killer makes sense. Not unless the three cases aren't connected."

"But all three were killed by the same toxin," Jay explained. "They must be connected."

The team regarded Jay in silence for a moment. Even Mason was nodding.

George was stuck. Both Luke and Jay were correct in their

thinking. But they were missing something, something huge. And George wasn't sure what it was. "We need access to Harding's emails." He turned to Jay. "Did you get the password from Penelope?"

"No, boss. She didn't know it. Plus, I doubt he would have used his usual email. I wouldn't. Not if I were blackmailing somebody." Jay shrugged. "There's no way of getting into that email without getting a hold of that laptop."

"Shit!"

"DS Fry has already gone through Harding's work email, boss, and there's nothing there. We expected that, like. Who'd blackmail somebody using their work's email address?"

"Somebody stupid."

"Exactly."

"And our culprit isn't stupid."

"No, boss."

"Shit!"

"Anyway, we're waiting on DNA and prints to come back for the two suspects we have in custody. We could get lucky. The issue is, if Rodríguez's prints and DNA are found at the house, he could easily explain them away as we know he's been in the house recently."

"I guess we have to hope their prints and DNA are on the whisky glasses then, boss," Jay said.

"True that, DC Scott. Still, the question remains, why would Gruber or Rodríguez want to kill Cole, Flathers and Harding?"

"Maybe they didn't, boss," Jay said. Once again, the team regarded Jay in silence. "Just hear me out, but I've been thinking."

"Oh, I bet you struggled with that, didn't you, son?" Luke Mason said, a grin already forming on his face.

CHAPTER THIRTY-TWO

"What if the fourth person involved in the Lena Schneider case, the unnamed individual, is our killer?"

"Could be, son." Mason stuck out his tongue. "Or maybe he's next," Luke added.

"Either of you could be right," George said. "We need to speak with Johnathan Duke."

* * *

"Ah, Inspector Beaumont, how are you, my friend? It's been a while."

George was always impressed by the sheer presence the six-foot-five American gave off. Though George guessed that was because he had to look down on most people. That, and the Falstaffian man's girth, blocked out most of your peripheral vision.

Johnathan Duke was waiting for them at a table in the corner of the Starbucks. As George approached, a broad smile formed, his rich American accent bellowing across the room. "Detective Inspector Beaumont, hello, how are you?"

George held up his hand and nodded his head in greeting.

"Please come and sit down," Duke said. He looked at Jay Scott. "No Detective Sergeant Wood with you today?"

"Not today," George said with a smile. "No Paige McGuiness?"

"She has left our establishment, I'm afraid," Duke advised. "Such a shame." He twisted in his seat, a troublesome feat for somebody so tall and wide to get an employee's attention. "We'd like to order now, thank you."

George smiled. The man hadn't changed a bit. Nor had he treated George any differently despite not speaking since the

Cross Flatts Snatcher case. Of course, they hadn't exactly been on speaking terms since, but clearly, that was water under the bridge.

After ordering, Duke grinned and said, "How can I help you?"

"We're here for some information on an Austrian woman named—"

"Lena Schneider," Duke said, cutting George up. His grin stretched. "It was getting to the point where I thought I was going to have to call you, Detective Inspector." Duke settled his weight in his chair. "But here we are." His fingers were at his lip, giving away his addiction to nicotine.

"One of my detective sergeants found the articles you wrote where *you* named Paxton Cole and Andre Harding as potential suspects that the West Yorkshire Police spoke with."

Duke smiled, and his cheeks turned rosy. "If I recall, I was the only journalist to post such information."

"I'd agree with you on that, Mr Duke."

"Oh, give it over, Detective Inspector," Duke said as the staff member came over with the tray of drinks Johnathan had ordered. She stood with a card machine in her hands, but Duke ignored her. So, George removed his wallet from his coat, pulled out his card and tapped the device. "How many times have I told you to call me Johnathan?"

"Who was the fourth?" Jay asked.

Duke regarded him with a strange sort of suspicion. "The puppy finally speaks."

Jay furrowed his brows. "Excuse me?"

"Oh, I apologise, young man," Duke said. "I jest, I jest." He took a sip of his coffee. "Tastes better in America." Johnathan pushed the mug away from him. "You want the identity of the fourth person they questioned?"

CHAPTER THIRTY-TWO

"Yes, the one you couldn't name for legal reasons, Mr Duke," Jay said.

"I see, so I was correct?"

Jay furrowed his brows again. "Correct about what?" He took a sip of his own coffee, the sweet caramel sauce mixed with the bitter coffee a sensation on his taste buds.

"My intuition is telling me you think the person I couldn't name due to legal reasons is responsible for the deaths of the other three." He smiled as Jay's eyes bulged. Duke thought the young puppy would never make a good poker player.

"The other three?" Jay asked.

"Don't pretend you don't know, Detective Constable," Duke said. "Paxton Cole, Edmund Flathers, and Andre Harding."

Jay shook his head. "I think you have your information confused," Jay said. "Have you read the press releases?"

George had. They had said very little. That was apparently policy regarding suspicious deaths, especially with Paxton Cole and his celebrity status. Juliette Thompson had done them without even asking George for any input.

"Thompson is an excellent liaison. By that, I mean she doesn't give anything away." Duke reached for his mug, and then as if thinking he was putting his hand inside a crocodile's mouth, he immediately pulled his hand back. "According to Thompson, HMET is investigating three separate deaths, but it doesn't take a genius to link them together." He tapped the side of his head. "Especially with the information I have. And the fact that your boss, Detective Inspector Beaumont, is SIO on all three."

As if defeated, Jay looked at his boss.

"We would appreciate your discretion," George said.

He grinned. "I thought you might."

"What do you want in return?"

The grin stretched as high and wide as Tim Curry's in Home Alone 2. "I'll give you what I know about the Lena Schneider case, and I'll hold off on publishing my article. In return, I would like exclusive access to case information."

"You know these are ongoing investigations, Johnathan," George said. "I can't give you much."

"Not officially, no. But unofficially, you can." Duke turned to Jay. "Close your ears if you must, Constable because this is how men do business."

"I can't," George said. "I won't." He stood up, and so did Jay. "Thank you for inviting us here so I could pay for your coffee, Johnathan."

Duke raised his right brow, and his face contorted. "I'm not asking for much."

Blood flushed through George's veins, and he clenched his fists. George knew how awkward Duke was but also knew just how much he liked to protect his reputation. "Need I remind you what I said last time you were being awkward." He was referring to the threat he had made to bring Duke down to the station when Duke was withholding information during the Cross Flatts Snatcher case. "I'm sure whatever paper Paige McGuiness works for now would appreciate a heads up." George scratched his chin. "What did I come up with last time?" George paused for a moment, the tension palpable. Then he clicked his fingers so suddenly that Duke recoiled in his seat. "A reputable editor gets brought in by police for questioning."

George let the words hang in the air.

"There's no need for that, Detective Inspector," the Falstaffian man said. George could hear the worry in Duke's tone, despite his attempts at hiding it.

"I don't appreciate being blackmailed, Johnathan," George explained. "So, the choice is yours."

George's words were greeted with silence.

"This is your last chance, Johnathan," George said. Menace laced his tone. "I have three dead men, and I think you have the answer I need, so I suggest you tell me now, or I'll get the 'puppy' here to arrest you for obstruction."

Chapter Thirty-three

Later that afternoon, DI George Beaumont held up an envelope for his team to see and said, "Incident Room, please. We've got the film back!"

Once his team were all huddled around a desk in the Incident Room, George opened the envelope and looked inside, then tipped the contents out before them.

The images fell face down, so George randomly picked one and flipped it over. Unfortunately, it was a terrible picture: out of focus and taken from behind a tree that showed a familiar Range Rover parked up in a secluded car park. The owner—Johann Gruber—didn't seem to be inside the vehicle at all, though the angle made it difficult to be sure.

The next photo showed the Range Rover—with its recognisable private plate—driving up to the car park, and this time Johann was clearly visible behind the wheel. There was another car there, too. One he recognised but couldn't quite put his finger on why. It was a pink, and white Mini Cooper adorned with the Adidas logo. Where had he seen it before?

Wood turned over the next picture. The Range Rover again. This time the driver's door was open, and Johann was out of the car, standing beside it, a smile on his face. He certainly looked different when they'd interviewed him yesterday.

CHAPTER THIRTY-THREE

She turned over another photo. In this one, Johann was not alone. The team regarded it in silence for several seconds.

Jay was the one to break the silence when he said, "Holy shit!"

With a trembling hand, George flipped over another picture. This picture had been taken up close through the back window of the parked Range Rover. The seats had been folded flat, and a blanket had been spread out, creating a bed-sized space.

But it wasn't just the blanket that had been spread. The blonde-haired woman who was in the previous photo was now laid on her back with Johann on top of her. Neither was fully naked, but they were well on the way to getting there.

Jay picked up the image. "She's noticed the person taking the picture." He pointed towards the blonde's face. "Look, she's staring right at him!"

In quick succession, George turned over the other photos, hunting for the next part of the story unfolding before them. However, it seemed that this was the last image in the sequence. There were other photos, but they looked like pictures of handwritten letters.

Most of the other photos were quite damning in terms of Johann Gruber's reputation and relationship, but that final one was damning in a whole different sense. The blonde knew Andre was there, and if the blonde did, then so did Johann. And that meant his dirty little secret would get out, and his marriage would end up in ruins. So what would a powerful, charismatic man like Johann Gruber do to protect his secret? His reputation? He was a decorated Austrian international football player. So George thought there probably wasn't anything Johann wouldn't do.

That was motive enough for George.

He checked his watch. They only had two hours before they needed to charge or release him. He turned to Luke Mason. "Mason, go and speak with DSU Smith. Explain the images to him, and ask him to contact the CPS. We're going to need an extension."

Mason nodded and left the Incident Room immediately.

"So Gruber has a motive," Jay said.

"Looks that way to me, Jay," George said.

George then looked at the other images they had, which looked like pictures taken of handwritten letters. George squinted at them, then passed it across to Wood to read. "I can't read it, can you?"

She studied the page. "Shocking writing. Like he was in a hurry?"

"Maybe he was. Can you make anything out?"

Wood brought it closer. "' I demand five million pounds or I will... Don't fuck with me. I will... send them to... press.'" She looked up at George. "A similar message to the text messages."

"Aye." He turned to Jay. "Speak with Yolanda and sign the journal out of evidence. We need to see if the handwriting matches."

"Boss," Jay said, leaving the Incident Room.

"'I have given you enough time to answer me. But for some reason, you have...' Christ, what's that say? Ignored?" George nodded. "Ignored. 'But for some reason, you have ignored any contact from me. Because of that...'" She screwed up her eyes and peered closer. "'Because of that, you leave me no choice but to share your dirty little secret.'"

"So we're looking at letters that Andre sent to the footballer?"

"Looks that way, George."

"Let's leave it for now and see whether DSU Smith will get us a handwriting expert. It'll help when this goes to court as the expert can match the letter's handwriting to the journal's."

"But that's definitely a threat. We can be sure of that," Wood said.

"Aye," George said.

"But what makes it worse is the blonde woman in the photos. The affair clearly means they have the motive to kill."

"I agree. Their motive is obvious." George nodded. "The footballer and the wife..." George said. "Sounds like it would make a good film."

"Or a good novel," Wood said.

* * *

"You remain under caution, Mr Gruber," DI Beaumont said after all the usual interview spiel was reeled off and the tape was started. Gruber glared at him, and George smiled. "As we have already disclosed to your solicitor, the Crown Prosecution Service has provided an extension so that we may hold you for up to thirty-six hours. Do you understand?"

Johann Gruber said nothing.

"You need to indicate for the recording that you do, or do not, understand, Mr Gruber."

"I understand, but I don't fucking agree with it!"

Wood slid information packs across the table to Johann and his solicitor, and then they started.

"See document ninety-four in your packs." He waited for them to look at the image. Johann closed his eyes and looked down at the table. "Do you recognise the people in this image, Mr Gruber?"

"I do."

"Ah, good," George said. "We're on the same page for a change. Please name the people in the image, Mr Gruber?"

"You know who we are. Does it really matter?" He turned to his solicitor, who spoke in Austrian.

"English, please," George said. "Unless we need an interpreter for the recording?"

"My client asked me if he needed to answer that question."

"You already know you don't have to answer any questions, Mr Gruber. That is your right. However, I would advise against it." George held up his hands. Johann had already provided them with a 'no comment interview', which was frustrating, to say the least. "This interview is for you. It's a chance to explain yourself and your side of the story."

"Please provide us with the names of these two in the image."

Johann gritted his teeth. "No comment."

George shook his head. *Fine.* They could return to that question later; he hated it when criminals got their way. "Please see document ninety-five."

"I can explain this," Johann said once he looked at the image. It was the one Andre had taken through the back window with the blonde on her back, looking up.

"The floor's yours," George said.

"I'm addicted to sex, OK?"

"Go on."

"I love my wife, but she can't satisfy me. No woman has been able to. But she..." He pointed at the image. "She satisfied me." His foot began to bounce up and down on the ground like a popular Disney rabbit.

"I'd appreciate it if we could deal with this... sensibly. I mean, this could ruin me. It could ruin my career, my family, and my entire reputation. Basically, everything I've worked so hard for since coming over here as a teenager."

When George and Wood said nothing, Johann said, "Please."

"Having an affair isn't a crime, Mr Gruber," George said. "But she's just lost her husband, a husband we believe was murdered." George paused. "So I'm going to ask you very clearly. OK?" Johann nodded. "Did you kill Paxton Cole, Edmund Flathers and Andre Harding?"

"I did not." He looked down at the table. "Just because I was shagging his wife behind his back didn't mean I killed him."

"We know all about the blackmail," Wood said. They hadn't disclosed this evidence to the solicitor, and he frowned as George slid across another envelope. "Do you recognise these messages, Mr Gruber?"

Gruber shook his head. "Nope. Not a single one."

"Have another look," Wood said.

"I don't need to. I didn't send or receive any of these messages." Johann turned to his solicitor. "They have my phone, right? So they could have checked this for themselves."

"That's correct," George cut in. "These messages were from a phone found at Andre Harding's property."

"So that smarmy bastard's been blackmailing somebody else, has he?" Johann grinned. It looked genuine, but George knew it was fake. Just like his words.

"We don't believe that, Mr Gruber. We believe he is talking to you." Wood then paused and stared. "We also believe the woman mentioned here," she explained, pointing at a highlighted extract, "is the woman you've been having an affair with."

"I've no idea who they are because I did not send those

messages." Johann flashed his pearly whites.

"Do you actually have any evidence that will help you charge my client?" the solicitor asked. "Because if you ask me, you don't. You have..." he paused, then spread out his arms. "This. Which my client strenuously denies are his messages. And then you have CCTV footage which is easily explained."

There was a booming bang on the door, and DS Luke Mason slipped his head inside. He had an envelope in his hand, which he offered to George. Mason smiled and nodded his head. George turned to Johann and his solicitor. "We have some new evidence to disclose," he said.

"For the tape, that was Detective Sergeant Mason at the door. He handed Detective Inspector Beaumont an envelope containing DNA and fingerprint evidence."

George grinned and slid four documents across the table, indicating Johann and his solicitor should take two each.

He watched Johann's face drop as he read it. "Fucking women!" he said. "This is what you do, isn't it? Us men have no fucking clue how you do it, but somehow, you whisper sweet little nothings in our ears whilst wearing a short skirt. You might change that up, you know, and flash a little cleavage or make some flirty little comments." He stood up, and so did George. "Then you've got us all eating out of your fucking hands, haven't you?"

Wood said nothing. She couldn't. The fear was back. It was like Ethan Miller was staring at her. He reached closer and grabbed her, and then Wood, like a broken computer, shut herself down.

She wanted to fight back. To scream. But she couldn't. She watched as Gruber grinned as he leered at her. Her body refused to do anything.

CHAPTER THIRTY-THREE

"I've fucking confessed to fucking her! OK, I've fucked her more than once." Wood could feel his breath on her face. It paralysed her once more. "We did it in her fucking husband's bed. But you have to believe me when I say it was all because of her. To start with, she was the one who wanted it—gagging for it, actually! And yet, look at what you're doing because of it. Because of her. Because of that fucking glorious flower between her legs." He took a breath. "Andre knew about it. And he had photos. And because he had photos, you're going to make out that I killed him. And then you're going to link that fucking murder to the others and blame me for those, too!"

The raised voice brought Wood back to her senses. Ethan Miller was in prison, awaiting trial. He couldn't hurt her any more. And nor was Gruber anywhere near her. Instead, he was across the table.

She shook her head and stood up. "Sit down, Mr Gruber!" Isabella instructed. "Before we make you!"

It was like a spell had broken. "What?" Johann said, looking around at the three faces watching him.

"I'm so sorry! I'm sorry!" he cried, covering his head with his hands. "I'm innocent. Please believe me."

"Yet this evidence, Mr Gruber, certainly suggests otherwise!"

Chapter Thirty-four

Tashan and Jay pulled up at the curb outside Jürgen Schmidt's house on New Lane in Middleton, their stomachs fluttering from nerves. Jay, especially as he knew all about Schmidt's operation from his time as a Uniform. That and the stories he'd heard were pretty horrific.

Jürgen Schmidt opened the door, a cigar wedged between his teeth. He wore a sharp suit with black pinstripes, a white shirt open at the neck, and shiny black shoes. His moustache was ridiculous, greying at the edges, just like his hair that was pushed back in a pompadour, exposing a forehead with various scars from old knife wounds. Jay wondered what kind of life the loan shark had had, wanting to ask him about the scars but not daring to.

"DC Scott and DC Blackburn," Jay said as both detective constables held out their warrant cards.

"Beaumont sent his kittens this time, did he?" Jurgy sucked his cigar, then plucked it from his mouth before saying, "What do you want?"

"We'd like to come in and ask some questions if that's OK with you, sir?" Jay said.

Dark, dangerous eyes narrowed at him. "About what?"

"About Paxton Cole and Edmund Flathers," Jay explained.

CHAPTER THIRTY-FOUR

"For fu—" Schmidt took a deep breath, then sucked on his cigar once again. "Fine, detectives. Five minutes, then you can fuck off! Alright?"

"Thank you, sir," Jay said as they followed Jürgen into the house.

"Aye, well, at least I know my taxes are being fucking used. Though used isn't the word I'd use. Fucking wasted is what I'd use. You know?"

Jay didn't know but said nothing. Not until he screamed, "Fuck me!" when the sound of scratching and barking came from his right.

Schmidt laughed and gestured for the detectives to head towards the kitchen directly at the end of the hallway. "Kittens don't like dogs, do they?"

Once in the kitchen, Jürgen gestured for the two detectives to take a seat and even offered them a coffee from his machine. It was one of those posh ones you put pods in. Jay looked at Tashan, who shook his head.

"Thank you, but we won't be bothering you for long," Jay said with a smile. Jürgen remained standing, his arms folded across his chest. "We were wondering whether you've heard of scopolamine before."

"What?" Jürgen asked.

"Scopolamine."

"What's that when it's at 'ome." The German almost sounded Yorkshire. He grinned.

"We're being serious with our questioning," Tashan said. "Please take this seriously."

"Oh fucking really?" Jürgen looked between the young men. "So ask me a fucking *serious* question then."

"We were wondering whether you've heard of scopolamine

before."

"Never heard of it," Schmidt said rather a bit too quickly for the detectives' liking.

"You're sure?"

"I'm sure." Schmidt pondered for a moment. "What is it?"

"It's the name of a tasteless and odourless drug, commonly made by grinding down the seeds of plants or shrubs named Angel's Trumpet," Tashan explained. "When the seeds are ground down, inhaled or consumed, they can eliminate a person's free will and can be fully controlled without inhibitions. It can wipe people's minds and turn them into a zombie-like state. It's horrifying stuff."

Jürgen Schmidt's grin stretched from ear to ear, exposing nicotine-stained teeth. "Whilst it sounds terrifying, it's not my style."

No, breaking legs and torturing people is, Jay thought. "Is there anything else helpful you can tell us, sir?" Jay kept his tone light.

"No." Schmidt got up and gestured towards the door.

* * *

Johann Gruber's earlier aggression had been replaced by a stunned confusion. Had he not been sitting, George knew the man would be pacing up and down. Or that's what his foot, which was hammering up and down on the floor, suggested. But he was answering their questions. Right now, that really mattered because George was fed up with all the 'no comments' Gruber was giving them before.

"Before we discuss the evidence we've just disclosed," George said, "I think we need to discuss your relationship with

Edmund Flathers, Paxton Cole, and Andre Harding in some more detail."

"What relationship?" Johann asked some of that old fire returning. "I already told you I don't fucking know who Edmund Flathers is!"

"You see, we have new information that suggests you did know who Edmund Flathers was," George said. "Tell us about Lena Schneider."

The look Johann gave George told him everything he needed to know and put him directly in the frame. They had their killer now. George was sure of it.

"What about her?" Johann said, his voice quivering. All his media training, charm, and confidence leaked out of him.

"So you don't deny knowing her?"

"No. Why would I do that? She was a fellow compatriot, correct?" Then he clicked, and George thought the lightbulb moment looked genuine. "Edmund Flathers. Our old mate Eddy." Johann shrugged. "He got cleared, though." Then Johann's face contorted. "Am I next?"

"Excuse me?" Wood asked.

"I've just understood the connection," Johann explained. "All three of them are dead. Murdered. And I'm next."

Wood shook her head. "No, Mr Gruber. We believe you murdered them."

"I didn't, honestly."

"Prove it, Mr Gruber," she retorted.

"How am I supposed to do that?" He turned to his solicitor.

"My client has strenuously denied all accusations during the time you've had him locked up here. You have very little evidence, so I would argue you have to prove my client murdered those men rather than my client prove he didn't."

George thought that was fair enough, especially as that was their job. "Tell me what you remember about the night Lena Schneider died."

"Considering it was over a decade ago," Johann said, "I don't remember much." He looked down at the table. "I remember going out with Paxton, and despite being like fifteen, swigging beer. Paxton was pissed up. I didn't really know Andre or Eddy that much. They were more Paxton's mates. I don't mind admitting I followed Pax around like a lost puppy that night."

"Did you provide Lena Schneider with the drugs that killed her?"

"Of course not."

"Do you know who did?"

"Honestly, I don't."

"So you aren't involved in a coverup?"

"Why would you accuse me of such a thing?"

"We're trying to figure out why Paxton, Andre and Edmund have been murdered. But, as you've already realised, Lena Schneider is the only thing that links all three."

"And you're the fourth chain in that link," Wood added.

"So I either killed them or I'm next." Johann pulled at his thick, blond locks, the shock threatening to completely consume him. "Fucking hell."

"And as I have already advised," Wood said, "we believe you killed them."

"Prove it!" Johann demanded, clenching his jaw.

The Austrian connection was obvious, but they weren't convinced Johann was Lena Schneider's brother. They were awaiting a call from the Bundespolizei, the Federal Police of Austria, who would be able to, they hoped, shed some more light on Lena Schneider and the family members that survived

CHAPTER THIRTY-FOUR

her.

So they went back to the prints and DNA, George explaining the truth of it all. He watched the disbelief become horror, then despair, then another surge of rage that saw Johann twist and wrench at the DNA profile analysis, tearing it in half, before he sprinkled it to the floor.

"How do you explain the presence of your DNA and fingerprints on the glasses found at Andre Harding's house in Rothwell?"

"Well, I can't explain it because they aren't mine!" Johann insisted.

"But they are," George confirmed. He pointed towards the sheet that sat in front of Johann. "We took your DNA, used that and matched it against DNA found on a glass in Andre's house. We also took your prints and found them on the same glass."

"Harding's prints and DNA were found on the other glass," Wood said.

"Harding has CCTV above his door," Gruber said. He was breathing erratically now, his chest rising and falling like his lungs were doubling in size with each frantic inhalation.

"Check it. You'll see I wasn't there the day he died."

"You're admitting to visiting Andre Harding at his home before?" Wood asked.

"He's mates with everybody on the team." He turned to his solicitor, who was being tight-lipped. "Why aren't you saying anything."

"I've already given you my advice, Mr Gruber. It's their job to prove your guilt, not your job to prove your innocence." The solicitor edged his chair away and then turned to George. "I'd like a break to speak with my client."

Chapter Thirty-five

Gruber and his solicitor were waiting quietly when the detectives sat down without a word. DS Wood handed out the document folders whilst George started the Digital Interview Recorder.

"Interview of Johann Gruber in the presence of his solicitor by Detective Inspector Beaumont and Detective Sergeant Wood." He added the date and time and then asked each participant to identify themselves for the DIR.

"You remain under caution, Mr Gruber," George said. "So far, you've denied being involved in the murders of Paxton Cole, Andre Harding, and Edmund Flathers."

Johann nodded. The room was far too hot for his liking, and sweat dripped down his face. "I'm innocent."

"So explain to us why you lied about knowing Edmund Flathers," Wood said. She had a steely glint in her eye.

"And explain why your DNA and prints were found on a whisky glass we seized from Andre Harding's property?" George asked.

"I can't explain," Gruber grunted. "Well, I can. I stopped talking to Eddy after the case went to court. I didn't want to be associated with criminals. But I can't explain the whisky glass."

CHAPTER THIRTY-FIVE

"Do you drink whisky, Mr Gruber?" George asked.

"Yes, I love whisky. Especially of the Japanese kind. But that doesn't prove anything."

At least he was beginning to incriminate himself, George thought. But admitting to enjoying whisky wasn't enough by a long shot. "Have you ever drunk whisky with Andre Harding before?"

"Yes," Gruber replied. "That doesn't mean I killed him." The man was on his last legs, volunteering information rather than them having to put pressure on him.

"When was the last time you two had a drink together?"

"Weeks ago." He shrugged. "I don't remember the exact date."

"So how do you explain the presence of your prints and DNA being found on a whisky glass seized from Harding's property the day he was murdered?"

"Could it have been an old one?"

George knew for sure it wasn't an old glass because the Submissions Team at Calder Park had carried out an environmental profile. They determined the whisky glass hadn't been in that location for very long.

"Having been to Andre Harding's house, how would you describe its cleanliness."

Johann looked towards his solicitor for help. Clearly, he knew Andre Harding suffered from OCD and needed his house to be clean.

"You're aware of Harding's OCD, then?" George asked. Johann nodded.

"For the DIR, Johann nodded," Wood explained.

"Do you know what an environmental profile is, Mr Gruber?" George asked. Gruber shook his head. "Environmental profiling detects tiny amounts of carpet fibres that as residents walk around their properties are thrown into the air and settle on objects which show you how long the objects have been in the locations."

Johann looked taken aback and unsure how to proceed.

"In essence, Mr Gruber, if that whisky glass had been sat on the side for any length of time, then fibres from the environment, like dust or clothing, would have settled on it."

"But the report from the lab suggests no presence of any fibres," Wood explained.

"Which means that glass was fresh, brought out of a cupboard on the day Harding was murdered," George said.

"And your prints and DNA are all over it," Wood explained.

"I'm being framed."

"By who, Mr Gruber?" asked George, his brow raised.

Silence greeted George.

"I think you're making all this up," George finally said. "We have you. We've got evidence that links you to the murder of Andre Harding. We also have dashcam footage that links you to the murder of Paxton Cole. As all three murders are linked, the CPS has advised we have enough to charge you. So..." George said, taking a breath, "I'm going to give you a chance to give us your side of the story." He let those words linger for a moment. "Maybe you killed Paxton out of lust for his wife and then came up with an elaborate plan to get rid of Harding because he was going to sell your secret to the press."

"But you needed it to be convincing, and because you knew about Lena Schneider, you decided to kill Flathers, too," Wood said. "Then I figure you come down here and pretend to be a victim." She turned to George. "He said earlier he believed he was next, right?"

CHAPTER THIRTY-FIVE

George looked straight at Johann. "Correct, Detective Sergeant."

"You have the motive, the means, and the opportunity. So, confess," Wood said.

"I really don't. If you're linking all three together, then it's obvious I didn't fucking do it!" Gruber was getting angry again. "I haven't seen or spoken with Edmund Flathers in years, and from the evidence you've disclosed, you have nothing that links me to him!" The dark rings under his eyes were getting bigger and darker, as were the enormous sweat patches under his arms. There was a sour smell coming across the table.

Johann was right, of course. They had very little to go on regarding Flathers' murder. But that didn't mean Johann didn't do it.

A loud knock on the door interrupted George's thoughts. George turned to find Tashan. "For the DIR, Detective Constable Blackburn has entered the room."

"Sir, DS Mason needs a quick word with you about the search." He handed George his phone.

"For the DIR," Wood said as George left the room. "Detective Constable Blackburn has replaced DI Beaumont, who has left the room."

Johann Gruber, a grim look on his face, asked, "What's that all about?"

"Your solicitor advised you we were doing a full search of your property, correct?"

Gruber nodded.

"I would suggest then that DS Mason and PS Greenwood have found something," Wood explained. "I would tell us now. It'll make things easier for you in the long run."

"I haven't done anything," Gruber said.

"So you weren't at Paxton Cole's house the morning he was murdered because you wanted to kill him?"

"No!" Johann exclaimed, uncoiling his hands and raising them emphatically. George entered the room again, replacing Tashan, just as Gruber said, "I didn't kill anyone! I'm being framed!"

"Tell us the truth, and spare their families a long trial. Come on, be a man and own up to what you've done!"

"Stop trying to antagonise my client, Inspector," Gruber's solicitor said. "I'll be making a complaint regarding your interview technique."

George grinned. *It wouldn't be the first time.*

"I think that's enough," Gruber's solicitor said. "I must insist we move the interview on. My client has answered your questions about the disclosed evidence, repeatedly denying your accusations."

It was clear from the solicitor's obstructions that Gruber would soon break. George didn't particularly like this way of interviewing, preferring to chat about the evidence, but this case was unusual in that there was a lack of it. So, he had to ensure Gruber couldn't get his composure back.

"Okay, Johann, this is your last chance," George said. "And I mean it. Why did we find a whisky glass covered in your prints and DNA the day Andre Harding was murdered?"

Johann's voice held an edge of panic. "I don't know!" Gruber looked at his lawyer, who looked at George with a furious stare. "My client has already explained he does not know. Move the questioning on."

George ignored the solicitor. "Tell us about the scopolamine we found inside your house, Mr Gruber."

When Gruber said nothing, George continued. "During a

CHAPTER THIRTY-FIVE

legal search of your home tonight, forensic officers found this." George passed his phone to the solicitor, who scrutinised the image, before handing it to Johann. "Confess, Johann. It'll be easier for you. Think about their families and friends. About what you're putting them through. We have so much evidence against you, such a strong case." He waited, pleading for Gruber to confess.

"Where did you get the scopolamine from?" George demanded.

But Gruber remained silent.

"No? Okay. Johann Gruber, the threshold test has been passed; therefore, it is my lawful right to charge you for the murders of Paxton Cole, Edmund Flathers and Andre Harding. Is that understood?" George asked.

"No! No!" Gruber screamed, banging the table with his hand. He stood to get up, but his solicitor gripped his arm. "Do your fucking job!" Gruber shouted at the man. "I'm being fucking framed! Whatever those fucking drugs are that they've found aren't mine!"

"Interview terminated," George said.

"Wait, I confess."

George spun on the spot. "What?"

"I'll confess."

George turned to Wood. They weren't expecting this.

"Continuation of interview with Johann Gruber in the presence of his solicitor. DI Beaumont and DS Wood are in attendance." He turned to Gruber. "Please, can you repeat what you just told DS Wood and me as we went to leave the room?"

"I want to confess," Gruber said.

"The floor's yours," George advised.

"I gave the drugs to Lena Schneider," Gruber panted. "The

ones that killed her."

Chapter Thirty-six

The shock on George's face was unmistakable. It then turned to anger. "Stop messing us about, Mr Gruber!"

"I'm not messing you about, Detective Beaumont. I'm next. I have to be. Everybody else is dead."

"Did anybody know it was you who gave Lena the drugs?" Wood asked.

Gruber nodded his head. "Paxton did. To protect me, he paid Edmund to take the fall for it."

George scoffed. "So Paxton paid Edmund to take the blame to protect you. And what do you do in return? Shag his wife! Then kill him!"

"I didn't kill him." A tear dropped from Gruber's eye. "I'm next. I must be. The final link in the chain." More tears fell from his eyes. "You must find out who killed them because I'm next. Please."

"I'm not sure that I believe you," George said. For all he knew, Johann was trying to get out of triple murder. So it made sense that he'd prefer the conviction of supply of a controlled drug and manslaughter. "Prove it."

"I can't prove it, Detective," Gruber said. Then he began to plead. "I did it. It was me. I'm confessing. Arrest me and throw away the key. Please!"

"We need to terminate the interview whilst I speak with the CPS," George advised. Both Wood and the solicitor nodded. "Interview terminated." He got up, turned off the recording devices, knocked on the door, and a custody officer opened it.

* * *

Whilst George called the Crown Prosecution Service, Isabella made for Detective Superintendent Jim Smith's office to explain Gruber's confession.

"We've got a confession from Johann Gruber," Wood explained.

Smith raised his brow. "A confession?"

"Correct, sir." She paused. "But only that he supplied the drugs that killed Lena Schneider."

"I see, and he keeps denying murdering Cole, Flathers, and Harding?"

"Correct, sir."

Smith paused. "The CPS said you met the threshold test to charge him for the murders, right?"

"Right, sir."

"Where is George right now?"

"Talking with the CPS to see if we can charge him using his confession."

Smith nodded. "OK, they'll most likely advise George to add it to the list of charges. I'm happy for you to proceed." He checked his watch. "When is he being transferred?"

"In a couple of hours, sir."

"OK, give Gruber an hour to stew and then interview him again. See if you can't tease another confession out of him."

Isabella got up to leave when Smith stopped her. "The search

CHAPTER THIRTY-SIX

at Amanda Cole's house turned up something interesting," Smith explained. Wood raised a brow. "Uniform's bringing her in as we speak."

* * *

Joshua Fry looked up from the laptop as George entered the interview room where the DS had holed up. "Perfect timing, sir; I was just about to call him."

George checked his watch. They didn't have long before Gruber was remanded in HMP Leeds, and he wanted to speak with Johann before he left the station. "What's his name?" George inquired.

"Jakob Bauer, sir." Josh tapped away at his keyboard. "He's now our contact in the Bundeskriminalamt, the Austrian Criminal Intelligence Service, the equivalent of our CID.

George nodded. "Thanks for this; I appreciate it."

"As far as I can tell, Bauer's rank is the equivalent of yours, sir. Kontrollinspektor."

George settled in an uncomfortable chair beside Josh, who hit the call button on his laptop. A video of the two detectives sitting side by side appeared on the screen.

Then another video popped up beside theirs.

A man in his forties or fifties stared at them. He was pale, had short, black hair, and a wiry moustache. But his eyes were a light blue. Though extremely intimidating. Kontrollinspektor Bauer scrutinised the two detectives for a moment before saying, "Hallo." His voice was firm and stern and heavily accented, unlike the other Austrian, Johann Gruber, who they had been dealing with recently. Gruber's accent had all but diminished due to the length of time he'd lived in Leeds.

"Hello, sir," George said.

"Hi," Josh offered. He smiled and said, "It's nice to see you in person, Kontrollinspektor Bauer. Next to me is the Senior Investigating Officer of a trio of murders we believe relates to Lena Schneider, Detective Inspector George Beaumont."

"Good afternoon, Detectives," Bauer said, nodding.

"How are you?" asked George.

"Very busy, but very well." He smiled, though it did not meet his eyes. "I trust you two are well also?"

Both detectives nodded, and DS Fry then cleared his throat. "The purpose of today's call is to introduce ourselves and discuss Lena Schneider's family."

"Let us get on with it then. What would you like to know?"

"We know her mother and father are dead, but there's a brother. Can you give us his identity?" George asked.

Bauer nodded. "Her half-brother?"

"Half-brother? Does she not have a brother with the same parents?"

"No, Inspector," Bauer explained. "Lena's father was actually her stepfather. Unfortunately, he is no longer with us. And neither is her mother."

George nodded, trying to keep the shock from his face. He knew both parents were dead, but not that Lena's father wasn't her biological father. "So, who is her biological father?"

Bauer grimaced. "We don't know that," he said.

George scowled. "What do you mean you don't know."

"Exactly that, Inspector. We only require the mother's details when registering a birth in Austria," Bauer explained. "It is the same in your country, no?"

George nodded. He'd gone with Mia to register Jack, though, so they were both on Jack's birth certificate. Emilia Alexander – Teacher. George Beaumont – Detective Inspector of the West Yorkshire Police.

"But you do know the identity of Lena's half-brother?" George questioned.

"Perhaps," he said lightly, offering nothing.

"This is important, Bauer," George said. "We need all the information you have." Then he added, "Please."

"So you do have manners, Inspector," Bauer said. He did not show any emotion at all.

George, however, was gritting his teeth. "Please."

"Fine. We know he was named Maximillian Steiner. He'd taken his father's surname, as did his mother once they were wed.

George had never picked up on this when reading the articles. Perhaps the British press didn't even know. "So, whose name is Schneider?"

Bauer tipped his head from side to side. "Lena's mother's... what do you call it – "

"Maiden name?" Josh cut in.

"That is it. Yes. Maiden name."

It certainly made sense Lena's mother would have given Lena her maiden name, especially if Lena's mother and stepfather weren't married – or even together – at the time.

"So, where is Maximillian Steiner now?" George asked.

"In England," the Kontrollinspektor explained. "But I believe he changed his name because we don't know much about him. I have my team researching him as we speak."

"Thank you," George said. "Do you know the reason he came to England? And when?" George wondered whether the Austrian had come over to get revenge for his half-sister specifically.

Bauer considered his reply, pursing his lips. "He moved over a very long time ago to pursue a career as a football player."

George and Josh looked at each other. Could Johann Gruber be Maximillian Steiner? If George considered revenge as *the* motive, then it would make sense that Johann Gruber was Maximillian Steiner. It would make sense why he changed his name. Everything was becoming clear.

"Are you aware of the Austrian footballer named Johann Gruber?"

"Of course."

"Could he have been Maximillian Steiner?"

Bauer shrugged. "You're asking an impossible question, Inspector. Unfortunately, Maximillian changed his name in England, so I suggest you do your share of the work and let *us* know whether he's Johann Gruber."

George raised an eyebrow. "Well, how many Johann Grubers are there?" He suspected the answer.

Bauer confirmed it. "Millions, Inspector. Think of Gruber as your Smith, the most popular surname in Austria. And Johann is just as popular for boys."

Shit!

Bauer considered for a second. "My advice would be to get in touch with whoever regulates name changes in the UK," Bauer said.

Josh was already scribbling notes on his pad. He could trust the detective sergeant to do a decent job of it.

"Is there anything else you could tell us about Lena Schneider and her family?"

"I'm told they were very religious. Mr Steiner was an extremely hard-working individual who worked on the Baroque castles in Vienna. He was well-respected." Bauer smiled. "I have my team researching Maximillian, Inspector. They're also looking at people who knew the Steiners so they can go and question them. Trust me when I say we're working hard."

"Thank you, sir," George said. "Here's hoping you find something for us."

"Now," Bauer said, grinning genuinely for the first time, "what can you tell us about Lena Schneider's death?"

George smiled. "The footballer, Johann Gruber, admitted he was the one who supplied the drugs to Lena Schneider."

"Excellent. And Gruber is to be charged?"

"Correct. But it makes no sense if you ask me."

Bauer frowned. "And why not?"

"Because if Maximilian Steiner is Lena Schneider's half-brother, then that means he killed his half-sister."

Chapter Thirty-seven

Amanda Cole had never been in trouble before. Not the sort of trouble that brought her into a police station. She was intimidated by the stark white walls that surrounded her. The fluorescent glow from strip lights forced her to squint.

She swung her legs, dangling them over the edge of the bed, her slender pins not long enough to reach the floor. Despite the blanket around her shoulders, she was shivering. They'd already taken prints and DNA. They did it first thing after the custody sergeant booked her in.

It was a woman with strands of greying hair trying to escape by her ear came to take the prints. She wore no jewellery, and her face was free of makeup. The woman was a complete contrast to Amanda Cole

Amanda didn't like how the woman held her hands and fingers whilst she took the prints, and she had to fight the urge to yank her hands away from the officer's grip. The woman had tried to offer a kind smile when they'd first met. The ex-glamour model had learnt to tolerate the invasion of personal space over the years, but she still didn't like being touched. Even now, she would shrink away if somebody brushed past her or stood too close.

CHAPTER THIRTY-SEVEN

And as for hugging people. Amanda Cole did not do that. Not even with the other WAGs. Or Paxton's family. He'd once flown them to the Caribbean so she could meet some of his relatives, some of them having been deported during the Windrush scandal. Specifically, Paxton's mother, Paulette, who was legally invited to move to the UK by the British government in 1968 when she was 10. Because she had never applied for a British passport and had no papers proving she had a right to be in the UK, she was classified as an illegal immigrant and sent back. It was shit what the government had done, or so Amanda thought.

All of this had started because Paxton had told Amanda he was spending obscene amounts of money on a specialist solicitor to try and help get her back into the UK, but Amanda knew the truth. He was a gambling addict that had thrown all their money on slots and horses. And that had brought a loan shark into their lives.

The woman repeatedly pushed her glasses up her nose and explained why they'd taken swabs and prints, but Amanda wasn't listening. Instead, she was picking at her trembling nails, biting the skin near the cuticles. "OK," Amanda eventually said, her voice barely a whisper. Her throat was on fire from the swab, and the ringing in her ears was deafening. She dreaded how she would feel once the adrenaline left her system.

Eventually, Amanda was moved to a cell where names of former occupants and unimaginative insults had been scratched into the walls. It was a waiting room, a holding pen whilst the police put their evidence together. She could smell a weird odour in the air, one she remembered from her teens, a combination of piss and sweat and shit.

The outfit she'd been given to replace her clothes did little to ward off the chill in the air, although they'd let her keep the blanket, which she'd draped across her shoulders.

To Amanda, the minutes feel like hours. It didn't help that the bench was hard, making her arse numb and impossible to get comfortable. No matter which way Amanda tried, a different part of her body throbbed. So instead, she sat on the floor, her legs curled into her chest, her chin on her knees, and the blanket draped around her, all in an attempt to keep the warmth in.

The flickering fluorescent light made it difficult for Amanda to do anything, and whilst she wanted to sleep, there was no chance of that, especially when the other prisoners began shouting; she jumped out of her skin. It was Saturday, so she should have suspected that the custody suite would be busy. She'd read about the regular drunk and disorderly arrests the police had to make during the weekends and the domestics and assaults.

Eventually, Amanda realised there was a worse noise than the shouting or the humming of the fluorescent light. Instead, it was the sound of metal on metal as the officers constantly opened and shut the viewing hatches.

Amanda soon calmed down, using her breathing exercises. She knew she needed to tell the truth to survive. Well, part of the truth, anyway. Even if she was still alive, and Cole wasn't, she was the true victim. But she did worry how long it would take until somebody connected the dots.

* * *

"How did your chat with the CPS go, Detective Inspector?" Gruber's solicitor asked once they were back in an interview room.

"It was fascinating, though not as interesting as the chat I had with Kontrollinspektor Bauer," George said. He'd walked Wood through his earlier chat with Bauer and the possibility that Maximillian Steiner was Johann Gruber. She immediately understood the gravity of that possibility, that Gruber could have supplied the drugs that killed his half-sister.

Both Austrians narrowed their eyes, recognising the term.

The solicitor broke the silence. "And why have you been in contact with Kontrollinspektor Bauer?"

"Because we wanted some background information on you, Mr Gruber," George explained. "Tell me, do you have any siblings?"

Gruber turned to his solicitor, who nodded. "No, I am an only child."

"And where were you born?"

"Vienna."

George grinned. "Can you tell us your date of birth?"

Gruber provided it. They already knew it, of course, or the one Gruber used, anyway. After speaking with the CPS, they let Gruber stew in his cell whilst they did some research. They found out that foreign nationals living in the United Kingdom can change their name by Deed Poll. They were awaiting information from the Royal Courts of Justice to see what Maximillian Steiner had changed his name to.

Though, if George were a gambling man, he'd bet there would be no such record, and Gruber's identity documents were fake.

There was no way to prove it—not without a confession.

"Make a note of those details, Detective Sergeant," George said. "We'll run them past Kontrollinspektor Bauer."

"Why?" Gruber asked.

"Because we believe your real name is Maximilian Steiner and not Johann Gruber."

If that name rattled Gruber, then he was an incredible actor. That, or he was so used to being called Johann that he didn't react to his original name. Which wasn't easy, George knew. If somebody in the supermarket said George, he'd be looking up at the sound of *his* name, whether he thought the person was speaking to him or not.

"How ridiculous," Johann said, looking at his solicitor. "Can they do this?"

The solicitor nodded. "Remember, this is your interview. Only answer questions you want to answer."

"The name Johann Gruber is suspicious, is it not, Detective Inspector?" Wood asked.

"I think it is, aye," George confirmed. "It's the Austrian equivalent of John Smith. Or so I'm told."

"That's nonsense." He turned to his solicitor again. "If that were the case, I'd be called Max Musterfrau, right?"

The solicitor nodded.

"Then why aren't you called Max Musterfrau instead of being called Johann Gruber?"

"Because that's my name!" Johann raised his brow and scoffed. "It's your job to disprove it!"

"Oh, don't you worry, we will."

"I think it's because it's too similar to his original name," Wood cut in.

"That makes so much sense, Detective Sergeant. Thank you." George turned to Gruber and grinned.

"Who is this Maximillian Steiner, anyway?" the solicitor asked.

George pointed at Gruber, who snarled. "Your client's real name."

"You know that's not what I meant, Detective Inspector." The solicitor shook his head. "How is Maximillian Steiner relevant to the case?"

"Because Maximillian Steiner is the name of Lena Schneider's maternal half-brother."

"That's preposterous," the solicitor replied. "You insinuate that my client has killed his half-sister?"

"Your client denied having any siblings," Wood pointed out.

"Exactly!" the solicitor said.

The two detectives and the solicitor turned to Gruber.

"I don't have a sister, and my name's Johann Gruber."

"The problem with that, Mr Gruber, is that you didn't exist for a very long time," George explained. "There are no records of a Johann Gruber attending school in the UK that matches your date of birth. So you appeared out of thin air at age seventeen after you were signed. Which is suspicious."

"No comment."

"We've checked border control records, and nobody named Johann Gruber with your date of birth has ever entered the country. So if you are who you say you are, then you're here illegally."

"So you can understand why we think you got fake documents once you were already over here," Wood explained. "Is that why you killed Cole, Harding and Flathers? Because they knew you as Maximillian Steiner?"

"No comment."

"Because we think you're lying about giving the drugs to Lena Schneider. We think Cole or Harding supplied them, and Flathers' was paid to help cover it up," George said.

"That, or you did kill your sister and are only now confessing to it to try and get away with triple homicide," Wood said.

"Which is it, Mr Gruber?"

"I told you that Pax paid Flathers' to cover it up so I wouldn't get in trouble."

"And you're sticking to that?"

Gruber nodded his head.

"This is your last chance, Mr Gruber," George warned. "Is there anything else you can tell us?"

"I've told you my story, but for some reason, you choose not to believe it!"

"So you're telling me you had no accomplice?"

"I didn't fucking do it!"

George stood. "Johann Gruber, the threshold test has been passed; therefore, it is my lawful right to charge you for the murders of Paxton Cole, Edmund Flathers and Andre Harding. Under advice from the CPS, I'm also charging you for the supply of a controlled drug and the manslaughter of Lena Schneider. Is that understood?" George asked.

"I didn't kill Cole, Flathers or Harding. Please," he whimpered, "you have to believe me."

"You need to indicate for the DIR that you understand Mr Gruber," George explained.

"No! No!" Gruber screamed. "I didn't kill them. I'm being fucking framed!"

* * *

Eventually, they took Amanda to be interviewed; she had lost all sense of time. She remembered a stocky sergeant had stood at the front desk. He looked her over, clearly recognising her,

CHAPTER THIRTY-SEVEN

his accent very strong as he enunciated every word. Amanda knew how to play being weak, knowing she needed every advantage she could get, and she played on it.

"Amanda Cole, I am arresting you on suspicion of murder. You do not have to say anything. But, it may harm your defence if you do not mention when questioned something which you later rely on in court. Anything you do say may be given in evidence."

Before a sergeant took Amanda to the custody suite, she was offered free legal representation, which due to having no money because of her fucking husband, she accepted. Within twenty minutes, a fat man with a bald head and coarse beard knocked on the door. An officer opened the door to let him in, and the man introduced himself as Nile Milner.

After asking questions about the case and listening to Amanda's replies, he simply told her to say 'No comment' to every question.

Then the pair sat in the interview room in silence until two detectives, a blond male and a brunette female, entered. The male detective introduced the both of them. He was Detective Inspector Beaumont, and she was Detective Sergeant Wood. She'd had run-ins with them already. Both were wearing crisp, white shirts. His blond hair was styled loosely, a bit long for Amanda's liking, whilst the female detective's curls were pulled into a bun.

Detective Sergeant Wood smiled at Amanda and pushed a mug of coffee across the table, a soft smile on her face. Amanda grabbed it, knowing she needed the caffeine now that the adrenaline was out of her system.

"Right then, Amanda," the male detective said before reciting a practised spiel about who was in the room and that they were recording everything.

She was expecting the first question but was expecting it from the man, not the woman.

"Why did you kill your husband, Mrs Cole?" Detective Sergeant Wood asked.

Amanda's legal aid patted her arm, and so she did as was advised. "No comment."

Chapter Thirty-eight

After an hour of Amanda answering every question with 'no comment', the two detectives decided to have a break and re-evaluate their questions because they were getting nowhere.

Isabella had noticed that every time she mentioned Johann Gruber, Amanda seemed to sink into her chair slightly. Or begin tapping the table with her nails. Everything she did when his name was mentioned was a nervous tick of some sort.

And Wood wanted to know why.

"So, during your relationship with Johann, did you ever think that maybe something was not quite right about him?" Wood paused. "Especially around Paxton?"

"Johann had a way about him that was very..." Amanda paused, not maintaining eye contact. "You wanted to please him."

"Because he was charming?" Wood asked.

Amanda's eyes met Wood's, and Isabella recoiled. "*Because* he was kind."

"Can you tell us what you witnessed the morning of Paxton's death?" George asked. "Specifically, regarding Paxton and Johann."

Amanda nodded. "Paxton had found out about the affair, so I

invited Johann over so we could chat about how we were going to proceed. As you can imagine, Paxton was furious when he found out, and I really needed Johann there for moral support. But..." Amanda's face contorted as tiny tears began to gather at the corner of her eyes. "I'm sorry..." She bit her lip, the tears in her eyes overflowing by the second. "I'm sorry..."

"It's OK, Amanda," Wood said. "Take your time."

"When Johann arrived, Pax..." She took a tissue from the centre of the table and dabbed her eyes. "Paxton got really angry."

"Why was he angry?" George asked.

"And then things got out of control," Amanda said, ignoring George, "and Johann just hit him. Hard. Then Johann was on top of Paxton." She paused to dab again. "I screamed. I–I tried to stop him, but Johann was like... like a different person."

George frowned. Dr Ross had not concluded that Paxton had been beaten before his death.

"I managed to get between them. I–I grabbed Johann around the waist. He got off Pax, turned, and looked into my eyes." Amanda began to sob then, harder than before. It took her almost a minute to finally say, "and I couldn't...I couldn't see anything but darkness."

"OK. How much more?" the solicitor asked.

"Just a few more questions," Wood advised. "Do you know what scopolamine is?"

"No, should I?" Confusion clouded her features.

"It was the toxin found in samples taken from your husband during the post-mortem."

"Wait, he was poisoned?"

"Yes," Wood explained. She slid across an image of an Angel's Trumpet. "This plant is highly toxic. Do you recognise

CHAPTER THIRTY-EIGHT

this plant?"

Amanda nodded her head. "Can we stop, please? I'm exhausted."

"Of course."

* * *

"What did you think of her?" George asked Wood once they were back upstairs.

"I think it's all put on if I'm honest. If you were having an affair, and your husband found out, I'm sure the last person your husband would want to see would be the person you were shagging."

"I agree," George said. "What are you thinking?"

"It's a set-up." She bit the inside of her cheek as she thought. "Maybe Johann or Amanda drugged Paxton at the house before allowing him to leave in his McLaren. Then the toxin kicked in, which caused him to crash."

"That's pretty much what I was thinking, especially if we consider the CCTV evidence."

"True," Wood said. "But we have no idea how long Johann had been there for. For all we know, he arrived after Paxton left, and Amanda's lying." She shrugged. "Yolanda's still working on getting the timings of Johann's route." She puffed out her cheeks.

"Aye, we really need the timings to see who's telling the truth and who's lying."

* * *

"Johann wanted Paxton dead so we could be together," Amanda

Cole said. "He was worth more to us dead than alive. It was better than a divorce as I got full custody of our daughter and a huge life insurance cheque. Or that's what Johann kept telling me. He loved Alicia like a daughter. He wanted to be her dad." Amanda burst into tears again.

"So, how did Johann kill Paxton?" Wood asked once Amanda had calmed down.

"I said he wanted him dead, not that he killed him," Amanda explained. "I've no idea who killed Pax."

"But you said you know about the scopolamine. And that Johann wanted Paxton dead. Surely you can put two and two together."

She shook her head, her eyes glistening. "I can, but you arrested me because of the two Angel's Trumpets I have in my house, right?"

"Right."

"Johann gifted them to me but told me never to let Alicia near them. I was also told not to touch them." She frowned. "It's why they're by the fire because none of us really went near there."

"So you knowingly had toxic plants in your house?"

"I didn't know they were toxic until you told me earlier. I can't believe Johann didn't warn me about them." She looked Wood in the eye. "I did not kill my husband, nor did I kill anybody else. Could it have been an accident?"

"An accident?" Wood narrowed her eyes.

"Could he have touched the plant, then touched his mouth? That kind of thing?"

"We don't know, but unless Edmund Flathers and Andre Harding had been in your house the day they died, I doubt it was an accident," George explained. "Did Johann kill those men?"

"I really don't know." She wiped a tear away. "I'm sorry." Amanda rubbed her eyes. She didn't have to pretend to be tired. The exhaustion was clear to everybody.

"What time is it?" she asked.

Wood glanced at her watch. It's a plain, leather strap, no-frills design.

"Half past three. Can I get you anything? Tea? Something to eat?"

"No, thank you, I just want to sleep," Amanda said as she yawned, having to hide her amusement as she watched Wood turn away to do the same. "Though I could do with a wee."

Wood nodded, and the interview was paused while she was escorted. The custody officer waited outside. It had been a long time since she'd had so little privacy, she realised as she washed her hands in the sink, trying to ignore her reflection. The woman looking back at Amanda terrified her.

The room was warmer when Amanda returned. Too warm. Both detectives were watching her. Waiting. But for what?

The two detectives suddenly got up and left the interview room, the solicitor hot on their heels. Amanda remained seated whilst a custody officer guarded the door.

* * *

"We need to release Amanda Cole," Detective Chief Superintendent Mohammed Sadiq said.

"What?" George asked. "Why?"

Sadiq raised his brows. "Because all of the physical evidence points to Johann Gruber. We've tied the three cases together with the scopolamine. We found the drug inside Gruber's property. We found a whisky glass at the scene of Harding's murder with Gruber's prints and DNA on them. *And* we know Gruber was at the Cole household the morning Paxton Cole was murdered. That man had the motive, the means and the opportunity. So give it up!"

"They could be in it together, sir." George said. No matter how pissed off he was, Sadiq was still his superior. He'd better start behaving. "Or Amanda could have been manipulating him."

"I've watched the recording, and I'm happy Gruber manipulated Amanda Cole. He bought her those plants as a way to get away with his crimes. We're lucky we found the other evidence."

"But—"

"And we have Gruber's confession of providing the drugs to Lena Schneider on tape, alongside a scared, pretty blonde girl who has a history of suffering physical abuse." Sadiq shrugged.

"He also said nothing about an accomplice," Sadiq said.

"But he also said he didn't do it. So we can't believe a word he says." George shook his head, the anger evident on his face.

"Look, George, I am not saying that you're wrong. Amanda could have been involved, but if she was, then she was manipulated into it. Johann was the mastermind. Think how a jury is going to think."

George was about to answer when Sadiq cut in. "Put yourself in their shoes. I guarantee you will see it the way I do."

"Let us speak with the CPS, see if they'll allow an extension, sir," George asked.

"It is over, George." He stood up, and opened DSU Smith's door. "Go home, and get some sleep." But George didn't move. "Now, Detective Inspector!"

CHAPTER THIRTY-EIGHT

* * *

"What are they doing?" she asked.

But the custody officer didn't reply. Instead, he did nothing but look down at the floor.

Were they looking at some new evidence they'd found? she wondered. *Did they even have anything?*

She'd been so careful not to get involved.

As Amanda waited for the detectives and the duty solicitor to come back, she noticed the ache in her head was getting worse. The ringing was getting worse. She wanted to scream. She wanted to sleep.

Then suddenly, the female detective came back in and spoke to the custody sergeant. "Please release Mrs Cole on bail."

* * *

A round of applause greeted George and Wood as they walked into the shared office after announcing to the press they had charged Johann Gruber for the murders of Paxton Cole, Edmund Flathers, and Andre Harding. They'd left out their theory about Gruber being Maximillian Steiner and his confession of supplying the drugs that killed Lena Schneider.

All of that would come out in court.

"Speech!" yelled Luke, grinning at him. "Speech!" The euphoric atmosphere and sense of accomplishment George felt seemed to go above and beyond solving a usual case. He supposed it was the complexity of the case and the fact that they'd had nothing to go on for a while.

His head hurt from the conversation with DCS Sadiq, and he felt angry that he'd allowed Amanda Cole to walk free. There were large sweat patches under his arms. And he felt like he could sleep for a few days straight. But otherwise, he was as delighted as his team.

"This is your victory," he said as he gazed at the team and support staff. "Without you, we wouldn't have solved this case." Jay looked up at him, beaming from ear to ear. Tashan was smiling at him, clapping, as were others who'd worked hard on the case.

He scanned the room to find Luke was still grinning at him, and Yolanda was clapping hard. Every piece of evidence, every interview, all the late nights, and ridiculous hours they worked were all integral to the charging of Johann Gruber.

He'd thank Sergeant Greenwood and his team of Uniforms when he got the chance, too. George also owed Lindsey Yardley and her SOC team. Without either of those two and their teams, they wouldn't have such strong evidence linking Gruber to the crimes. And as such, they wouldn't have solved the case.

"Speech!" yelled Luke once again. "Speech!"

"Fine! George said with a grin. "To you all. To the SOCOs, and the Uniforms, for without whom we wouldn't have solved this case!"

Another roar of cheering erupted all around the room.

"Who fancies buttys from the van across the road?" George asked.

Wood took orders from smiling, clapping detectives and support staff. The food truck across the road in the ice rink car park did incredible hot and cold sarnies.

George was rather partial to their sausage and bacon butty slathered with brown sauce.

After about twenty minutes, the pair returned to the station with bags filled with foiled, greasy buttys, and soon, the squad room carried the fragrance of bacon, egg and sausage mixed with tomato and brown sauce.

All went silent as everyone tucked in.

Chapter Thirty-nine

Two Days Later

Tap, tap, tap. The rhythmic sound of George's keyboard joined the others. He liked leaving his door open and being approachable to detectives working in the open office. Though other than the keyboards clacking, the office was quiet for a rare and blessed moment.

Johann Gruber had been to court that morning and, like his interviews, had denied everything because he had pronounced himself as 'not guilty'; they were finalising all the paperwork they needed for the court case.

Johann was remanded in HMP Armley until his trial. Johann did, however, admit to the drug-related charges, which was something at least, even if George thought he was lying. But George was sure they had enough evidence that a jury would convict Johann of killing Harding, Cole and Flathers.

The entire case had been a bittersweet mess. Yes, they'd managed to get justice for Lena Schneider, but three men had suffered for something they'd had no part in. Especially Harding. George was still livid that Paxton Cole had paid Flathers to take the flack. That's what Gruber had told them, though his statements were unreliable. In truth, they weren't sure what happened, and would never know because the

CHAPTER THIRTY-NINE

other three witnesses were dead. He wasn't going to suggest their deaths were punishment worth their crimes because they weren't. George didn't think they should have paid the ultimate price for their actions. He didn't believe in the death penalty and believed in the justice system.

It was exactly why the sticky, wet crunching sound haunted his dreams most nights. He'd denied families justice because of his temper. And that wasn't on.

George was still struggling with why Gruber had killed Flathers. If they believed Gruber had supplied his own sister the drugs, then Edmund had taken the flack for *his* crime. As far as they knew, the two men hadn't spoken with each other in years. The only reason George could fathom was that Johann wanted the three deaths to be linked; as such, Edmund was a sacrificial lamb. That or Flathers knew Gruber's original identity.

Austrian CID, the Bundeskriminalamt, were still searching for Lena Schneider's biological dad but had gotten nowhere.

The press had been ravenous since George had announced to the press that they'd charged Johann Gruber. Everybody apart from Johnathan Duke had been trying to contact George through their office manager. Juliette Thompson had dealt with them, leaving George to cross the t's and dot the i's.

* * *

He may have gotten away with his crimes this time, but it had been close.

Too close.

But the plan had worked. The planted burner phone was a genius addition, as was planted whisky glass.

And the scopolamine, what a boon. It was lucky he had the footballer in his debt, as those 'broccoli extracts' from Colombia were incredibly potent. It also helped the Colombian had managed to gift Gruber two Angel's Trumpets.

That idiot Austrian had been so easy to frame, so easy to manipulate.

But he'd have to be careful not to draw attention to himself in the future. But his work wasn't over. It was merely a setback. A hurdle. A blip on the road of revenge.

Because there was still work to be done—revenge to be dealt. Lena needed to be avenged. As her biological father, it was the least he could do. Because that's what fathers did, they protected their children.

Everything would take time, but it would be worth it, and like before, he would see it through—his master plan.

He would continue the mission, whatever it took.

And if people continued to get in the way, they would have to be dealt with, too.

So he got out his finest pad of paper, his best fountain pen, and wrote down a name.

George Beaumont.

Then he wrote another.

Isabella Wood.

He wrote down the other names of easy enough people to strike against, especially as they'd nearly foiled his plan.

Luke Mason.

Tashan Blackburn.

Jason Scott.

That done, he returned the pen to its case, blew lightly on the paper to dry the ink, folded it, and placed it in the envelope. Then his phone pinged. The money Amanda Cole owed him had arrived.

She had settled her debt with him, but Jürgen Schmidt was not done with the detectives.

Not by a long shot.

***

Whilst Jürgen Schmidt was writing down names using his finest fountain pen, George was holding Isabella's hair back as she spewed into the toilet.

George had never seen anything so disgusting come from a woman of such beauty before but continued to hold back her hair as she released the entire contents of the tea he'd cooked specially for her.

He fought against his own nausea as chunks of chicken and undigested pasta flew from her mouth, splattering against the little blue disc. George had never seen Isabella in such a state before and then panicked at the thought that she, too, had come into contact with a toxin. "Do I need to call an ambulance?" he asked.

She shook her head and wiped her mouth with her hand. "Help me get up." When he did, she asked, "Can you pass me my phone?"

He handed it to her and saw Isabella look through it, a confused look soon spreading across her face. That confused look then turned to a look of terror. Then to a look of happiness.

"What's going on?" George asked.

"I'm late."

"Late?"

"Yes." Isabella put a hand on her belly. "I think I might be pregnant, George."

Afterword

Thank you, reader, for reading my new novel. I always struggle to write these afterwords, which is hilarious considering I write novels for a living, but my good friend Mandy reassured me many of you like hearing from the author.

I strayed away from Middleton this time and hope I have written the other areas of Leeds well and given them justice.

The idea for this novel came after watching a documentary named *The Footballer, His Wife, and the Crash* about the death of real-life footballer Jlloyd Samuel. It was a fascinating documentary, and I advise anybody interested in football and/or crime documentaries to watch it.

George returns to Middleton in May in The New Forest Village Book Club before investigating a murder in Rothwell in August called The Killer in the Family.

As always, if you enjoyed this book, I'd really appreciate it if you could leave a positive review and comment on Amazon. As a self-published author, reviews are the only way I get readers, and having readers means I can write more books.

Take care,

Lee

Also by Lee Brook

The Detective George Beaumont West Yorkshire Crime Thriller series in order:

The Miss Murderer

The Bone Saw Ripper

The Blonde Delilah

The Cross Flatts Snatcher

The Middleton Woods Stalker

The Naughty List

The Footballer and the Wife

More titles coming soon.

Printed in Great Britain
by Amazon